Praise for *The Trip*

'Completely gripping - strong holiday read recommend!'
Beth Morrey

'Luminous. Evokes a sultry and febrile setting with
luscious detail'
Louise Dean

'A rich and evocative story about a holiday that's supposed to
be perfect and secrets that are meant to stay buried'
Nicola Gill

'With such beautiful, evocative writing and a page turning plot
at its core, this is truly a perfect summer read!'
Carys Jones

'A gorgeously written and heart-tugging emotional deep dive
of friends in their forties'
Harriet Walker

'Masterfully crafted, wonderfully evoked settings,
I'd recommend for your next holiday read!'
Matt Cain

'An exquisitely written meditation on the way the choices we
make in our twenties ricochet throughout our lives. Nuanced,
perceptive, heartbreaking, and so true'
Kate Maxwell

'Absorbing, vibrant, emotive and utterly compelling.
I couldn't put it down'
Gillian Harvey

'The descriptions are exquisite, the characters rich, never letting
up with the pace and intrigue of the best psychological thrillers'
Caroline Corcoran

Rebecca Ley is a journalist, writing for various newspapers including *The Times* and the *Guardian*. She is a graduate of the Faber Academy and lives in London with her husband and three children. *The Trip* is her second novel.

Also by Rebecca Ley

For When I'm Gone

THE
TRIP

REBECCA LEY

ORION

First published in Great Britain in 2022 by Orion Fiction
an imprint of The Orion Publishing Group Ltd
Carmelite House, 50 Victoria Embankment
London EC4Y 0DZ

An Hachette UK Company

1 3 5 7 9 10 8 6 4 2

A CIP catalogue record for this book is
available from the British Library.

ISBN (Paperback) 978 1 4091 9559 7
ISBN (eBook) 978 1 4091 9560 3

Typeset by Deltatype Ltd, Birkenhead, Merseyside

Printed in Great Britain by Clays Ltd, Elcograf S.p.A.

MIX
Paper from
responsible sources
FSC® C104740

www.orionbooks.co.uk

For Ellie, sister extraordinaire

'It becomes still more difficult to find
Words at once true and kind,
Or not untrue and not unkind.'

from 'Talking in Bed' by Philip Larkin.

'There is really nothing in the world that can
be compared to red shoes!'

from 'The Red Shoes' by Hans Christian Andersen

Star

6 a.m.

Star's final twenty-four hours begin. She surfaces from sleep and – for thirty woozy but delicious seconds – has no idea where she is. She opens one eye, and then both, to see a counterpane of dawn sky stretched overhead, gold percolating blue. She's outside?

Star blinks and the previous night's excesses intrude: lager, wine of different colours, a shot of tequila and a creamy cocktail studded with a maraschino cherry that she told herself would pass for supper. Her brain is sodden two-ply tissue and her intestines twist, familiarly enough: Star is not unused to mornings after nights before. But when she swallows, the back of her throat is raw, and her right arm throbs.

Ah, yes. The door. That's right. Star rolls onto her side on the sunlounger where she has slept and looks over at the bifold doors, a concertina of glass. It's still shut. Locked from within, the wide handle turned upwards. Star falls backwards with a groan.

Last night, after she realised she was trapped outside, she made more fuss than she ever has before in her life. She howled and hammered her hands, eventually throwing her full weight against the glass, bruising the skin of her upper arm. But nobody came to set her free and eventually she had to conclude that the remaining party guests couldn't hear her over the music – thudding hip-hop that spilt like oil into the night.

Eventually, she gave up and returned to the sunlounger where earlier in the evening she'd had that awful conversation with Cal, and lay down, tipping into unconsciousness.

Now, a new day unfurls. Her surroundings are stupidly luxurious: a penthouse roof terrace of property daydream, on top of one of the city's most desirable high-rises, with its exclusive views of the Opera House and Harbour Bridge. It's the tallest poppy in the skyline, not overlooked by anyone, aside from wheeling gulls. Star is twenty floors up, lodged in the sky, with the salted breeze and tender strips of pink cloud.

Along with the sunlounger and its twin, the roof terrace hosts a selection of sculptural plants in tubs and an enormous barbecue, its exoskeleton as glossy as a beetle's. Star reclines on cushions stitched from outdoor fabric in an indeterminate beige that she thinks of as Corporate Oatmeal. She is unwitnessed, a most unusual state for her. She stretches her arms, points her toes inside the sparkly tights that encase them, rolls the back of her skull against the black cradle of her hair.

Above her, a plane tracks across the purplish sky, tail lights on, jewels in the dawn. Star watches its underbelly for a second and sits up suddenly, with another groan. How could she have forgotten? Later today she has to catch a flight herself and her future depends on it.

She stands, heads back to the door and tries the handle again. It's still locked from within and she presses her forehead against the glass. She can't see anything. After Cal stormed back inside and shut the door, he pulled the curtain across, and the interior of the apartment is hidden by a wall of heavy, lined fabric in yet more Corporate Oatmeal, that tonal spectrum favoured by the rich.

If nobody comes soon, she will miss her flight home. That would be a disaster. She'd like to think that Lucas will understand if she doesn't turn up, but she knows Lucas and he won't. He is too clever to have made his words sound like the ultimatum they were, but Star understood the meaning that lay behind them.

This is her last chance.

I

Riad Mousseline, Marrakesh

Friday afternoon
Twenty years later

From where she lay, sprawled on her back, Molly could see
a spray of bougainvillaea and a slice of sky, framed between
the interstices of unfamiliar buildings. The sky was a different
type of blue from at home – purer, more trenchant – and
she was tempted to continue lying on the dust looking at it.
Perhaps forever.

The moped had come from nowhere, a mosquito-whine
along the narrow, high-walled alleyway, causing Molly, in
wedge espadrilles she had bought especially for the weekend,
to reel, then topple backwards. The youth who'd felled her
hadn't stopped, merely glanced over his shoulder with an
apologetic wave and grin.

Molly rolled to her side and clambered up, reddening at
her own absurdity. She brushed her palms over her clothes

and smoothed her hair, relieved that nobody had seen, then reached for her wheelie bag, surrendered as she fell. She closed her eyes for a second, letting her shoulders sink and her heart rate normalise. London was already starting to chill, leaves crisping, but this city's air remained syrupy. Despite the anguish of the previous week, the indignity she'd just suffered, she had vowed to register any splinters of pleasure that presented themselves.

She must almost be at her destination; the dot pulsing on her phone was just round the corner. Left, or was it right, at the end of this alley? Once there, she could regroup.

The side street that she turned onto was nondescript, and Molly made her way to an arched, wooden door, dotted with studs and set into the high, putty-coloured wall. To its right, a discreet brass plaque pronounced *Riad Mousseline*. Her destination appeared unremarkable, but Molly knew that this must be deceptive. Lucas and Alice didn't stay anywhere but the very best and this trip had been planned for almost a year. She reached her hand to the doorbell and took a step back to wait as it chimed deep within.

'*Mol!*' Alice swung open the heavy door as if she owned it, extending her arms in greeting. The colour of every part of her seemed dialled up: tanned skin, a kaftan in grassy silk, and her hair, the roots near black, the tips a yolky blonde. Molly knew herself to be washed out in comparison. Alice wasn't quite beautiful – the length of her face and pronounced arch of her brows made her look like a naughty caricature – but she had a quality, always had, of drawing the eye. 'You made it! Lucas is upstairs on the roof terrace, but I'd just nipped downstairs to talk to the cook. Fatima. She's making *fattoush* for later. Where's Noah?' Alice looked up the alleyway beyond Molly. For a second, Molly followed her friend's gaze as if she might be surprised by her own husband.

'Last-minute change of plan,' said Molly, gathering herself. 'A work thing tonight. He'll probably come tomorrow.' She pressed her cheek against Alice's clavicle, scented with the sort of figgy, expensive perfume that verges on the unpleasant: that way, Alice couldn't see the expression on her face.

'No problem,' said Alice, not missing a beat. 'It's just so wonderful to have *you* here.' She squeezed both of Molly's upper arms, making eye contact. Molly submitted to the familiar thrill of Alice's appraisal. 'You look pale, Mol. Was the journey a pain? Come in, come in. You must just dump your bag and head straight up to the roof. This place is incredible,' added Alice, taking Molly's right hand and drawing her inside.

'But I wouldn't expect anything less,' said Molly, the comment sounding less playful than she intended.

She followed Alice into the dark corridor, the floor soft with a *millefeuille* of rugs, the walls covered with reportage-style photographs of spice stalls and date palms in the very streets Molly had just walked through. The passage opened into the razzle-dazzle of a central courtyard, in which stone pillars wrapped in jasmine surrounded a compact fountain, its water a dribble of glitter. On the left, an orange tree bore bright globes, while to the right its counterpart was a fig, curvy leaves as wide as dinner plates. There were several different seating areas, wicker chairs set around low tables on a floor covered in black-and-white tiles, a chessboard smoothed by the footsteps of all those who had come before.

'Wow,' said Molly, impressed. 'Would you look at this? It's such a contrast to how plain it is outside.'

'Not bad, is it?' said Alice, looking around and then up, hands on hips, to the sky above the courtyard, a square this time, of the same unknowable blue. Then, in a familiar tone of affectionate dismay, stepping forward to pluck a twig from Molly's back, 'Mol, you look like you've been rolling on the ground. What *are* you like?'

A corner of the courtyard concealed a staircase to the next floor, the building unfolding as an Escher maze; all unexpected alcoves, chaises begging to be prostrated upon, shelves lined with the well-thumbed, yellowing paperbacks of earlier guests. On the landing they emerged onto, there was a heavy smell of incense, a stick glowing to ash from a small alcove in the wall.

'This is your room. Just come and find us upstairs when you're ready,' said Alice, as they arrived at a door, a smaller version of the heavy one at the riad's entrance, with the same pattern of studs.

'Don't I need to check in or something?' said Molly. Alice laughed, shook her head and walked away with her familiar sway.

Molly turned the handle. Inside was a four-poster bed made of dark wood, inlaid with sprigs of bone flowers. Through the open door to the bathroom, she glimpsed a sunken bath, set in a sheet of burgundy marble and almost big enough for doggy paddling. A window to the street outside was cracked open, letting in a thread of exterior air, and the white sheets were strewn with rose petals, as if for honeymooners. Molly relinquished her bag. She was almost glad that Noah wasn't there to see such splendour. The contrast between the room's sensual possibilities and the reality of how they would inhabit it would bother them both in different ways. For Noah, sex was like plastic bread, a staple he could consume with reliable, yet profound, enjoyment.

Molly exhaled. The space was hers alone. It surprised her what a relief that was. She eased her feet out of the espadrilles, which had started to rub against her heels, leaving discs of carpaccio skin, and launched herself face-first onto the snowy bed linen. She pressed her features onto the cotton and let out a muffled roar, her shoulders shaking. An observer might have struggled to tell if she were crying or laughing.

After ten minutes, Molly stood and made her way to the minibar, located in a carved cupboard opposite the end of the bed. It took some effort to ignore the miniatures, but she chose a packet of crisps, which she took back to the bed with her and munched, her legs stretched out in front of her, contemplating those feet, so veiny now that she sometimes caught a glimpse of them and couldn't believe they belonged to her.

* * *

The roof garden was larger than Molly had anticipated, segmented by trellises and cacti, alternately skinny and bulbous.

It was also full of surprises – a terracotta urn, mirrors, a wire sculpture that looked like a toddler's scribble and several small pools laid with mosaic tiles – and offered a view of Marrakesh's Tetris skyline – blocky buildings stacked upon one another in the Rose City's regulation brown-pink. Molly wove towards the sound of conversation.

'*Molly.*' Lucas stood to greet her, courteous as ever, leaning in to kiss her on both cheeks. Lucas: marathoner, senior partner, committed father, aesthete. Alice didn't rise, for she was ensconced in one of the pools in a bikini, a glass in her hand stuffed full of ice cubes and torn mint. 'Where's Noah?' Lucas added, gesturing for Molly to sit down. His sandy hair was clipped close and he wore a T-shirt with a picture of a skateboard on its front and pristine trainers, air bubbles pinioned in their soles. The older Lucas got, the more youthful his clothes; a corporate lawyer who had scarcely seen natural light for the last two decades, but who favoured streetwear in his downtime, his rimless glasses perhaps the only tell. His body had also become markedly leaner as the years passed. Once a bear, he was now – thanks to a gruelling regime of running to and from the office – something rather more sinewy and insubstantial.

'Last-minute change of plan,' said Molly. 'He'll come tomorrow.' She was grateful for the sunglasses shielding her bloodshot eyes. She wasn't certain if Noah was going to come at all. Or even if she wanted him to. After the week they'd endured, Molly had hardly felt like it herself, but couldn't see how she could let Alice down – after the months of planning and anticipation – without grievously injuring, possibly

9

ending, their friendship. Despite everything, she didn't want to do that, Alice too significant a figure in the landscape of her life. But she always found the date of Lucas and Alice's anniversary difficult anyway, even after all these years.

As for her husband, she could try laughing off Noah's absence, but the others knew them too well. She and Noah seldom argued. Or not in public. Of course, their relationship had a hidden side – which relationship that had lasted for more than twenty years didn't? But in front of others their inter-actions had always been characterised by a calmness she prized – another reason she had made her choice all those years ago. Noah brought out the best in her, or at least he always had.

'Have a drink,' said Lucas, gesturing at the glass on the low table in front of him. 'We're on cocktails already. The most amazing margaritas you've ever had, I swear.' Everything Lucas did had to be definitive.

'No booze just yet,' said Molly, sinking to a cushion on the banquette and glancing across at Alice. She hadn't drunk any alcohol for a week, since the night she had found out: the evening that Noah had made his broadcasting debut. Molly shut her eyes for a moment. She had drawn blood with her fingernails, tiny rubies mixed with the stubble on Noah's jaw. She had never committed such an act of violence, not even in the days when her life had been so much more exciting.

'Really?' said Lucas. 'No trouble. I can get them to make you a non-alcoholic one.'

'Sure, OK then,' replied Molly. She knew Lucas would want her to sample the riad's splendour in full. Her role was to be wide-eyed at the luxury to which Alice had long grown inured.

Lucas tinkled a brass bell, and a young, unsmiling man appeared.

'Mohammed. A non-alcoholic version of this, please?' said Lucas, lifting his glass. 'No alcohol,' he repeated.

Mohammed nodded and disappeared. Five minutes later, he was back with a drink for Molly. She smiled in gratitude and took an extravagant suck from the straw, but it was disappointingly sweet, grains of sugar grazed her teeth.

'What a place, eh?' said Lucas. As if he weren't the one paying for the weekend. Mousseline, a courtesan, opening her thighs for the highest bidder.

From the muezzin in his tower, barely twenty metres away, the call to prayer. The three paused their drinking for a moment, heads cocked. Mindful for a minute, Molly imagined, or perhaps pretending to be, of the difference between their afternoon and that of so many others. Alice glanced down at the water; Molly twisted her face towards the minaret, while Lucas let his gaze rove over the roof garden.

Molly wondered how long it was appropriate to wait before taking another sip.

'Come on, time to get in.' Alice let out that whoop that Molly knew so well, and flicked a skein of water that sizzled on the sun-warmed tiles. Lucas smiled, habitually indulgent towards his wife, ever the firestarter.

'Nope,' said Molly.

'Spoilsport,' said Alice, but chuckled, evidently satisfied, and submerged her two-tone head under the water. The pool wasn't large enough to swim in, designed only for wallowing; it held jasmine flowers whisked into it by the wind.

'Give me a chance,' said Molly. The truth was, a dip was exactly what she wanted after the previous night. So many interminable hours next to Noah wondering who exactly he was, this man she had lain beside for so long, who had twice sieved her shit out of a birthing pool and brought her a cup of tea almost every morning for decades, but had recently proven himself unknowable.

After unexpectedly coming to Marrakesh on her own and navigating her way on foot through the narrow streets, she ached for release, longed to wash away the particulate pollution of her own city, the streak of sweat in the small of her back, her own confusion.

But she didn't fancy the casual scrutiny. She was accustomed to seldom thinking about her body any more, beyond servicing its basic needs. Most of the time, this was a blessing. The gnawing sense of her own shortcomings had dissipated, even as her midsection had expanded. This, then, was a rude reminder that her form could still be objectively judged, that so could the rest of her, outside the carapace of family life, in which a certain quality of translucence served her best. She was there, but not completely as herself, for her children.

They shouldn't care, these old friends. They were changing, too – slipping and creasing despite their astonishing stamina, all the boot camps, the intermittent fasts, the chunky watches slapped on wrists, recording every step and exhale. And yet.

Molly paused. In the previous week's looping debates, Noah had returned often to her lack of spontaneity. As if it were a *crime*.

'Oh, go on then,' she said. 'Let me get my cossie.'

* * *

The water was blood temperature and, once she was safely submerged and beyond scrutiny, Molly felt her muscles soften.

'See?' said Alice, grinning at her expression. Molly nodded. 'I told you you'd like it.'

'You did,' said Molly, resting against the side of the pool. Alice was always up for it, their fulcrum. Molly had always been grateful for Alice's certainty, happy enough to be bullied into new experiences, although in recent years her friend's drive seemed more frenetic, as if all the things she'd acquired and the memories she'd accumulated still weren't enough – a committed seeker, not in a spiritual sense, but the experiential.

This weekend was one of her most lavish yet. Some party! Two nights in Marrakesh for her and Lucas's twentieth wedding anniversary. No dependants allowed. An excuse for the friends to reconnect and relax, to let their hair down and remind themselves of how they had bonded in the first place, through a commitment to hedonism as keenly developed as their more conventional ambitions; their lodestars of pleasure and personal advancement.

There was that other thing too, that Molly knew Alice craved still: the desire to prove their alliance was legitimate. That how they had behaved hadn't been because they were inherently bad, just young and foolish. They were good people, the kind who stayed friends, who looked out for one another.

Best not to dwell upon those they'd lost.

'We just don't see enough of each other any more,' Alice had said. 'It's going to be amazing.'

As the years had passed, professional choices, initially almost arbitrary, had driven a wedge. It had been subtle at first, as Lucas and Alice moved to a different area, less multicultural, replacing chicken shops and sirens and fossilised vomit splatters on the pavements with hushed, tree-lined avenues and shops that sold glittery notepads. Then they had defensively announced that they were sending Edward to private school, despite what Lucas had long argued during late-night discussions, an abrupt volte-face that they made clear was never to be discussed.

'When it comes down to it,' Alice had said once, half-cut, 'everyone is just going to do what's best for their child. And if they don't – they bloody well *should*.'

As time had gone on, extreme wealth – and the absence of it – had shaped identities: politics, diets, dress senses and educations. You are what you do.

As if the Mousseline herself weren't enough of a lure, Alice had jokingly promised A Big Surprise for the main party on Saturday night, by which point the others should have arrived.

'What kind of surprise?' Molly had asked, on her mobile in the staffroom, tapping her pen on the Formica tabletop in front of her. A parade of imagined delights had cartwheeled into her brain, in contrast to the shabbiness of her familiar surroundings: the stained carpet, the fridge full of colleagues' Tupperware, the stale reek of coffee and endeavour.

'Oh, you'll see,' Alice had said. 'You won't believe it. Truly.'

And so. Here they were. Back in the realm of towels folded into swans and afternoon massages, a place that had once fleetingly seemed Molly's birthright as a twenty-something, now a tentative dry run for the years ahead, perhaps, when her children had left.

'Have you got sunscreen on?' asked Alice. Her skin was already that rich teak from some other holiday.

'Yes,' replied Molly. She was careful these days. Her freckles had recently transfigured, treacherously revealing themselves to be blotches of pigment.

'Noah would *love* this,' said Alice, twisting herself.

'He would,' agreed Molly. Noah was usually the first to enter any body of water.

Molly turned her face up to the sky. The thrum of the Jemaa el-Fna, out of sight but startlingly close, was muted by the heat of the afternoon. Yet there was still a coil of smoke rising, the sound of drums, an occasional shout. The *phut-phut-phut* of all the little mopeds ridden too fast along narrow streets, like that one that had knocked her over.

Molly wondered what it would be like if Noah were sitting next to her in the pool. Away from the cluttered lower maisonette they had lived in for so many years, from the streets so familiar they scarcely saw them, the corner shop where they bought emergency milk, the local park with its leggy rose garden and wrought-iron railings. Perhaps she would even reach for his hand. Maybe a weekend like this would put everything back on track.

'We are going to have *so much* fun,' Alice said. She lifted one of her feet out of the water and dropped it back down again, the splash emphatic punctuation.

'Definitely!' said Molly, trying to project enthusiasm. In truth, she would consider the weekend a success if she could get through it without breaking down. Flashes of the previous week had surfaced intermittently, both on the plane and during the taxi ride from Menara Airport to the medina, where she had been dropped to make the last bit of her journey on foot. The view of Noah from where she had slumped against the dishwasher; the unsure planes of his face from that angle. The tone of her own voice as she had repeated, 'I don't know any more. I just don't know.'

Yet such upset retreated against the magnificence of her current situation: the breeze carrying its rasp of nearby desert, the rhomboids of sunlight falling through the trellis onto Lucas's shoulders, the swill of warm water around her skin.

Perhaps she would be able to enjoy herself a tiny bit?

'Viv is getting here tonight,' said Alice. 'With Iona.' Viv only latterly having come out, this her first proper girlfriend, certainly the first she'd introduced to them.

Alice leant her head back, replete, shutting her eyes against the sun. But only for a moment.

'Lucas. Take our picture,' she instructed.

Molly grimaced. She knew that the photograph would promptly be uploaded, Alice's competitiveness finding a perfect outlet in the modern requirement to vaunt one's life. Alice would come out of it looking exceptional, while she, Molly, would be the foil of ordinariness.

It was always disconcerting to recall the accident of their

coalescence. University, then the flat above the Vietnamese restaurant which served as a focal point, although Molly herself had never actually lived there; that dingy palace replete with a rodent problem, the floating smell of *pho*, the view of the abandoned railway track which had rewilded itself into a kind of Elysian garden, full of fronded grass, foxes and only the occasional topless, staggering drunk.

But, with hindsight, it was what had happened to Star that had really cemented them, a sense of free-floating complicity linking them in perpetuity. She was one of them, whether they chose to admit it or not. Star's fate had been so shocking and unlikely that even people who hadn't known her remembered the story twenty years on. Something about the circumstances had stuck in the public imagination, or perhaps it was just Star's cabaret beauty; in death, she achieved the renown she had so longed for in life.

Molly had found herself running past the old flat a few months earlier, on one of her long Saturday afternoon routes, upping the mileage in the desperate quest for endorphins. Since having Bella, she had avoided the area. It was too painful, too redolent, its bustle and throb the antithesis of parenthood's more measured pace. It was best not to recall how thrilling life could be, Molly had found, or memories could taint your early nights and family suppers with an unproductive yearning.

The restaurant still existed, but its frontage was smarter, the whole area sanitised, as if it was finally aware of its proximity to the Square Mile. Molly had paused, panting, outside.

After a minute, a young woman had emerged, clopping

onto the pavement and neatly shutting the door behind her. She was dressed for attention, a short shift and cork-heeled clogs, the backs of her knees vulnerable. The girl glanced either side of herself reflexively, wondering who had noticed her now. Molly, Star and Alice had been just like that, once. Just waiting to be noticed. Chosen.

Startled out of reminiscence, Molly had run on, not mentioning to Noah where she had been when she got home.

'And what about Tommy?' said Molly to Alice, then, touching upon the absentee that it was acceptable to mention. Their scapegoat.

'I asked him, of course.' Alice was casual. 'He was non-committal. Said something about showing for the party tomorrow night. I think he's actually off it all at the moment, would you believe?'

'He is,' said Molly. 'Almost a year.'

'Impressive,' said Alice, with a nose wrinkle that suggested otherwise. 'I'll still be amazed if he shows up. There is still one room unaccounted for, but I think it's unlikely. You know what he's like. But we had to ask him, of course.'

'Better for everyone if he doesn't,' added Lucas, taking a sip of his drink, one arm stretched out expansively. In front of him on the table was a slim edition of *The Waste Land* that Molly knew he would soon pick up and frowningly read. Lucas's wealth now surpassed even his own wildest dreams, but he still earnestly hoped for credibility in other regards, both sartorial and literary. Noah would have certainly teased him for the book. Ribbing Lucas was a well-rehearsed routine, usually received in good humour. Yet in so many ways,

Lucas had had the last laugh – graciousness just one of the many things he could afford.

'Luc,' said Alice, standing out of the pool and shaking herself, like a terrier. 'Don't be mean. It would be great for Tommy to come. But I can hardly twist his arm.' She strode over to the seating area and took a sip of her husband's drink. 'Nobody can make Tommy do *anything*.'

'It would be a bit hard on him. That's all I'm thinking,' said Lucas, shrugging. Lucas had always worked hard at not letting Tommy get to him.

'I don't know about that,' Alice countered and unfurled a yoga mat that had been leaning against the side of a seat. 'Leaving him out is worse, surely? And if he really is doing so well ... Although I'll believe that when I see it.'

Alice moved through a sun salute. Then she put her elbows on the mat and placed the crown of her head between them, shifting her weight forwards and then drawing up into a headstand, muscles flexed beneath the fabric triangles of her bikini, toes projected towards the sky. Inverted, Alice's breasts were neat gelato scoops, her hair a caramel puddle.

Molly rolled her eyes but looked; it was hard not to. After a few minutes, Alice scissored her legs above her head and dropped out.

'Show-off,' said Molly.

'You should try it, Mol. It's so good to get that head rush,' Alice replied, grinning, pulling on her kaftan over her head. 'Anyway, now. A walk? To the square? Come on. Let's explore.' She had always had to keep moving, Alice, chasing something she might miss. It was the quality she'd had in common with Star. So similar in some ways, yet so different when it came to it.

'I'm going to nail this,' said Lucas, picking up his book.

'As long as you don't end up doing work emails,' said Alice. 'Molly?'

'Yeah, all right,' said Molly. She didn't mind being instructed, had always found it soothing submitting to someone else's slipstream.

'I'll meet you on the ground floor,' Alice said, and Molly rose out of the water, swaddling herself swiftly in a towel.

Back in her bedroom, she removed her phone from her bag and placed it on the side table next to the bed. A statement of intent. She could go and explore without constantly checking it. If Noah wanted to get hold of her, he would have to wait.

That morning, her taxi five minutes away, she had gone to kiss her daughters' foreheads where they lay still sleeping in their teenage nests, before going down to the kitchen, where Noah was looking out of the window at the garden, the lawn quilted in end-of-summer brown and yellow. His Italian stovetop coffee pot, the one she always considered an affectation, bubbled on the hob. Neither had slept.

'You really aren't coming?' she had asked.

He had looked at her and shook his head. 'How can I, Mol?'

'This is important to them,' Molly had said. 'It's not about us, this weekend. Whatever is happening between us can wait. And you know what she's like. I'm the one who will get it in the neck if you don't turn up.'

Noah had rubbed his jawline but said nothing.

Star

Since waking up, Star has lapped the roof garden three times and finds herself well acquainted with every corner of it, so different in daylight: the oiled decking, the plants, the sunloungers. She sits down again. The inescapable fact is that there is nowhere to go; the terrace is surrounded by a glass balustrade topped with a railing of tubular steel. To get out of here, she is reliant on the flat's owner — a middle-aged man called Pete — rousing himself and opening the doors. If he's sleeping off his hangover, that could take hours.

Star still feels a little drunk herself, but she knows that — soon — this soft buffer will start to wane. She glances at her watch and runs her tongue along the front of her teeth. They are starting to fur; her mouth is sour. The sun has definitely risen now, but it's chilly. She hears that they are having an extended late-summer heatwave in England — just in time for the wedding, trust Alice's luck – but in Sydney, it's winter. Luckily, she wore her jacket when she came out here last night, or she would be freezing.

Star pulls her collar closer and regards her and Cal's half-empty glasses, on the side table between the two sunloungers. Her handbag rests alongside them, a cotton pouch with an elephant embroidered on the front which she bought in Bangkok. It has spilt its contents: a golden lipstick cartridge, the keys to the house she shares, the strip of passport photographs of her and Molly that they took in Angel Tube station on their break and that Star has kept with her ever since.

Even here, Star has made a mess. But her possessions confer a certain normalcy. This is welcome, because as the minutes have ticked by, the seam of horror in her core thickens.

She should never have come to the party last night. It was a huge mistake.

Her flight is at four. Ideally, she would be at the airport by two, but Star is an expert at being late and she knows she will be fine as long as she is there by three and mounts a full-on charm offensive at the check-in staff. But she has to go back to her room first, in a run-down Victorian villa in Alexandria Park, to get her backpack and her passport – she estimates that the latest she can leave this penthouse and still get there in time is half past one.

It should be fine. Someone will definitely let her out before then, Star tells herself. She tries to relax.

If she catches her flight, she will touch down in Heathrow twenty-fours later, at 5 a.m. English time. Even if everything goes smoothly, that will only give Star a few hours between landing and the time that Alice is set to walk up the aisle, resplendent on her father's arm. A brief window to see Lucas and hear him out.

She will need to head directly from the airport to the hotel where he is spending the night before the wedding. If what Lucas said on the phone was true, he won't have slept and will be waiting for Star, consumed by the enormity of what he plans to do.

What they plan to do.

But if she misses her flight ... well, that doesn't bear thinking about. She has a horrible feeling that Lucas will go through the motions, not wanting to let down the querulous trifecta of Alice and his parents. Star shakes her head, dislodging the idea.

She focuses on her immediate senses, that old anxiety-quelling trick. She can see early boats with rainbow-coloured sails racing across the harbour, bath toys from this vantage point. The harbour bridge's fretwork soars above the water, waves capped with white crests. She can smell the ocean, a hint of car exhaust and the eucalyptus in one of the nearby planters, can hear a hum from the wind at such a height. She touches her fingertips to the silk of her dress, running them down to the rougher texture of her tights.

Star stands again and returns to the barrier at the edge of the terrace. She spots a jogger moving across the boardwalk, far beneath her. An ant in a luminous gilet. In this city, people run for pleasure in a way that remains incomprehensible to her.

'Hey,' Star calls, banging the glass. 'HEY!' But it's no use. She is so far up and invisible behind her protective, reflective screen, her voice whipped away by the wind. She is on her own.

2

Marrakesh

Friday afternoon
Twenty years later

'I'll give you twenty dirhams,' Alice said to the stallholder.

'Madame,' he said, with ersatz affront. 'They cost more than that to make.'

'Fine,' said Alice, placing the bangles back on the table decisively and sighing. 'Come on, Mol, let's get out of here.'

'How about thirty?' said the man, his palms turned upwards, his smile fixed. 'I can do them for that?' Molly admired his luxuriant moustache.

'OK. You've got a deal.' Alice pulled out her card. 'Have you got contactless?' He nodded, and as they finished the transaction, Molly leant back against the carpet that was hanging against one wall of the flimsy shop, the tufts of wool soft against her spine. She looked out at the souk. The stall opposite was full of replica football kits. Arsenal.

Tottenham. Real Madrid. Some were sized for babies, and Molly wondered about buying one for her teaching assistant, Mina, an unlikely but ardent Gooner, who was bovine in late pregnancy and about to go on maternity leave.

For so long, Molly had been jealous of pregnant women, about to have their first child; envious of all that milky bliss, the press of a bundle against the chest. But lately, as childbirth retreated in the rear-view mirror of her life, she only felt sorry for them. For herself. They had no clue what they were getting into. The older she got, the more courageous and foolhardy reproduction seemed. She had always assumed she would get to a point where she didn't constantly worry about Bella and Eve, was only recently starting to realise that perhaps it would never come. That her own mother's habitual detachment was probably a survival mechanism. She would choose motherhood again, she thought, most likely, but perhaps had been too quick to discount the importance of freedom in her calculations.

Star would never have made the same mistake.

Molly looked back at her other friend. Alice wore denim cut-offs, and her hair was pulled back in a plait under her baseball cap. Even at their age, she attracted glances from the people they walked past.

'Shakira,' someone had hissed, catching a glance of Alice from behind. Smooth calves and neat ribcage. That buttery, copious hair. Alice had turned, and he withdrew, bowed his head, backtracking at the realisation that she was old enough to be his mother. Alice had only smiled broadly, undaunted. Molly had watched her friend deal with male advances so many times. Alice had always been the one to catch attention. It never made her flustered; she took it as her due.

'Pretty, aren't they?' Alice said, holding her wrist out to Molly as they continued through the souk, past more stalls with floor-to-ceiling rows of leather goods: slippers, key fobs, belts and satchels, shiny as conkers and all emanating a strong smell of their curing solution.

'Gorgeous,' Molly agreed. Alice was a magpie. It didn't matter how many shiny things she had at home, she always, always wanted more – cheap bangles when she already had Cartier ones. 'They remind me of the kind of stuff Star used to wear.' Molly wanted to take the words back as soon as they fell out of her mouth.

'Oh yeah, you're right, I suppose,' said Alice, glancing down. Once upon a time, Star had been one of their favourite topics of conversation, arriving in their lives as she had, seemingly overnight. Star's style had been idiosyncratic: she favoured vintage clothes but had offset them with a riotous tangle of jewellery, dressed herself up, *like a Christmas tree,* as Molly's father, Alan, would have put it. A turquoise cocktail ring in bubblegum blue, friendship bracelets, an amber pendant around her neck which held a suspended prehistoric midge.

'I can't believe that it's been so many years,' said Molly.

'I know,' said Alice. 'How is that even possible? I think there's a rip in the space-time continuum.'

'Yeah, maybe.' Molly smiled, weakly.

'I'm just so pleased you're here,' said Alice. 'We've got so much to catch up on.' She squeezed Molly's hand before dropping it. 'We just don't get to see enough of each other at home.'

'I'm around,' said Molly, working to keep any defensiveness out of her voice. It was Alice and Lucas who were busy – with client dinners, skiing weekends, governorship committees, personal training sessions. The heavily diarised lives of the wealthy. Molly enjoyed teaching most of the time; it had been a better choice for her than journalism. Noah loved his research and, thanks to the documentary, was finally being rewarded with the attention he deserved. They stood by the decisions they had made. Yet sometimes, the sheer lifestyle disparity brought her up short. As they had left the riad, she had overheard Lucas musing about buying somewhere like the Mousseline for weekends in retirement, as if it was an imminent prospect. Work stretched ahead for years for her and Noah, perhaps forever. And yes, they enjoyed it. Mostly. But she was tired. The rewards for doing the right thing seemed scant. She had always imagined she was progressing towards something, some understanding, but had begun to realise this wasn't the case.

There was also the chasm between Molly's supposed intimacy with Alice, her old friend, and the reality. She couldn't be honest about the constant arguments with Noah of the preceding week. And, despite all the time that had passed, Molly knew that she and Alice wouldn't honestly talk about how they felt about what had happened to Star. Despite the performance of closeness, all the things they wouldn't discuss stretched between them.

With the afternoon shifting into early evening, the central

square was stirring into frantic life once more. *Jemaa el–Fna.* The place of annihilation. Shaped, actually, more like an octagon. The stink of horse pee, charcoal and sweat rose in the air; the pulse of drums and clack of castanets a background heart arrhythmia. There were stalls offering argan oil, henna tattoos, packets of mysterious herbal teas. Molly even spotted some dentures for sale on a table, proudly placed alongside a collection of combs.

Nearby, a troupe of acrobats worked their patch; dressed in red pantaloons and yellow waistcoats, they somersaulted and cartwheeled before stacking themselves into a human pyramid. To their left, in front of a fruit stall stacked with pomegranates, a monkey wrangler and his charge watched them impassively. Carts moved forwards containing piles of cast-iron staves and struts, steel grilles and trestle tables, pushed by youths hurriedly throwing together food stalls. A man stepped out in front of them with a laminated plastic menu.

'Ya, Gazelles!' Thirty-seven takes you to heaven!' he called out coquettishly to the women. He was much younger than they, wearing a Yankees cap and a basketball top, his arms heartbreakingly muscular and smooth.

'No, thank you,' said Alice. She squinted at the menu and smiled. 'Ox hearts. My favourite. We aren't hungry just yet.' Holding Molly's arm, she leant into her, a pulse of amusement moving through her torso.

'Come back later!' he said, a boy really, laughing eyes the palest brown. 'Remember, thirty-seven takes you to heaven!'

Molly couldn't tell what he thought of them. It had got

to that point now. She could no longer assess if she – or even Alice – retained any erotic capital for men younger than themselves. She rather suspected that they didn't, that they were increasingly the subject of a kind of sly primal mockery, their attempts to make themselves alluring – the smears of lipstick, multiple ear piercings, threads of gold looped around their necks – increasingly pathetic. This realisation induced panic for what lay ahead, for the mouldering and disintegration that winked at them. Molly had only grudgingly accepted middle age; she couldn't bear being truly *old*.

'You know what I fancy?' she said to Alice, pointing at a drinks cart in front of them stacked with glass bottles of fizzy drinks. 'One of those Fantas. They look as though they're so full of E-numbers they would glow in the dark.' Of all life's consolations, sugar seemed the most enduring.

'Great idea,' said Alice, as Molly had known she would.

The women stopped and bought their drinks, then chinked their glass bottles and lifted them to their lips, sipping in unison.

'Oh, that's lush,' laughed Alice. 'Well done, Mol.'

'Sugary drinks always taste better on holiday,' said Molly, grinning. 'The bubbles are going up my nose.'

They walked for a few minutes before becoming snagged in the small crowd beaded around an older man, blindfolded above his white beard. He stood on his tiptoes with outstretched hands, telling a story. Behind the strip of black fabric, his face was hashtagged with the grooves of someone who has spent a lifetime outside.

'And then the jinn snaps the lid on the bottle, and Abdul

is trapped,' he said, with a flourish. The audience applauded. 'Come back later for more,' the storyteller enthused. 'This is better than Netflix, I'm telling you.' He bowed with a sweep of his hands, gesturing towards the clutch of dull coins already in the tin laid out by his feet.

He looked up in the direction of Molly and Alice. Molly stepped back. Despite his blindfold, it was as if the man could see precisely where she stood.

'You want a story, ladies?' he called out indisputably to them. 'I tell good ones. The very best.'

'We're OK,' called Alice. 'Thanks.' She waved her Fanta bottle and turned to go.

'I'd like one,' said Molly, looking at Alice. 'Sorry. I won't be a moment. You go on if you want.'

'If you insist,' Alice said, shrugging, remaining on the same spot but angling her head to one side and regarding the man from a slanted perspective.

'OK,' the storyteller said, pleased, his face splitting into a radiant smile. 'You two women know about life, I can tell. You need something serious. No romance.' He grimaced under his blindfold, moving his hands in the air in front of his face. 'How about the story of the moon princess? She went on a magic carpet, but it flew too quickly, and she tumbled through the sky, past the stars, into—'

'Don't fancy that one, thanks,' said Alice, stepping away without looking back.

'Please come back, madame,' the blindfolded man called. 'I can do another.'

But Alice was gone, just like that. They had always framed

it affectionately: Alice didn't do things she didn't want to do; she told it how it was, lacked the people-pleasing gene. The irony being that people loved her for it, or did until it hurt them personally.

'Sorry,' said Molly. 'Don't worry about my friend.' She glanced at Alice's retreating back.

The man smiled again, reassured, his face turned directly towards Molly. 'So, not that one then ...' he said, softly.

'It's OK by me,' said Molly, gripping her glass bottle and wishing she could leave herself.

'I could tell you one about an indecisive queen,' he suggested.

'Sounds a bit like me,' said Molly. 'Apart from the queen bit.' She regarded her lurid orange drink, almost gone. It was a joke, but it also wasn't. She had always been indecisive, and like so many personal characteristics, this tendency had calcified with age. The older she had got, the more aware she was of the gaps in her own knowledge, of the life experiences which informed people's polarised viewpoints. The impossibility of objective truth. Certainty was like collagen: it nosedived after forty.

'Like many of us. Believe me,' said the storyteller. 'But not your friend perhaps.' He laughed conspiratorially. 'Anyway, this queen lived in Zanzibarrrr ...' He rolled the 'r' out with relish. 'She lived on the beach, on a diet of mangoes and lobster. She liked the meat in the claws best!' The storyteller pincered his fingers, his pliable, partially obscured face somehow semaphoring frightened crustacean.

'Sounds like an acceptable life,' murmured Molly.

'Oh, you might think so! But she was bored, this queen. So *bored*. She loved her husband, the king, well enough, but her children were growing, and Zanzibar is small. She would walk around the island, looking out at the waves and wondering if she was ever going to leave. She longed for an adventure, but she thought perhaps that was done for her. She had no more stories left.'

'Hmmm.' Molly cleared her throat. She scuffed an espadrille in the dust at her feet.

'One morning, the queen – her name was Zana – woke up and found herself unable to decide about anything. She couldn't choose whether to put on her pink robe or her yellow one. Whether to put her hair up or leave it down. To walk left or right on the beach. She was incapable of making those little choices. All she could do was sit, in her sleeping clothes, waiting for someone to decide for her. But nobody could. She sat in the same spot for weeks, ignoring her husband, her children, her friends. She simply stopped.'

Molly frowned. If this story was tailor-made for her, she wasn't sure she liked it. A small group of tourists had formed alongside her, but the storyteller kept his blindfolded face trained upon hers. She wanted to leave, badly, but was worried about causing offence.

'Everyone grew very worried about the queen, but the best doctors and magicians, none of them could offer a solution. And then, the wind changed and blew in a new boat to the island.' The man paused. 'And on this boat was an old woman who came and told the king she could help. He was so desperate that he agreed and let her speak to the indecisive queen. The old woman went into the queen's chamber and whispered something in the queen's ear. Then – and it was just like magic – the queen got up and washed and put on her pink robe and ate a mango and then a lobster and walked on the white sand and lived the life that she already knew how to live. And she never fell into indecision again, for she wasn't bored again.'

'Hang on a minute,' said Molly. 'What did the older woman say?'

'Ah,' said the storyteller, raising a finger to the side of his nose. 'I thought you'd want to know. You might expect it to be something really big or profound, but the old woman simply said, "*Pay attention.*"'

'What does that mean?' Molly rubbed the top of her arm, annoyed.

'She meant, of course, that our lives get dull when we don't pay proper attention to them. And that it's always wise to remember that,' said the storyteller. He didn't smile this time. His body seemed spent, as if his words had cost him.

'Here,' said Molly. She reached into her bag and took out a note. 'Thanks.' She placed the dirhams in the cap and backed away, draining the last of her drink and then looping back to return the bottle to the stall she had bought it from. She was disappointed that the parable had descended into the motivational. Even here, she couldn't escape the commands to live her best life. If only she knew what that was. Besides, the best people she had ever known had been the ones who hadn't paid attention, who let entire days and weeks slip through their fingers like water.

She circumnavigated the square, looking for Alice but unable to find her. Once she had gone full circle, she stopped and paused, breathed in and out, soothed a little by the clamour of people she would never know.

3

Flat 48, The Bacon Factory, Kingsland Road, Shoreditch

Twenty-two years earlier

It was a Wednesday night when Molly and Noah side-stepped from being friends into something different. They had found themselves on their own, for once, in the flat by the abandoned railway bridge, a warehouse loft in what had once been a meat-curing factory. Molly didn't live there – Noah shared it with Lucas and Alice – yet it was the closest place she had to a home, in the face of the city's indifference.

On a typical evening of full occupation, Alice would be moving around purposefully, Lucas frowning over some documents brought back from the office and Noah reading. Viv might be making tea, Star perhaps doing a handstand against the wall, exposing the pearly curve of her stomach, Tommy elongated along the length of the rug, occasionally making a sardonic interjection or falling asleep, smack bang in the middle of the room. While Molly would be watching, delighted by them, exactly the friends she had hoped for when she left home.

But that night, the open-plan room was quiet. Star, Tommy, Viv, Lucas and Alice were out somewhere, endlessly fascinated with one another. Molly and Noah had cooked pasta stirred with salty jarred pesto, satisfied with their own maturity. They were now drinking corner-shop Rioja and sitting on the sofa, plastic leather which squeaked against Molly's skin.

Outside, there was a thunderstorm, and they were distracted from the mediocre film they were watching – a romcom in which the beautiful heroine threw herself at an alternately sleazy and disinterested man – by the more dramatic show of rumbling and forks of burning light above the bridge outside the window.

'I love storms,' Molly said, standing to peer out of the window at the sky. She was aware of Noah watching her.

Molly and Noah assured everyone they were just friends. And most people believed them; they weren't each other's sort. Noah spooned through girls, but none of them stuck. As Alice put it, he was a 'literary lothario' – the type for whom academic tendencies and a rumpled citatory charm were a positive boon in terms of pulling.

And yet Molly herself had sensed the change in his attention towards her. She couldn't have told you how; he had never revealed himself. Yet, it was there, in the air between them, a hovering question mark. She hadn't decided what she wanted to do about it yet. She had always liked him, since the first time she had met him and Tommy in a seminar about *Paradise Lost*, the comprehensive boys comforting to her amongst the Old Paulinas and Harrovians. Noah, desperate to prove his intelligence but reddening a little every time he responded to their tutor, an academic with long, filed fingernails that he tapped on the table.

They had since become friends, and although their friendship was ostensibly tangential to the group, Molly had grown to rely upon it. She didn't want to jettison what they had for something temporary. She didn't think she could bear to spend time with Noah if he moved on from her, as he had from others.

There was also that other entanglement to consider. Noah, out of everyone, would be the most surprised at whom it was with. It happened away from everyone else and had a kind of stomach-curdling intensity that she had never experienced before but that made her entire body chime in ja-ja-jackpot recognition. So, this was what they wrote all the songs about. She had hoped the relationship, if you could call it that, was going to become a real thing, that could be exposed to the daylight and built upon, but lately it was dawning upon her that this wouldn't be the case, that the secrecy it was predicated upon had infected it, terminally.

This realisation had broken her heart. But there was nobody she could talk to about it because not a single person – not even Star or Alice – knew.

As she looked outside, it occurred to Molly that she would have to make a choice, fast – one she wouldn't be able to foresee the consequences of.

'Let's go out there,' said Noah, putting down his glass. 'Out on the bridge. We can do a rain dance.'

'We might get struck by lightning,' said Molly, hedging still. There was a full moon that night; Star had informed her earlier. Typical Star mumbo-jumbo, but she couldn't deny the sliding sense of transition vibrating in the very molecules around them. One of those nights – they'd had them before – when all the pieces got thrown up in the air and arranged themselves anew.

'Rubbish,' said Noah, still at the age of invincibility.

'I don't think it's a good idea,' said Molly. The bridge spooked her a little, even in the day, when the rising tussocks of grass and astonishing yellow poppies could almost look pastoral, if you ignored the glint of discarded cider cans, the drunks making crop circles as they slept. Alice and Star had no such qualms and liked to sunbathe out there, bikinis on bath towels; little and large.

'Come on.' Noah already had the window half cracked open, and he disappeared outside. The sound of a thud as his feet hit the ground. Molly hesitated for a full second before joining him, hoisting her thighs over the edge of the windowsill and squeezing herself out into the warm darkness before dropping down. As her feet landed, the sky above her cracked open with a flare of light, followed almost immediately by a low roll of thunder.

'The storm must be right above our heads,' said Molly, as a warm raindrop landed in the centre of her forehead, like a mother's kiss.

In the darkness, the railway bridge was an unknowable landscape, and she shuddered to think about the creatures curled in the weeds. On the mornings after she had spent a night asleep on the leatherette sofa, she would sometimes look outside at the bridge and notice all the spiderwebs, early sunlight embossing the dewdrops; appreciable from a safe distance.

'Shall we go right? Towards the City?' asked Noah. The skyscrapers were still illuminated, like docked cruise ships, hundreds of bright windows which probably contained people still working. People like Lucas in ties and shoes which shone like black glass.

'I don't know. No. The others will be back soon. And it's pretty wild out here,' said Molly. She shivered, although it wasn't cold.

'Come on,' said Noah, reaching out his hand for hers, the first time he ever had.

'All right,' said Molly, still reluctant, but intrigued by the turn the evening was taking and the revelation of his skin – his palms didn't carry even a hint of clamminess. She had so nearly stayed in her flatshare that night, a two-bed she shared with a Kiwi called Jenn. Jenn of two 'n's was the ideal flatmate – she didn't endlessly co-opt the washing machine (Alice) or play music late at night (Star). But they weren't like friends, more like colleagues, keeping the tiny top-floor flat clean and co-existing. 'I'm just wearing these stupid sandals, and I don't want to cut myself or stand in shit or something.'

'You'll be fine,' said Noah, and she saw his teeth in the gloom as he smiled to himself.

So, they walked, hand in hand, along the path worn by the others who had dared to venture that way. Beneath the bridge, they could hear cars, people singing and shouting as they moved between sticky-floored bars on Kingsland Road, the cut and thrust of the city night. Affixed to the bridge's metal girders were fluorescent lights in the shape of birds, neon-pink shapes fixed in futile flight, trying to reach the clouds above in that milky urban orange.

Molly could see through the windows of other flats, the fairy lights and peace lilies of people she would never meet.

'You know they are planning to extend the line,' said Noah. 'Turn this back into a railway track again?'

'When?' said Molly.

'Next year, I think. These flats will be impossible to live in, including ours,' said Noah. 'The noise. Eveyone is going to have to move out.' His hand was still in hers, but his face turned towards the sound of the traffic. Somewhere out there were their friends. Maybe in the bar on the square, embarking upon those spirograph conversations that had no end, and that they picked up again every time they drank, overlapping circles that took you nowhere. Star and Alice might already be dancing; they were usually the first.

'Really?' Molly said, twitching as something slinked past her ankle, and letting out a muffled moan of instinctive horror. 'I think a rat just ran past me. Ugh.' The recollection of fast-moving fur.

'Are you sure?' Noah's voice slid up the register. He hated vermin, Molly knew.

'I am sure. I want to go back now. Come on.' Molly tugged his hand.

'I can carry you back?' he said, an apparent effort to disguise his own discomfort. 'If you want.'

'What?'

'Seriously. Get on my back,' said Noah.

Molly looked at him and then at her feet. She climbed onto his back, looping her arms around his neck, her legs around his waist. Noah wasn't as tall as Lucas and Tommy, but he was more densely packed, possessed of a pleasing muscularity. He didn't look like an individual who spent hours every day in the library, who had embarked on an obscure PhD in textual differences between different folio editions of Shakespeare's plays. She clung on, legs dangling.

She wondered what the other man she was seeing would think if he could see her. He wasn't the sort to casually proffer a piggyback or indeed to demonstrate any kind of physical attention in public. Only in private, he held her with a reverence that alternately thrilled her and made her uneasy. It was hard to believe that someone else was interested in her too – if only she could have told the Molly of just five years earlier, so convinced of her undesirability.

'Giddy up,' said Molly, giggling, and Noah set off, jauntily, back in the direction of the window into the flat. After a minute, Molly rested her chin against the top of his head, the chestnut brown Astroturf of his hair cushioning the jolts of movement. Neither of them was to know that it was in exactly that same manner that their daughter, Bella, would one day do the same thing.

4

Riad Mousseline, Marrakesh

Friday afternoon
Twenty-two years later

Molly couldn't avoid further exposure. Alice and Lucas's weekend demanded the peeling away of layers; she may as well accept it. She was to be a piece of fruit; skin pared away with a serrated knife. A skinned rabbit. A winkle extracted from its shell with a pin.

In the alleyway which led to Mousseline's unprepossessing wooden door, she had encountered Alice also returning from the central square.

'Had fun?' asked Alice, her new bangles jaunty against her brown forearm.

'Yes,' said Molly. 'You were right to give the storyteller a miss though. It turned out to be a bit disappointing.'

'Thought as much. I bought some orange-blossom water,' said Alice, holding up a white plastic bag. 'Smells like heaven.'

She reached in and uncapped a small bottle, holding it to Molly's nose.

'That's incredible,' said Molly, obediently inhaling the scent, then sniffing again more deeply. It was like nothing else she had ever smelt before.

'I know,' said Alice. 'We should have a hammam now. Come on. It will get all the dust off. Make us feel scoured and clean. Your skin feels amazing afterwards – like silk. And after that, we're going to have a drink on the terrace. A proper one.'

Molly agreed, to the hammam at least. Its uterine warmth appealed, as did the idea of being touched by someone who didn't ask anything of her apart from money. But she was hoping to get away with another mocktail. After close to thirty years of casually equating enjoyment with oblivion, the previous week had brought her up short, particularly her expression in the sitting-room mirror after she had scratched Noah: one of blank, almost blissful, derangement. She had looked old and mad and revolting.

Molly went up to her room. She reached for her phone on the side table and pressed the home button. There wasn't a message from her husband, just the background picture of Bella and Eve on the broad step out to their back garden; arms draped over each other's shoulders. It showed them in the very spot in which Molly had sat herself with her daughters when they were newborns, wrapped up in the yellow waffle blanket she still had lodged at the back of her wardrobe at home. She never imagined that they would still live in the flat when the girls were teenagers. She had assumed that something would happen to transform her circumstances, but it never quite had. Perhaps now, with Noah's newly higher profile, it finally would, although Molly wasn't sure, the way things were going, that she would be a beneficiary. She paused with the device in her palm. Her apps beseeched her, but she placed it back down.

Was Noah really not going to come? It scarcely seemed possible that her husband, who sported his emotions capillary-close, was going to do something as cold as not show up. Besides, Bella and Eve knew they had planned the weekend for months – how would it look to them if Noah stayed at home? She didn't want to field off more questions from Alice, or cope with the frown on Lucas's forehead as he whirringly discerned something afoot. Her oldest friends. In one sense, she could always rely on them, but in another, she was so knotted into the past when she was around them that she could no longer tell what she thought about anything.

Molly went into the bathroom and looked at her expression in the mirror above the sink. She lifted the skin at the side of her temples with her fingertips and then sighed. She riffled in her sponge bag and found a foil strip of medication. She popped out a white tablet and swallowed it with a slurp of water from the gold tap. Sertraline. It helped her function, but it was no magic spell. She stared at her expression again, resignedly, and left the bathroom.

Alice had told her that the hammam was on the ground floor, tucked away behind the kitchen. Molly still hadn't seen Mousseline's owner ('A real *character*,' according to Alice), but she heard voices coming from what she took to be the kitchen, for it emitted a fragrant fug of rice, meat and sugar. A cat slinked its way across the courtyard, spotted like a toy leopard. Molly watched it meander past the orange tree, jump up by the fountain and pause, face inches above the water.

She turned and found what she presumed was the door to the hammam.

Behind it was a plump, watchful woman in a black T-shirt dress and flip-flops. She smiled at Molly, extending a cushioned hand, but a reserve to her greeting made Molly feel judged.

'Mol!' Alice was already there, wearing just her bikini bottoms, the stripes of her ribs visible, a piercing glinting in her navel. In place of the old T-bar, a ring encrusted with tiny diamonds, chips of trapped rainbow. Molly knew without asking that they would be genuine. 'You made it. I was starting to get worried you'd got lost. This is Camille. She is going to scrub us down.' Camille's expression was unreadable.

The hammam was a cave, the entirety of the small, hot space bedaubed in a smooth, flesh-coloured plaster, *tadelakt*. There wasn't a window, but a succession of circles at the top of the wall revealed the pale sky outside, shifting into an evening of yawning perfection.

Camille motioned for Molly and Alice to sit down.

'First, you steam, and then I'll ...' She gestured a scrubbing action with her fists in the air. The two women nodded obediently. 'Your skin is like a map,' said Camille. 'I can tell how you eat, if you are sad ... But, first, you need to get very hot.' She nodded and slipped out.

'It's boiling in here,' said Molly, sitting down on the shelf inbuilt into the wall. She could feel the sweat gathering in her armpits, pooling at the backs of her knees. She was self-conscious being in such a confined space with Alice, worried about the revelation of her own ageing body at such close quarters. She glanced up at the snatches of sky through the odd portholes.

'Yes,' said Alice, but with satisfaction. 'Lovely, isn't it?' Alice had always run hot. In the old days, she had had a soft spot for dousing herself with the kind of lotion that made you crisp like an oven chip. SPF 2. Alice opened one eye. 'Just lie down, mate. Give it ten minutes. You might even relax.'

'OK.' Molly untied the robe she had found in the hotel room and positioned herself at right angles to her friend. She shut her eyes and tried to silence her nakedness. The nipples from which Bella and Eve had dangled, the ghostly striations on her hips, the stubble along her bikini line. After a while, she started to drift, the warmth and sense of acquiescent exposure taking her somewhere else altogether. Another holiday, a long time ago. In those days when Lucas still hadn't chosen between Star and Alice, when she and Noah were new.

'Bliss, isn't it?' said Alice, who had positioned herself on the shelf on the other side of the small room. She touched her toes to Molly's, affectionately, and Molly forced herself back into the present. 'Everything OK, Mol?' added Alice. Molly kept her eyes shut. 'Seems a bit weird Noah isn't here yet?'

'It's fine,' replied Molly. 'It was just a last-minute rewrite he needed to do on his latest paper. Everything has fallen behind – with the show.' She knew how unlikely the excuse truly was. Yes, the documentary had taken Noah's career in a new direction, but he still set his own deadlines for his research, and this weekend had been in the diary for months. But Alice seemed satisfied.

'He's been working hard,' commented Alice. 'Noah. With the series?'

'Yup,' said Molly, pressing a foot against the seamless plaster of the wall. That part was accurate, at least. The programme had taken over Noah's life. *Shakespeare's Compulsions*. A chance for Noah to charmingly expound, much as he had been doing to his undergraduates for many years, on his favourite subject: textual differences between the tragedies. Noah's ebullience made him a natural on camera, and he had drawn instant approval on social media after the previous week's debut episode, for his corduroy jackets and professorial enthusiasm. It helped that he hadn't lost any of his nutmeggy hair, that his face retained a boyish appeal despite its creases.

Molly was pleased for him; of course, she was, although she had a slight sense of disbelief at the cliché of it: that men were allowed this second act, to become sex symbols in middle age. Her husband's abiding passion for his subject also chafed. Molly's convictions about the critical importance of her job, comforting for so long, had been ground down by years of closely monitoring seven-year-olds' grasp of subordinate clauses when all she wanted to do was try to get them to love stories. Increasingly, she saw herself as a kind of butcher, moulding sausages into links.

Molly debated for a second about saying more to Alice,

pausing on the threshold of having an entirely different week-end to the one she'd planned. *I think my marriage could be over*, she could say. *I'm not sure we'll be able to get past this.* Instead, she resorted to the safety of well-worn complaints.

'It's made the housework situation even worse. He's like a water-skater on the pondlife of our house.'

'Ha,' said Alice, grinning.

'You know Marcel has diabetes now?' said Molly, relieved to have found a conversational route. 'Well, Noah says there's no way he can inject the cat. It's too visceral apparently, he might actually *faint*. I don't know what he thinks I'm going to do.'

'Honestly, if men had to do something as medieval as childbirth – or menopause – the world would be a different place,' said Alice, with a cackle. 'We're tougher.'

'It's more than that though. I always imagined that we'd change as we got older,' said Molly. 'And I suppose in some ways we have ...' She gestured at her body, ruefully. 'But in a certain sense, we've dug down into our positions more than ever before. Noah really likes continuity – he wouldn't especially mind if we never move from our flat, or if we go to the same campsite in France every summer. I just want to do things that are different before I die, even if they don't turn out to be as good – the difference itself is worth it to me.' Molly stopped. She hadn't spoken these thoughts before. And what she said was true. Yet, in fact, it was Noah who was trying new things in his career, and life, not her.

'I think that's a good thing,' said Alice. 'An appetite for new things.'

'But I still don't want to spend a night watching a Coen Brothers' film, or listening to reggae,' said Molly. 'I can't go that far.'

'You don't like reggae?' queried Alice.

'I always assumed it would grow on me,' replied Molly. 'But I've realised that won't ever happen.'

'Novelty is fun, but people don't really change,' said Alice. 'You should definitely have understood that by now.'

Molly looked over, surprised at the sudden sadness of Alice's tone. But then they were interrupted by the shuffle-slap of Camille's flip-flops against the plaster. The younger woman held up a plastic tub of gooey blackness, gesturing that Alice and Molly should sit up. Molly folded her arms across her exposed chest.

'Now for this,' Camille said. 'It's a soap made from olive oil. It helps to exfoliate the skin.' She drew out the words. Again, she gestured that Molly should hold up her arms. Camille dolloped the black substance on and worked it into Molly's skin. It looked like tar but was slimily detergent against her skin.

To begin with, Molly felt stupid and revolting, an uncooked pork joint, but she relaxed into it as Camille's soft hands stroked her muscles, working daubs of the strange soap over her. Camille performed the same routine with Alice, and then she scrubbed the women down, washing the soap away with a showerhead. Then she rubbed their exposed bodies with a rough mitt, producing shocking curls of skin on their calves, upper arms, the smalls of their backs. Removing their rind.

'This is much healthier,' she said, noting Molly's self-disgust with a smile. 'It will help your body to breathe. It's good for purification.'

Molly nodded. Who would have imagined that her skin could shed itself so easily?

Camille smelt of mint and perfume and cigarettes, and Molly could see the tiny black hairs on the other woman's upper lip. Despite the workmanlike nature of the movements Camille made, the intimacy was more exhausting than she had predicted. She wondered what Noah would think of the scene. Would he find her remotely desirable if he could see into this space, so womblike and shadowy and damp? She honestly couldn't guess. She hadn't offered herself up physically like this to anyone for so long and yet had to pretend that it was no big deal.

'Look at this stuff all coming off. Dead skin,' said Alice. 'Gross.' But she was satisfied. Alice hadn't practised law since Olivia had been born. As her refracted wealth had increased, she had become the kind of woman for whom maintaining herself was vocation enough. The bleach at the tips of her hair was splashed on with painterly artistry, her eyebrows enhanced with individually tattooed strands, her skin starting to assume a certain taut lustre. Even Alice's Cupid's bow had that telltale ridge that Molly saw on so many women now on public transport, many of them not much older than Bella. Alice was fighting the dying of the light with every means at her disposal, her doll-like face ossifying into a counterfeit of what it had been when she was twenty-five.

Perhaps if she had done the same, things between her and

Noah would be different, Molly thought. It would have been a financial stretch, but she could have tried to go down Alice's route of technologically advanced maintenance, instead of merely adding creams that promised to restore radiance to her supermarket shop and begrudgingly dying her hair from a box.

In truth, she knew that how she looked wasn't the issue. The problem was that she and Noah couldn't objectively see each other any longer. They were too close and too far away.

Skin scoured, they showered and covered up again. Camille disappeared after telling them to drink plenty of water. Relieved to have her robe on again, Molly was suddenly giddy.

'That was fun. Good idea,' she said to Alice. 'I feel ... clean. Really clean. And light! I could float away.'

'There's so much filth on our skins from the city,' said Alice. 'It's good to get it off. Like a detox. A detox before a retox.' She winked.

Back in her room, Molly fell on her phone. She hadn't had any contact with Noah since the morning, the longest they had gone since getting smartphones. She wanted a jokey missive, a return to normality. But there was nothing. Instead, a message from Mina about Braxton Hicks. Was it quite normal to get so many?

Yes, totally normal, texted Molly, recalling the sensation of her stomach hardening into drum-like tautness. That sense of expectation. Just a prelude. A warm-up for the real thing.

Another from Bella, asking what the riad was like, to send her a picture. Molly frowned. Her daughters had no idea of what had happened between her and Noah, of course. And every time she thought of what came next, she saw their faces, so like their father's. Impossible to unpick it all.

She stood up from the bed and took a picture of the room. The pattern of petals on the sheets would satisfy Bella's hunger for romance and adventure. She was an ungainly, bookish girl whose extensive reading had afforded her nuanced insight into affairs of the heart, without any lived experience. Molly had been surprised at how difficult she found Bella's gaucheness, her strapping form, the tender rolls of puppy fat that larded her waist. She hadn't expected to be that kind of mother. But then, she hadn't expected her daughter's adolescence to remind her so unhelpfully of her own. At fourteen, Eve was a different proposition, already possessed of a knowingness, an instinctive sexuality, that relieved and intimidated Molly. As the message whooshed away, Molly lay back on the bed, then turned her face into the pillow.

Something about the trip, the twenty years, and the rupture with Noah had brought Star to the forefront of her mind in a way that she hadn't been for so long. The guilt, that she had got so good at squashing, had mushroomed. Molly hadn't met anyone else like Star, in all the years that had come since. Although Star had pursued an acting career, her ambition had been curiously non-materialistic. Star had sought applause, the coruscation of a spotlight; she hadn't been bothered about the spoils. Molly couldn't imagine her caring about kitchen splashbacks and sofas, like all the other forty-somethings she knew. If only she had aged alongside them, Molly knew Star would have been a welcome corrective.

It was Star who had convinced Molly to leave journalism

when everyone else was advising her to stick it out. After extensive work experience, Molly had scored the editorial assistant role at a newspaper supplement, a dream starting point, but she'd struggled with the urbane bitchiness of her colleagues, the obsequious PRs, the endless mound of products she had to corral for photographic shoots, desirable to begin with, but after a while just more stuff. She had been overwhelmed by a conviction that she ought to do something more worthwhile with her time.

'Fuck it. Leave,' Star, who had just moved in with Alice and Lucas, had said. 'You've only got one life.'

'But it's an amazing opportunity,' Molly had said, repeating the ricocheting words in her head that her mother, Alice, and even Noah, had voiced.

'Not if you hate it,' Star had replied.

'If I stick it out for another year, then I should be able to get a great job.'

'Do you want to be like your boss?' Star had asked. 'That's the question you should ask.'

Molly had considered her editor; a woman convinced – possibly correctly – that her power correlated directly to her unfriendliness and who was so time-poor that she was often to be found jogging along the newspaper's corridors in her kitten heels, a stack of page proofs held against her chest.

'Nope.'

'So, leave. Write your own stuff. Or do something else. Screw them and their cushions.'

Star's counsel had helped Molly summon up the courage. The plan had been to pursue her writing, but the teaching career she had chosen as an adjunct had increasingly consumed her energy.

Star hadn't been there to see her grow disillusioned with that too.

There was a soft knock at the door. Molly turned, imagining it to be Alice, looking to borrow deodorant, to gossip, to summon her up to the roof to enjoy herself.

'I'm not ready yet, Al—' said Molly, as she swung open the door. 'Oh, sorry ...' For it wasn't Alice, but a tall woman, at least a decade older than Molly, with a nimbus of pewter hair and fortunate cheekbones. She was dressed entirely in black, an elegant crow.

'Sorry. Don't want to disturb. I just wanted to introduce myself,' said the woman, with a French accent. 'I'm the Mousseline's owner. Lilith. I like to say hello to everyone staying here when I get the opportunity – my guests. I'm just sorry not to have done it sooner, but I've been working away in my office downstairs. And I like to allow everyone to settle in without my breathing down their neck.'

'Molly,' said Molly, extending her hand, feeling absurd in her robe, her indolence.

'Did you enjoy our hammam? Did Camille look after you?' asked Lilith, peering at Molly's face, as if the answer would be apparent there.

'Oh yes.' Molly touched her damp hair. 'Incredibly relaxing.' She smiled.

'Fantastic,' said Lilith. 'This is what it's all about at Mousseline. Relaxing. That is what you are here for.' She blinked; her lids were covered in iridescent eyeshadow, the shimmering green of dragonfly thorax. Her desiccated glamour chimed with Mousseline's own. She was an heirloom, like one of the pieces of antique furniture, the hanging brass lanterns, the hand-loomed rugs.

'This whole place is just …' Molly trailed off.

Lilith nodded, accepting the implicit praise. 'A total wreck, she was, Mousseline, when I bought her. *Une femme d'un certain age*. A bit like me.' She laughed heartily, dirtily. 'Restoring her has taken years. I was living in Paris to begin, but then I moved. Committed. Anyway, dinner is at eight. I just wanted to say hello. And I look forward to meeting your husband. He come tomorrow?'

'Yes, tomorrow,' Molly said. 'Unless work takes over.'

'Oh, work. Yes, I see,' said Lilith, looking at Molly with something close to sympathy.

It was only after the door closed that Molly started to cry. Softly at first, but then stingingly. It was all wrong. She had resolved not to ring first, but she could no longer resist.

She dialled Noah's number, saved as 'Home'. For so long, that's what he had been. The phone rang and rang. There was no answerphone message. She had to decide for herself that he wouldn't answer and hang up.

Star

8 a.m.

On the roof, Star is thirsty. She fantasises about fat splashes of grimy London rain on her outstretched tongue, the brook at the end of her mother's garden, running through the valley like a vein. Finally, with a grimace, she takes a slug of Cal's abandoned drink from the previous evening. Melted ice cubes and lemon, a vodka afterburn.

She was trying to do the right thing in coming here last night. She owed it to Cal to say a proper goodbye before leaving Sydney at such short notice.

The party was held by their mutual boss, Pete, an entrepreneur whose varied interests included a stake in the restaurant they worked in, so it provided a perfect opportunity to see Cal one last time. And even though it was her last night, and she wasn't heartbroken to be leaving Sydney – a city she knew, deep down, wasn't for her – she was also intrigued to see Pete's rumoured penthouse, so different from the hostels and shared bedrooms she has spent months staying in.

It had been a thrill to travel up twenty floors – twenty! – in the lift and emerge into the minimal space, a millionaire's bachelor pad, with nary a pop of colour, just those many shades of beige, parquet floors that shone like syrup and a modern chandelier, tessellated glass fixed in a circle. On closer inspection, the penthouse wasn't to Star's taste. It had the look of a show home: no books anywhere and the arid kitchen of someone who seldom cooks. Star prefers a place to look as though somebody occupies it. Still, she had exclaimed over the undeniable opulence, exhaling sharply at the view of Sydney, spread dials of light, through the glass bifold doors which ran along one wall. She hadn't imagined quite how much time she was going to have to contemplate it.

Pete, at least twenty years older than the majority of his guests, had spent the evening on the sidelines, paunch warping the pinstripes of his shirt: the sort of vampiric middle-aged person who draws energy from the young. Pete gave Star the creeps, but she started to enjoy herself nonetheless. A few drinks helped. She reasoned that the long plane journey back to London would give her plenty of time to sleep off a hangover.

Star rests her forehead against her bare knees. Someone must come soon. She just has to keep her cool. Lucas wants her back. He actually rang and then put money in her bank account for the flight. Perhaps the pain of the last year – her friends lost and ambitions shelved – will be forgotten. She can return to London, and things will revert to how they were when life seemed rich with colour and possibility.

She frowns. There is a problem with this line of thought. Alice *is going to be so ... furious. Her parents will have spent a fortune on the wedding, because that's the kind of people they are. The marquee is undoubtedly already erected between the rose bed and the greenhouse in their Kent garden, in the shadow of the village church. The caterers will be booked, Alice's dress adjusted to encase the tidy cylinder of her gymnast's body perfectly. Still, even Alice's anger – that white-hot rage that Star has long sought to avoid – will be worth it.*

At the realisation of ebbing time, Star goes back to the glass door and beats on it again, as she already has so many times.

'Help,' she calls. 'I'm stuck out here. Let me in.' But her voice is reedy after so much shouting. Nobody stirs.

5

Riad Mousseline, Marrakesh

Friday night
Twenty years later

By the time Molly had showered off the residual grease on her skin and returned downstairs, Lucas and Alice were installed in a corner of the dining area, which opened off one side of Mousseline's central courtyard. Viv had arrived with Iona and sat opposite. Swatches of silk in clashing jewel shades of sapphire, emerald and pink hung on the walls, a style that Molly was starting to realise originated from Lilith rather than being authentically Moroccan. On the low dining table, tea lights flickered between ceramic bowls of olives and pistachios, robed in their shells.

The sound of conversation overlaid the trickle of water from the fountain. A savoury animal smell nosed out from the kitchen, mingling with the slightly faecal perfume of jasmine. Alice had told her earlier that, alongside the *fattoush*, they were to eat pigeon dusted in icing sugar. A speciality that Molly suspected got wheeled out for bored tourists rather than the genuinely hungry.

As she approached the others, Molly hoped that her face didn't reveal the way that she had spent the previous hour. She had tried to call Noah again, to no avail, and had ended up balled on the four-poster, replaying what they had said to each other over the previous few days. They had made it this far. It had been fair to assume certain things. Yet it was almost as if she had been waiting for this since they had got together and she had first deceived him by omission. How provisional it was revealed to be, this edifice they had built.

Eventually, she had pulled herself together, threaded hoops through her lobes, dried her hair, applied her customary piratical ring of kohl around her eyes. She might not spend the hours that Alice did maintaining herself, but she remained attached to her eyeliner as a tribute to her former self, even if, these days, it immediately transferred onto her eye socket, forming sad spectres on her lower lids.

They had planned the weekend for months. A *minibreak*: the very word spiking chemicals in Molly's bloodstream. She had pored over the clothing catalogues that she usually ignored, choosing outfits for the Friday meal, the Saturday brunch, the main party on Saturday night. That new swimsuit, architectural in its boning. A wide-brimmed hat of supple straw. Spending more than she usually did, could afford. The anticipated sensation of warmth on her back, of the souk's hustle and sway, of not having to rinse out cereal bowls and pour biscuits into Marcel's bowl.

But the trip was no longer shimmering on the horizon. It was actually happening, shorn of its anticipatory glow. Molly had told herself she wanted to get away, that she would be able to see her life more clearly from a distance. Now she was here, and this presumption seemed risible. She felt stupid and exposed in the new muslin dress, simple as it was. What had she been expecting? To desire and be desired, perhaps, again. To feel that flame sputter in her chest like a flicked lighter. To feel that her life contained more than full stops.

Lucas and Alice were already in session, heads leaning attentively as they talked to the new arrivals. Molly could tell, even as she walked towards them, from the solicitous way they held themselves, that they were assessing Iona, taking in every single detail, from her fingernails to her hair. They would be doing so in that scrupulously polite, relentless way of theirs.

They had all assumed that Viv was asexual. In the warehouse years, she hadn't had so much as a hint of a boyfriend. Then later, as her career had taken off, she had always claimed not to have the time. In the face of their lemming-like domesticity – bar Tommy – she had been resolute in her aloneness. A wonderful friend and aunt, who owned her own flat, a triathlete, a serial trustee. They had stopped expecting anything else. Viv had never formally come out, but when Alice had sent out emails about the weekend, she had said that there was someone she wanted to bring: a woman she had met at work.

What Molly noticed about Iona was her youth. This was the defining thing. Molly couldn't guess at how old she was

– somewhere between late twenties and early thirties, her cheeks bouncily undemanding.

'Mol!' Viv reached over the table for Molly. 'It's so good to see you. You look great. This is Iona …' Viv beamed, and Iona smiled too. She might have been young, but she wasn't remotely shy. She was established, her bosom a coastal shelf, her grey eyes appraising and unafraid, a pennant of ruler-straight, light-brown hair hanging down her shoulders.

'I'm just so delighted to meet you, Molly. Viv has told me so much about you.' They shook hands then, laughed at the incongruity of it.

'It's so great to meet you too,' said Molly. She slipped in next to Viv and nodded at Lucas and Alice.

'You look hot, Molly,' remarked Alice. 'Doesn't she look *gorgeous*, Lucas?'

'Thanks,' said Molly, touching the panel on the front of her dress, a triangle of black sequins rough under her finger-tips. She knew that Lucas wouldn't think she looked good. He never had for a second found her attractive, even decades earlier. She intuited this, and the feeling was mutual. She had never understood what drew in Star and Alice. Lucas was clever, yes, and capable, but he was too concerned about what others thought of him. Noah, despite his job, was a man rooted in the corporeal, someone for whom taste and touch held sway rather than other people's judgements. This she had always loved about him, even if she now struggled with its consequences.

She reached forward for a pistachio and denuded it with her thumbnail. She thought of how Noah ate nuts, cramming them in. He would already have a pile of shells on the table in front of him, would be taking great slugs of lager, warming to a theme.

'Starters should be out soon,' said Alice, looking in the direction of the kitchen. 'Well, this is *fun*, isn't it? Iona was just telling us about her *work*.'

'Drama workshops,' said Iona. 'For kids usually. But sometimes corporate too.' Her accent was luxuriant Estuary.

'She came into our office to do one,' said Viv.

'I was dressed as a clown,' explained Iona. 'Green wig, face paint, a red nose ...' The words summoned comedy, but she said them laconically, her expression regal.

'Wow,' said Molly. 'I never knew you had a thing for ... clowns, Vivi.' It was a half-hearted joke, but they all laughed, the vision of Iona as a clown a little terrifying.

'Neither did I,' said Viv. Her face was transcendent with love, softened and transposed. She looked prettier than Molly had remembered, her eyes a hitherto unnoticed tawny gold. They had assumed that Viv didn't need what everyone else did; they had been wrong. 'Turns out she made an excellent clown,' added Viv. She and Iona smiled privately at each other and touched hands. Molly imagined that Iona could make a compelling clown; she had a true performer's dense, agile presence, that black-hole attention-suck.

'Drink?' said Alice, looking at Molly.

'Going to stick with soft,' replied Molly.

'Don't be boring!' sang Alice. She placed a hand on Molly's arm. 'Please.'

'I'm not. It's just ...' Molly rolled her eyes. After scratching

Noah's cheek and catching sight of her reflection, she had grabbed a candlestick and smashed it against the gilt-framed mirror hanging above the mantlepiece, the one into which they tucked invitations or favoured photographs. She had been hoping for the sound of shattering, a percussive crescendo for her anger. But she had merely cracked the glass so that her pathetic reflection had been further distorted.

'A glass of wine isn't going to do you any harm,' said Alice. 'Get red. It's good for your microbiome.'

'What will they come up with next? But no – I'll have one of those ones I had earlier,' Molly said. 'It was delicious.' That wasn't true. The drink had set her teeth on edge, but she knew that once she succumbed to wine, it would be like backflipping off the high dive. The truth, or some version of it, would spill out before she had finished her first glass.

'Hey, where's Noah, Mol?' asked Viv.

Molly tried to keep her face composed, blood throbbing in her ears. She didn't have the sunglasses any more. She would probably be OK with Viv. It was Alice she worried about.

'He got held up – work thing in the department. One of the old guard is retiring. He should be here tomorrow.' She looked down at the tablecloth so as not to see if Viv was still looking at her or not.

'I thought you said it was a paper,' said Alice.

'A bit of both, really,' said Molly, not meeting Alice's gaze.

The hummus arrived shortly afterwards, followed by the *fattoush*. Then the sugared pigeon. It was sweet and savoury, delicious and disgusting all at once. After the group had eaten it, they were brought *baklava*, by Lilith, on wide silver trays. Tiny, sticky pillows soaked with syrup and dusted with cinnamon.

Noah would have demanded the recipes. He was a committed gourmand who liked to prepare weekend feasts; Catalan fish stews and gyoza dumplings – technical cooking which used every pan in the kitchen and required the purchase of unusual jarred ingredients, the remains of which would fester at the back of the fridge in perpetuity. But they weren't the kind of couple in which only one person cooked. It was just that Molly took on the more everyday stuff, although increasingly the sheer relentlessness of meal production had got to her. It just disappeared. All that effort just gobbled up as if it were nothing.

'I hope you are all having fun,' Lilith said, clapping her hands together. She had teased her hair into a beehive and wore a velvet dress as if she, too, were a guest.

'Wonderful, thanks.' Lucas stretched his arm along the back of Alice's chair so that his watch glinted against the golden hairs of his forearm. That discreet but eye-wateringly expensive watch that Lucas had once explained was part of the unwritten dress code at his firm. 'This place is amazing. That meal was sublime. Thank you, Lilith.' He spoke as if they were old friends, not paying customer and host.

'Oh, you're welcome. Perhaps head up to the terrace now for some air? More drinks?' said Lilith. 'I'll get Mohammed to bring them up.'

Everyone murmured their thanks, gathered themselves and headed back through the courtyard. The stars were splashed across the sky above them and the breeze carried the smell of the city's tannery quarter, a raw undernote of animal skin. Somebody had turned on fairy lights concealed in the trees, bestowing electric blossom.

Molly could see that the others were already on their way; talking more loudly, limbs looser, cheeks coloured, eyes sparkling. She longed to join them in that familiar whooshing and slipping away; the delectable numbing.

You would have thought that they might have given it up by now, pushing fifty, their joint craving for oblivion. But there didn't seem to be any sign of that. As their lives had taken on more responsibility, the yearning to step away, to get mashed, had taken on an almost spiritual urgency. The evening would take its course, wherever they were. The conversations getting more disjointed, sloshier. At some point, someone would start dancing, smoking, crying. They would remember who they had been, forget about who they were becoming. The nights they had spent together over the years joined in one long line. In a sense, they were all the same night.

Molly had talked about it with Alice once, when they were walking away from a Pilates class they had taken together at Alice's gym.

'Do you ever think about not drinking?' Molly had asked, curious. 'I mean, giving it up for good?'

'Oh, I couldn't,' said Alice, her top unzipped so that her astonishing mint all-in-one remained visible. 'Too boring. I'm not dead yet. Besides, I look after myself. Life is all about balance, it doesn't pay to go to extremes. Moderation in all things, Mol.'

Perhaps Alice's internal organs were pickled, despite her carefully maintained exterior. Still, Molly knew what her friend had meant. Sometimes survival required moments of chemical transcendence. How else to achieve them in middle age?

Alice and Viv paused in the courtyard to admire the moon, fatter and pinker than at home. Molly approached them and rested her head on Alice's shoulder from behind.

'Hey,' Alice laughed at the display of affection, leaning back into Molly.

'Dinner was even better than I thought. Thanks for bringing us to such a stunning place,' said Molly, wrapping her arms around Alice, suddenly grateful for her formidable energy, her standards. 'And for forcing us to make the effort, as usual.'

'I'm just pleased we're here together,' said Alice.

The women stood together for a few minutes, loosely tethered by Molly's arms.

Star

Star keeps sentry by the locked glass door. She longs to slump on the sunlounger again, but if she does, she fears she'll fall asleep — and then she will definitely miss the plane. Her body jangles with unmet need — thirst and a contradictory need to wee.

She has spent the last ten minutes calling out again, amplifying her voice as best she can. It seems incredible that Pete hasn't heard her.

Then a horrible understanding descends — what if Pete isn't actually in his flat? Perhaps he has left early for work, in the time she was unconscious, or ended up spending the night somewhere else, with one of those other waitresses from the restaurant that he was so attentive towards? The apartment had an unlived look; perhaps Pete only uses it for his parties.

Star whimpers. No, that can't be right. She is scaring herself.

She had meant to tell Cal about her unexpected flight home as

68

soon as she arrived. After all his kindness towards her, she owed him that. But she put it off. She was sheepish about leaving, that was the truth. She had complained often enough about Lucas to Cal – this was a pivot that she was going to struggle to explain. So, she drank cocktails and chatted to the other guests, delaying the inevitable.

When it got to midnight, she realised that she couldn't postpone it any longer. It was high time she exited, to finish packing and get some sleep. She had asked Cal to step outside onto the roof terrace – despite the evening's chill – so that she could explain her decision in private.

She had known Cal wasn't going to like it, but not for a second had she anticipated his reaction. They hadn't so much as kissed! She had spent hours talking to him about Lucas! She supposes she has been grateful for Cal's attention, the validation of it. She may have flirted with him a little, out of sheer habit, in the months that they had known each other, but she had always been absolutely clear that her heart lay somewhere else.

Obviously though, in retrospect, Cal had started to hope something was going to happen between them. After he had stormed back inside, she had remained outside on the roof terrace for ten minutes, gathering her thoughts. If only she could want Cal, her life would be so much easier, but it was Lucas. For so long, it had only been Lucas.

Eventually, she had stood and tried to go back into the apartment. It was only then that she realised that Cal must have pulled the bifold door shut as he left, accidentally locking her out. She had started calling out, assuming that it would only take a minute for someone to get her. Then she had progressed to shouting – then screaming. She hadn't bargained for how drunk the remaining guests were, how loud the music, how the thick interior curtain hid her from view. In the angry state he was in, Cal had probably left the party immediately, not staying long enough to realise she hadn't re-emerged. He must have travelled downstairs in the mirrored lift, crossed the marble lobby and returned to his flat.

She is forgotten. Cal will assume she is heading for the airport. He won't be worrying about her whereabouts, he'll be trying to scrub any vestiges of her from his mind. And if she doesn't get out of here soon, she'll lose the second chance that Lucas has offered her. Forever.

* * *

It was the morning before that everything had changed.

'Star! It's for you.' One of her flatmates, Rachel, had held the phone out as Star wandered out of her bedroom and into the hall. Star had been dressing for the lunchtime shift at the restaurant, buttoning up the white blouse with the tiny lobster above the breast pocket.

'Hello?' Star had answered in confusion. Only her mother had the landline number for the house she shared with four other British backpackers, and they'd already spoken that week.

'Star?' Lucas's voice in her ear, as if he were just next to her, instead of across continents and oceans.

'Lucas?' Star had been incredulous. A spurt of something in her chest that she had almost forgotten how to feel. Hope.

'Yes. I rang your mum and got your number. I needed to talk to

70

you. I miss you so much.' A pause. 'I'm so sorry. For not believing you. I made a terrible mistake.'

Star hadn't answered. She had wanted Lucas to apologise for so long that the sound of him actually saying the words didn't seem real. She took a deep breath and fixed her gaze on the corkboard in front of her, covered with flyers for takeaway pizzas, dance classes and reflexology sessions.

'I want to make it up to you. I can't go ahead with this—'

'The wedding?' Star had returned to herself, biting her lip.

'You need to come back. Before it happens.'

'Luc ... it's Thursday morning here. I'm just getting ready for work. You're marrying Alice on Saturday. What are you talking about?' Fury had closed Star's throat. It had been more than a year since she had moved out of the flat she shared with Alice and Lucas. A long and lonely year for her, but a fruitful one for her former flatmates: they had bought a property and planned a wedding, with remarkable speed. Yet, despite how busy he'd been, Lucas could surely have found the time to get in touch with her. That he should do so now was completely unacceptable.

And yet, and yet ... this was the call she had dreamt of every day of her travels when, no matter what she did or whom she was with, the heartache didn't shift.

'Give me your bank details and I'll put the money for a ticket in your account. Get the plane tomorrow. You'll be back before it begins and then I'll have the courage to tell her I can't go ahead with it.' Lucas's voice had sounded different from usual, imbued with the emotion that he was usually so good at covering up. 'I need you here to give me the courage.'

Star had been silent. It was true that she had been mostly

miserable in Sydney, but she was building a new life, fashioning it out of sunblock and sand and tips tucked into the front pocket of her apron and chats with Cal about her mistreatment.

'Star. Please. I messed up so badly. I've realised I can't live without you. Please.'

'OK.' Star exhaled the word down the phone. OK. OK. OK. He hadn't needed to ask twice. She would be furious, but she would forgive. Of course, she would. After she had hung up, excitement rose up her body like a drawing bath. Lucas had chosen her. For that, she would give up her dingy houseshare, her waitressing job, her tentative new friendships, the Aussie sunshine. For that, she would give up anything.

Now, on the balcony, Star thinks of Alice: her charm, her entitlement, the background which will have enchanted Lucas's awful parents. She looks around the roof terrace with fresh determination. There has to be a way out of this place. There just has to be.

She frowns. If she doesn't escape soon, then Lucas will be a married man. Tomorrow.

6

Kefalonia

May
Sixteen months earlier

In retrospect, Lucas's choice seemed so obvious, it was hard to imagine that he might ever have taken a different course. But at the time, his decision hung in the balance.

Along with his precocious maturity, his Chilean mother, his graduate job in the entrails of a corporate law firm, the intellect he polished and maintained, Lucas, reserved himself, had a taste for clamorous girls, the extroverts who compelled everyone's attention. Star, like Alice, was such, although her attention-seeking was less modulated; she couldn't help herself.

She hadn't arrived from commuter land like the rest of them. From the cosy confines of Hertfordshire or Kent, that semi-detached Shangri-La of piano lessons and frozen pizza. Instead, she had grown up in Devon with a single mother, leaving school early – unthinkably before even taking GCSEs – and living an entire lifetime by the time the rest of them had graduated.

It was Molly who met her first, at Petit Soleil. A summer job for Molly, but Star had been there far longer, weaving through the gingham tablecloths in her studied get-up; pressed-powder skin, arterial red lips and Kirby-gripped curls. Molly had been charmed by her instantly. She had never met anyone like Star before, and before long, Star was indispensable.

Hard to understand the group's chemistry. There had been so many people, but something about them *worked*. Noah was childhood friends with Tommy. The rest of them, bar Star, met at university, but after graduating, they really cleaved together, around the flat, shared initially by Alice, Lucas and Noah, but then by Alice, Lucas and Star.

Lucas was still floating between the two women, his flat-mates, on that holiday. Molly could see him vacillating. He and Alice had briefly gone out together in the third year but had split to concentrate on their finals and had been scrupu-lously only friends ever since, yet now Lucas seemed to juggle the chance to restart things with her – or strike up something new with Star. Molly pitied her friends but could grudgingly understand how Lucas felt – trying to pick between Star and Alice was a little like trying to choose between the moon and the sun.

Kefalonia: a paradise overrun with stray cats. One of their first grown-up holidays, when hotels and ouzo and deciding which taverna to pick for dinner were all still novel. When all options were still open to them, paralysing and exhilarating in equal measure. They stayed in a three-star hotel, a starter hotel for their starter lives.

There had been a day on a perfect crescent of a beach situated at the end of a steep, curving descent; white pebbles, parasols striped white and lemon-yellow, sunloungers facing the lambent water. Everyone went, aside from Tommy, who was recovering from the night before in the darkened hotel room he was sharing with Lucas. Star and Alice, who were sharing a room, had argued about a towel.

'I carried it down,' said Alice.

'It's mine from the room,' said Star.

Eventually, Star had flounced off into the water, telling Alice to take it, the silly bitch, and had swum out towards the horizon. Star, a strong swimmer, kept her crawl languid and technical, despite her anger. Molly had pretended not to watch the argument but had stared at Star's departure – at first, relieved that the quarrelling between her friends had stopped, then a little disturbed as the girl's head grew smaller, a burr on the horizon. Alice and Star had always got on well, Star wouldn't have been admitted if they hadn't, but they shared a far more frangible relationship than Molly did herself with either of them. She shied away from confrontation, whereas neither of them did.

'Do you think she's OK?' Noah said to Lucas, who had looked up from his book.

'She'll be fine,' Lucas replied. 'She's the best swimmer of all of us. It's completely flat. She's just looking for attention.' The last sentence half-admiring.

But Star hadn't emerged. And eventually, they had stirred themselves into a disbelieving kind of half-baked panic. Lucas had enlisted the help of the bored teenage coastguard, sitting on his high chair, who had frowningly looked through his binoculars. Alice had started berating herself, loudly, for the argument.

'I should have just let her take it. You know what she can get like,' Alice said, shaking her head. 'Now it's my fault if she drowns.'

Noah had waded into the water and then started to swim, eventually returning and emerging from the water, panting but shaking his head. The teenage coastguard had called the help of an older man.

'This young woman – is she a good swimmer?' the older man had asked.

'Yes, very,' said Lucas. Alice stood closely at his side. They looked like the couple they weren't yet.

'Had there been any kind of disagreements?' said the coastguard.

'We'd argued a bit,' said Alice. 'Sometimes we do though, it doesn't mean anything.'

'We will keep an eye out, but meanwhile, you might like to check at your hotel,' said the coastguard. 'Let us know if you find her.'

They walked back from the beach, dazed. Their bodies sun-drunk and relaxed, despite their anxiety. And, sure,enough, they found Star there, sitting by the pool drinking a cocktail with Tommy, a strawberry daiquiri that clashed with the stripe of sunburn on her chest.

'Oh, you weren't worried about me?' she had said, eyebrow raised. 'I just went for a swim and came back here to chill with Tom. I assumed you'd realise.'

She had swum round the headland to the next inlet and sauntered through the small town in her bikini, much to the delight of the fishermen arriving back with the afternoon's catch sparkling in the bottom of their wooden boats. But somehow, instead of being furious with her, they had been merely relieved she was safe, and enchanted by her bravado, her drama, her beauty. Especially Alice, who had forgotten all about the towel and was ecstatic at their reunion, looping her arms around Star and laughing into her neck as if she hadn't been cursing her just moments before. In some ways, they were of a type, yet physically the two women could hardly have been more different. Alice a bantam blonde, Star tall and creamy and dark, like a pint of Guinness.

They had sat around the pool, eating thin, scantly salted European crisps and drinking too much. The last night of the holiday, before they all went back to their nascent careers, working out who they were going to be. Noah finishing his PhD, Lucas already making more than the rest of them combined at his firm, Alice with a different solicitor, Molly teaching in a primary school in Islington and Tommy a creative at an advertising agency. While Star was riding high on the success of a starring role in her theatre company's production of a fairy tale, *The Red Shoes*, and still doing shifts at Petit Soleil.

After a while, Tommy had stood, then dived into the deep end of the pool, sliding into the water. He erupted, gulping at the air.

'Having fun?' asked Molly, tilting her chair over to see him.

'Always,' said Tommy, hauling himself out, granting Molly one of his most radiant smiles.

He gave a good show of leisure, but Molly could sense something newly untethered in him. The latest news from his mother's consultant hadn't been good.

'How would you sell washing powder?' Tommy said to Molly, apropos of nothing, sitting down. 'You need to make it sexy, remember. Or sanitary towels?' He gave a childish giggle.

'I thought you were working on the Nike account?' said Molly.

'I *was*,' replied Tommy. 'We had a client weekend in Amsterdam, and I may have got a little bit carried away. My boss wasn't that happy, but the clients loved it at the time, I'm telling you.'

'You need to watch out, Tom,' said Molly. Tommy had become fluent in a language Molly didn't know, of story-boards, VO, pitches and accordion inserts, bleeds and blow-in cards, but his real progression had been in his blood alcohol tolerance, not to mention his threshold for other recreational drugs.

'Oh, thanks so much, but I'm OK.' Tommy took a sip of the beer in front of him. Molly suspected he had already had several before the rest of them had returned from the beach.

'How is your mum?' Molly knew that Tommy didn't want her to discuss his mother's illness, but she was also concerned that her developing relationship with Noah had unsettled him at the worst possible time. Noah and Tommy had always been so close. How could he not feel, on some level, that she had taken his best friend away?

'Still waiting for a bone marrow donor. We live in hope.' Tommy laughed hollowly.

'I'm so sorry. I really am,' said Molly, quietly, considering eye contact but finding that she couldn't bear it.

'Fancy a smoke?' said Tommy, lowering his voice.

'Wha ...?' Molly shook her head. Absolutely not.

'Brought some in my boxer shorts,' said Tommy, laughing at the expression on Molly's face. 'Don't be a bore.'

'You're mad,' said Molly, shaking her head. 'If you'd been caught ...' She thought of the policemen at the airport in Athens, with their machine guns and navy-blue berets.

'Star,' Tommy hissed. 'Smoke?'

Star nodded, and Molly watched them disappear.

* * *

'Who's more attractive?' Molly said to Noah later that evening as they lay under the floppy sheet, trying to ignore the tetchy sand that had worked its way into the bed. 'Star or Alice?'

'Seriously?' Noah shook his head. 'I can't answer that.'

'You have to,' said Molly, snuggling next to him. Her inhibitions had been stripped away by alcohol, salt water and sunshine. And, as cohabitees, they had got to the stage where supposedly nothing was off limits; answering such questions was proof of his commitment.

'OK, if I have to, then ... Al.'

'What! You fancy Alice?'

'I didn't say that, and I don't! Honestly. Neither of them is my cup of tea if I'm honest, but if I had to choose ...'

'But Star is so *gorgeous*,' said Molly, in the declamatory manner of women talking about the beauty of their friends.

'She is,' said Noah, 'I can't deny it, but ... just not my cup of tea.' He shook his head.

'OK. I get it. Alice is gorgeous too,' said Molly, lying back and looking at the ceiling. She wasn't jealous; she was satisfied by the intimacy. Noah had delivered a juicy titbit, like a cat dragging in a kill. She traced her fingertips along his chest. He tanned so much more quickly than she did, and his skin was like a hazelnut, in contrast to her freckled whiteness.

'How about you?' said Noah. 'Tommy or Lucas?'

'Yuk. I couldn't choose,' said Molly.

'You have to,' said Noah. 'I didn't make the rules.' He grinned and turned to rest on his side, propping his face up with his arm.

'Um ...' said Molly.

'Wait ... are you blushing?' said Noah.

'No!' said Molly, covering her face with her hands. Noah leant over her and kissed her hands, peeling them back and kissing her face, her cheeks, her eyebrows, the soft seam at her hairline.

'Answer me,' he said.

'I guess ... um. Lucas?' said Molly.

'Lucas?' Noah snorted. 'Surely Tommy? All the girls fancied him at our school. He's always had that thing ... I don't know, charisma.' He shrugged as if Tommy's light-bulb charm had never bothered him.

* * *

The next morning, Star and Molly walked on the harbour wall. Since moving in with Noah, she and Star had spent less time together than they had become used to, and Molly had suggested it.

'Are you and Alice fine now?' she asked, taking a deep lungful of the warm, salty air.

'Oh yes, it was just a silly row.' Star seemed distracted, looking out across the livid turquoise of the sea. 'I can't believe this island. It's so beautiful. I've never been somewhere like this before.'

'I know,' said Molly. Star's mother's fear of flying meant Star hadn't gone abroad as a child.

But Star hadn't heard her. She had run ahead, her arms spread out like wings, a striking sight with her black curls and bare feet, wearing one of the Miss Havisham-style lace dresses she'd found in a vintage shop that would have looked peculiar on anyone else.

Molly caught up. 'You know, I left my aftersun by the pool last night and when I went down to get it, I saw you and Lucas. Kissing,' added Molly.

'Yup,' said Star, a huge grin spreading across her face, spots of pink on her cheekbones from the movement.

'I didn't think he'd be your type,' said Molly.

'Why not?' said Star.

'You're so different.' Molly searched for the words. 'He's so, um, by-the-book, I suppose.'

'It's refreshing to get involved with a grown-up for a

change,' Star shrugged. 'I like that he knows things. And besides, he's different from how he seems. When we're alone. He really listens to me.'

'How long has it been going on for?' asked Molly.

'A few months,' replied Star. 'Since he came to Devon for the weekend.'

'Don't you think you ought to tell Alice?' said Molly. Star scrunched up her face.

'No?' Star said, but with the expression of someone who knows they're putting forward the wrong answer.

'I think you owe it to her,' said Molly. 'They used to have a thing, and you're all living together, it could get messy. If you're honest, I think she'll settle down and get used to it.'

'Do you think so?' Star's face was radiant with hope. 'I've been so unsure how to react and Lucas has wanted us to take it slowly, living together and everything. I've been so worried it's going to ruin everything.' Star's face crumpled.

'Here,' said Molly, pulling Star into a hug. Star smelt of coconut lotion, and Molly was surprised at the feel of her up close, so soft. 'Everything is going to be OK. I know it.'

How Molly longed, in that moment, to confide in Star her own secret. She opened her mouth, so tempted, searching for the right words, but she looked up to see Alice, progressing towards them in chino shorts.

'Star! Molly! Bakery time,' said Alice. And the three left the jetty, thoughts turning to filo and another day on the beach.

7

Riad Mousseline, Marrakesh

Friday night
Twenty-one years later

'You're a teacher?' asked Iona. They were reclining on cushions under the sail of neoprene affixed above the seating area, intended as a shield against daytime sun. At the other end of the table, Viv, Lucas and Alice were talking about the referendum's outcome, still, in agreement with one another but mining seams of enjoyable outrage nonetheless.

'Yes,' said Molly. 'Year Threes at the moment.'

'I used to do an afterschool programme in a primary,' said Iona.

'Oh, we've got one of those,' said Molly. 'I bet you were great.' Iona smiled, gracious.

'So, I heard that it's not just Lucas and Alice's wedding anniversary? The date of this weekend?' said Iona.

'What do you mean?' Molly was hesitant. She wasn't sure

how much Viv would have said to Iona; their relationship was new.

'Viv said that there was a close friend of yours who died,' said Iona. 'On the same date as the wedding.' Even in this, Iona retained her unabashed confidence. Molly had found that most people avoided direct mention of the subject if they possibly could, while simultaneously trying to truffle out details. Iona's approach was unusual.

'That's right,' Molly answered. 'Star. Twenty years ago, tomorrow. You must have just been a kid.'

'Yes, I suppose I was. It caught my attention when Viv mentioned it because she said she was a wonderful actress,' said Iona.

'That's right,' said Molly, surprised that Viv had talked about Star like that. 'She was really talented.' Molly sighed and rubbed the crease between her eyebrows, a self-soothing habit she had fallen into after her mother had exclaimed at how deep the vertical lines on her forehead had become. 'We were friends first before she met the others. We met working in the same restaurant. But she wanted to perform – like you. She worked for a theatre company that staged productions in the weirdest places. She was brilliant and gorgeous and funny. And then she went away travelling, and I – *we* – never saw her again.' The words sounded OK, Molly thought. Palatable. They didn't reveal the shameful truth: she had failed Star, when it mattered most.

'Sounds like you loved her,' said Iona.

'Oh. I did,' said Molly. 'I really did. You know when you meet someone and you can't quite believe that that person exists? They seem so much more vivid than everyone else. That's how it was when I met her. She was so full of ...' Molly looked up to the patch of inky sky visible beyond the grounded sail, searching for a word that did Star justice, but failing to find one and electing to move on. 'She must have been about your age when *it* happened. Such a waste. Of course, as time goes by, you learn to get on with things, but something about it being twenty years has brought it all back, I've got to say.' Molly swallowed, close to tears. Still, she hoped that Alice hadn't heard what she'd said. The weekend relied on omission.

'I'm so sorry. Viv said that the circumstances were distressing,' said Iona. She leant over and placed one of her square palms on top of Molly's hand. Everything about Iona was broad and calm.

'They were.' Molly frowned. Was Iona going to press for more details? Molly wasn't sure she could bear that. The facts were ugly – the closed casket, the faux-sympathetic newspaper editorials, the conjecture about Star's final hours and her line of work, about the owner of the penthouse's questionable business decisions. Molly swallowed. 'We had no idea it had happened. Those two got married,' she nodded towards Alice and Lucas, 'and it wasn't until a few days after the wedding that we heard. News didn't travel quite so quickly back then.' Toasts, a cut cake, a crowded dance floor and a feathered, rainbow flock of fascinators, all when Star had already been cold. Not to mention the declarations of eternal love which Molly had found hard to stomach, even without knowing Star's fate.

'I'm so very sorry,' repeated Iona. She squeezed Molly's hand. 'If I lost one of my friends like that, I'm not sure how I'd ever get over it. My friends are everything to me – they're like the family I've chosen.'

Molly smiled weakly. The words were intended to be kind, but it was hard not to take them as a rebuke.

Star

Star stands on the edge of a cuboid pot belonging to a tall cactus. With the extra height this affords, she can pull herself up to look over the edge of the glass barrier surrounding Pete's roof terrace.

She glances down. The drop is unreal. She has never been particularly scared of heights. She even studied trapeze for a bit, when she was considering running away to join the circus. But to be this high, in the crystalline Sydney morning air, is something else entirely.

Her cheeks sting in the breeze. Ever since the hands of her wristwatch moved to 10 a.m., Star has been unable to stop the tears. There is still no sign of life in the penthouse and it has a shuttered, vacant look that confirms her worst suspicions.

If Pete isn't there, she has to find another way out. She just has to.

Star squints, assessing her options. From this perspective, she can clearly see the ledge which runs along the outside of the barrier around Pete's penthouse roof garden and, beyond that, to the left, a glimpse of the balcony belonging to the flat below. The block is covered in a thick lattice, like honeycomb. Perhaps she could climb onto the ledge and then shin down the lattice, dropping onto the balcony below?

She might be able to escape that way and make her plane in time, but it would be risky. Very risky, indeed. One stumble, one trip, and she will be toast.

Star swallows. She realises that her hands are shaking as she grips the balustrade. She's not ready to try something so dangerous yet. She would have to be really desperate.

She climbs down from the cactus and returns to her sunlounger, lying on her side. Her body bangs with adrenaline. Fight or flight. She feels an overwhelming yearning for her mother; things must be really bad. Star seldom longs for Moira – there simply hasn't been a great deal of point. Moira is a busy woman, with lots of people to look after, people far more vulnerable and deserving than Star. That's why, since she bought a one-way train ticket to London aged seventeen, Star has seldom gone home. But how she wishes she was in her mother's house now, tea towels hanging against the Rayburn, about to eat one of Moira's bowls of vegetable soup and a cheese scone. She would open the door to call for the cat, feel the outside air blow inwards with its wet, green smell, the tug of wild garlic and mud. She is so far from home.

She has been so angry with Moira for never putting her first. For all the lodgers. Or guests, whatever you want to call them. For her father's absence. And yet, how wonderful it would be to be back there right now at the mill house in Devon, instead of stuck *here on this roof. She would be so much more forgiving.*

There are so many places she would rather be. At Petit Soleil, the French restaurant in Islington where she worked for years, with its regulation checked tablecloths and candles melted into wine bottles. Or at Molly's flat, the one she shares with Noah, sitting at her kitchen table, drinking tea and gossiping. Or back at the Lucid Theatre in Dalston, with posters tacked onto black-painted walls and dust motes dancing in the stage lights, rehearsing for a new production.

Star can see how precious these places were now, how she took them for granted. If she can only get free from this roof garden, from this city, she'll never make the same mistake again.

8

Riad Mousseline, Marrakesh

Friday night
Twenty years later

More drinks. Music played through Lucas's portable speaker. All the old favourites they had been listening to since they first met. Massive Attack. Bob Marley. Groove Armada. Aural wallpaper.

Cigarette tips gleamed in the dark. The time of night for confidences, for spilling things apart, getting to the root of things. That sense of softening, of no longer caring. The sheer cartwheeling relief. You might think they had said everything they had to say to each other, but their endless appetite for rehashing things appeared undimmed.

A string of festoon bulbs along the side of the terrace swung slightly in the temperate, indigo breeze. In the half-light, individuals looked how they always had; their gestures were the same, their essence constant. Easy to pretend for a while that nothing had changed.

After the unexpected intensity of her conversation with Iona, Molly had allowed Alice to pull her up to dance, determined to prove she was capable of having a good time without drinking. If she kept moving, she could distract herself. Although, if Noah didn't turn up by tomorrow, her excuses would fall apart.

But how could she explain it?

I let him down constantly. I knew I was doing it. Not because of what I concealed when we got together. Instead, I failed him in a thousand smaller ways. I didn't want him to touch me, but I couldn't address it. I pushed him away because I don't know what I want. And then – finally – he let me down too.

Such sentences would need to be wrenched from her. This night might be the last she had before she had to define herself in a new way.

Lucas was holding forth to Iona, explaining how his firm might fund her performance collective for a season if she submitted the correct application form. He drew down on one of the cigarettes that Molly knew he still allowed himself on high days and holidays.

'Oh yeah, don't worry about it,' said Iona, who had one arm around Viv's back. Viv had leant into it, with her eyes closed, as if basking in the sun.

'We've got a generous charitable programme,' pressed Lucas. 'It really could be worth your while.'

'We don't tend to take corporate donations,' said Iona. 'It can all get a bit ... compromising. No offence.'

'None taken,' said Lucas, but he leant forward and took a hard suck of his drink. 'A hard way to make a living, but *rewarding*, I'm sure,' Lucas continued.

'Wonderfully so,' said Iona, undaunted.

'Well, remember the offer is there,' said Lucas. 'If you change your mind. So, are you living at Viv's in Stockwell?' Viv had bought herself a terraced house long before she had had anyone to share it with, as if she had always known that she one day would. She kept it intimidatingly clean, but Molly had always told herself it was because Viv didn't have to contend with any children and their attendant clutter like she did. At first, it had been plastic toys and bouncer chairs, but now Molly had to fend off trainers clogging the hall and nut-butter-smeared knives on the kitchen surfaces.

'Moving in next week,' said Iona, glancing at Viv.

'It's just so wonderful,' said Lucas. 'We are all so thrilled that someone has finally taken Vivian in hand.' Iona's rejection had made him more emphatic, Molly noted.

'I don't know about that,' said Iona. 'She seemed to be doing a pretty good job on her own. But we're happy, that's something.'

'It's not just something. It's everything,' said Alice from where she and Molly stood. They had stopped dancing. Molly, who had been looking at the floor, was surprised by the vehemence of Alice's remark and looked up. She caught Lucas glancing at his wife and raising his eyebrows. Intention was communicated between them, and Alice visibly reined herself in from saying any more. Instead, she raised her arms and wriggled out of her dress, dropping it to the area of tiles that had become their dance floor. She was entirely naked underneath, her pubic hair the slim landing strip of a remote jungle airfield. Molly averted her eyes.

'Jesus, Alice,' said Lucas. 'Do you mind?'

Alice just looked at him over her shoulder, her expression inscrutable, and walked towards the pool she had occupied earlier in the day. Her hair swung down, covering the top of her buttocks. Alice had always had long hair, but lately, it seemed exaggerated. Molly suspected discreet extensions, realising that Rapunzel hair was a stealth status symbol for a certain kind of forty-something woman. She had accompanied Alice on the school run once, dropping Olivia off from the tinted-window-comfort of Alice's vehicle, and witnessed how closely Alice's style mirrored that of the other mothers saying goodbye to their offspring: hungry-looking bodies in milkmaid blouses, slick skin, spidery eyelashes and those tawny manes.

'You lot are pretty crazy,' said Iona. She narrowed her eyes slightly. 'I've heard some stories from Viv. I wish I'd been born in Generation X – if only so I could have afforded to buy my own place.'

'Well, it had its downsides,' said Lucas. 'And we're all terribly sensible these days.' He stubbed out his cigarette, tented his fingertips above the tiny crocodile on the front of his polo shirt.

'I think we'd better crash,' said Iona. She gently pulled Viv up. Viv, who had always looked after herself so efficiently, seemed pleased to be shepherded.

'That's so nice to see,' said Molly, moving to sit down next to Lucas.

'Yeah. Until they split up, that is,' said Lucas. 'And Viv is left washed up and heartbroken. That Iona girl is only a kid.'

'You don't know that they will,' said Molly. 'This might finally be it for Viv. She deserves it.'

'Yeah, hopefully,' said Lucas, who had picked up his phone and was flicking through it. Molly knew he didn't have time for social media; he would be dipping into his work inbox, seeking a quick reminder of his significance.

'Don't be sour, just because she wasn't gagging for your outreach programme.'

'Fuck off.' Lucas didn't look up.

'Not everybody is solely motivated by cold, hard cash,' said Molly. She laughed to make it seem like a joke. She and Lucas had been having this conversation since they had first met, and as time had gone by, their positions had only grown more entrenched. In the beginning, Lucas had argued that it was incumbent upon anyone capable of doing so to earn enough to buy a house. After that, you could turn outwards, contributing more fully to those less fortunate. But the time had never been right, it seemed, for Lucas to enact the second step of his ideology. Molly knew the truth was that he enjoyed his work and was good at it. And why not? It was hardly his fault that he was so well remunerated.

'Sure, I guess.' Lucas was expressionless as he said the words, still looking at the screen. 'I was only trying to be helpful.' His tone was light. Once he would have tried to convince Molly of his morality, but it seemed he could no longer be bothered. Lucas had succeeded so well in his chosen profession that he had absorbed its precepts and could only see the truth as subjective anyway. 'It's nice to have some fresh blood. It's hard enough to keep things going, isn't it?' He looked up at her. Molly wondered what he knew, whether he had been in touch with Noah and had some idea of what had happened. Or perhaps he had just guessed that something was afoot with his customary sharpness.

'What are you saying?' asked Molly, sitting up properly. She felt herself reddening in the darkness.

'Nothing,' Lucas replied. 'We've all just been in this for ages, haven't we? An anniversary makes you realise how long we've known each other. Golly. A lifetime.'

'Not quite,' said Molly. She looked away.

'How are things with work anyway?' asked Lucas then, placing down his phone.

'Much the same,' said Molly, unable to keep the flatness out of her voice. 'I'm literacy lead now, which is good. But we've been cut to the bone, you know how it is. Everything is a struggle.'

'Literacy lead sounds terrific,' said Lucas. 'You know there's a brilliant new children's author you ought to get in for a workshop ... I'm just trying to think of his name. You must know – the chap with the beard. Brilliant retellings of fairy tales.'

'Thanks, but I'm pretty set for the next year.'

'So, will you stay at the school?' At their last get-together, Molly had admitted to considering leaving her job.

'I wish I knew, Luc,' said Molly. 'I'm not sure about anything these days.'

'Do you ever think about her?' said Lucas. His voice was

softer than before, and Molly couldn't make out his expression.

'Star?' said Molly. So, he had been thinking about her. With Lucas, you could never tell.

'Yes.'

'Of course,' said Molly. 'Every day.'

'She'd be old now, just like the rest of us,' said Lucas. 'Weird to imagine.'

'Yes, I suppose she would,' said Molly. Star had stayed resplendently youthful in her memory, her skin the texture of double cream.

'I tried looking her up once, you know,' said Lucas. 'Googled her and whatnot. Stupid, really, but I suppose I just wanted to see if she had left any kind of digital footprint at all.' He coughed.

'What did you find?'

'Nothing. You know, back then, we didn't live our lives online. It was as if she never existed.' He tilted his head, glanced at Alice.

'Do you ever wonder how it would have been if you'd made a different decision?' murmured Molly. Just another joke between old friends.

'Yeah,' said Lucas quietly. 'Sometimes. I very nearly did. A drink?' He rose. He was wearing crumpled linen trousers, that top buttoned right up to the collar, another pair of freshly unboxed trainers. Molly knew that, for all its studied casualness, the outfit would be costly and deliberate, like everything else in Lucas's life.

'Just a Diet Coke,' said Molly.

'I can get that for you,' called out a voice, rising up from the stairs.

For a second, Molly thought it might be Noah, arrived at last, and she stood, unsure. But the tall figure that loped up the stairs wasn't her husband. This man wore a fedora, an embellishment that would have made Noah squirm.

'Tommy!' she said. 'You made it.' Molly moved forward to embrace him, trying to cover her surprise.

'Hiiiiiiiii. Last flight from Heathrow,' said Tommy, removing his hat with a flourish. The hour was dark enough that you couldn't see the colour of his skin, and for that, Molly was grateful. With the garland lights dusting the top of his icing-sugar hair, he could almost be the old Tommy before it all went wrong. She knew that in daylight, she wouldn't be able to avoid the look which had crept into his eyes.

Lucas clapped him on the shoulder. 'All right, mate. I hear you're doing well. I'm so pleased.'

'Yes, well. One day at a time,' said Tommy.

'Tom!' Alice jumped out of the pool with a splash, her nakedness satiny in the lantern light, long hair hanging over each shoulder, sodden as a mermaid's, her areolae pink.

'That is quite a welcome, Alice,' said Tommy, laughing. He held that particular energy that Molly recognised but that she hadn't seen in him for so long: the anticipatory shimmer at the start of a night out.

Molly knew that they had been starting to think of their beds, even if they hadn't yet admitted it to each other. Of brushing their teeth, taking off their watches, draping their clothes on the chairs in their rooms and climbing into those sheets, gelid from the air conditioning, which would have been turned down by now.

But Tommy had arrived; the evening began anew.

Star

In her glass cage, Star has reached the point of avoiding her watch. She can tell, by the sun's relentless ascent, that the minutes are ticking past. The anticipation of soon being back in London has helped her to realise what a half-life she's been living lately. It doesn't matter how exciting it may have looked externally – mopeds in Bangkok, full moon parties, Tiger beers on the beach, green curries, the frilled turrets of Angkor Wat – on the inside, she has been painfully lonely.

There were many nights she cried herself to sleep, thinking about Lucas and Alice, imagining her former flatmates acting out the happiness montage in a romantic comedy – Alice tasting something Lucas offers her on a wooden spoon, the pair of them roller-painting walls in their new house, Lucas unzipping one of Alice's tailored work dresses with his look of absolute concentration.

It's not just Lucas. Star has also ached for Molly, whose gentle insight she misses, and for the career she had spent so long build-ing, which looked as though it was finally going to take off after The Red Shoes *did so unexpectedly well.*

Star should have fought for these hard-won things. She can see that now. Instead of turning tail and letting Alice win. But she had felt so beaten. By Alice's betrayal and Lucas's weakness. Molly's supposition. A sequence of disasters that had climaxed with the falling apart of her theatre company, which had been broken by success rather than made by it.

With so many things going wrong, Star had begun to feel as though escape were the only option.

Now, Star finally plucks up the courage to glance at her watch. She winces. The morning marches remorselessly on. Her hangover is asserting itself and her head thumps with metronomic regular-ity.

Lucas is on the threshold of the future that Alice has promised him. A life like their wedding list, consisting of cut-glass tumblers and dessert spoons and napkin rings and convention. The life she, Star, would never be able to give him. This, she reasons, is why he behaved as he did.

She knows that Lucas won't have told anyone he rang her. It will be another secret he's keeping, like the others. And if she doesn't get back to see him, he will lock it inside and move on.

9

Shoreditch

Fourteen months earlier

Star stood on the pavement outside the Vietnamese restaurant, in front of the photographic menu of dishes, with its tofu pancakes and summer rolls, a collection of swollen bin bags at her feet. One had turned on its side, and items of clothing were escaping onto the pavement: a jumper, a pair of velvet trousers, a T-shirt with a satin rose appliquéd on the front like a gunshot wound.

'Where are you going?' Molly and Noah turned up, hand in hand. They had been down to the market, looking at the racks of vintage clothes, the tables covered in paste jewellery, the bikes hawked by desperate men who had probably stolen them from other people's front gardens only the evening before. Molly and Noah hadn't bought anything aside from bagels filled with flaccid hunks of salt beef and Polystyrene cups of coffee.

'Moving out,' said Star, shivering. 'Just waiting for a taxi to take my stuff.' Her hair had lost its bounce, and her face looked pointed and pale in the morning light. Star was seldom up this early at the weekend. She wore a cardigan with a fur collar and a pencil skirt which revealed bruises on her calves in varying shades of development, from a wretched purplish-blue to yellow-green – the product of various drunken tumbles.

'You're *what?*' said Molly.

'I can't live with them for another second,' said Star. She knelt to try to stuff the clothes back into the overfull bin bag. 'Alice—' She bit back whatever she was going to add.

'Where are you going to go?' asked Molly. 'Are you completely sure?'

'I'll find somewhere to crash,' replied Star. 'I was only subletting. My name isn't even on the lease.'

'You can't do that.' Molly was aghast.

'Why not?'

'You're paying rent here. This is your home.'

'I can't stay. Alice made that clear,' said Star. 'This has been a mistake. I'm sorry, Mol, I am. It doesn't affect anything between us. Taxi!' Star raised her hand, and a black cab thundered to a stop. 'Listen, I love you. I'll ring you – yeah?'

She bundled the escaping clothes back into place and threw her bin bags into the belly of the cab before climbing inside, waving as it pulled off. Noah waved in return, but Molly just watched.

As they watched the taxi roll up the road, Lucas came into view, walking from the other direction with his hands shoved into his pockets and a pensive expression on his face.

'Has she gone?' he asked them both. He looked past their shoulders up the road.

'Yes,' said Molly. 'What happened?'

'She and Alice had a disagreement,' said Lucas.

'What about?'

'I think you should ask one of them,' said Lucas, frowning. 'It's really not my place.'

'Oh, I wouldn't say that,' replied Molly, a scintilla of accusation in her voice. She knew what Star had said in Greece. How hopeful she had been. The situation had been bound to end in disaster.

Lucas looked up the road as if he might be able to summon back Star's cab, but then he turned and put his key in the lock.

Upstairs, the flat was already subtly altered. The windows were all cracked open, and the washing machine was shuddering to the climax of its cycle. The door to Star's room hung open, and inside was stripped of all her fripperies: the silk scarf draped over the dressing table, the mounds of clothes, the saucers holding her collection of jewellery, all gone.

'Coffee?' said Alice, standing at the kitchen counter. She wore her running clothes; Alice was a person who liked to feel the burn before such a thing even became fashionable.

'What is going on?' said Molly. 'She can't move out. That's a terrible idea.'

'She couldn't stay here, Molly!' said Alice. 'It's OK for you

– you didn't have to live with her. She – well, let's just say she crossed a line.'

'What on earth are you talking about?' said Molly. 'She's our friend.'

'Listen, I don't want to get into it,' said Alice. 'Let Star tell you.'

'So, this isn't anything to do with Star and Lucas?' Molly said. The expression on Alice's face told her everything that she needed to know. 'I know what's been happening,' Molly continued. 'She told me in Kefalonia and I said that she ought to be upfront about it.'

'What, their fling?' said Alice, wrinkling her nose. 'I know about it too, but that's nothing to do with this, and besides, that's history, isn't it, Lucas?'

Lucas cleared his throat and looked uncomfortable. It was a moment where he could have become a different man, but he opened his mouth and then closed it again, consigning himself – and the rest of them – to an unhappier fate.

* * *

Star never came to the flat again. Alice made no effort to see her; Lucas was seemingly no longer allowed. Noah and Viv tried, but maintaining the friendship involved a level of effort that their busy lives could ill afford. Only Tommy and Molly saw Star regularly in the following months, turning up at the end of her shifts to sit at the bar in Petit Soleil and order carafes of the house red.

Alice and Lucas got back together soon after Star moved out and, staggeringly quickly, left the old flat themselves and became engaged, as if the legitimacy of their reunion was predicated on speed. Lucas's salary allowed them to buy a nearby former factory worker's cottage on Colombia Road, where visitors to the flower market thronged past the living-room window each Sunday.

'It's a start,' Alice had said, filling the small red-brick house with vast bunches of flowers bought cheap each week when the market was about to finish; stargazer lilies and delphiniums, rosebuds and overblown peonies. 'I want flowers just like this at our wedding.'

Star, always the least settled of them, the one without a clear trajectory, started to look different, too, as if it needed to be marked on her body. She got a decisive tattoo on her soft, white forearm, which Molly hated. A ringed galaxy, Andromeda, a stark counterpoint to the old-fashioned clothes she favoured.

'It took five hours,' Star said, holding out her arm proudly across the bar, one afternoon not long after she had left. 'Star by name, stars by nature.'

'It's really something,' said Molly.

'Do you hate it?' asked Star, with a half-smile. 'Don't worry, you can tell me. Lucas would fucking hate it.'

'What will your mum think?' said Molly. She could only think of what her parents might say.

'Moira wouldn't give a shit,' replied Star. 'She'd like it probably. Maybe. If she even noticed.'

'Have you shown her?' asked Molly. To her, the tattoo looked a little wonky, as though whoever had done it hadn't been concentrating correctly.

'Nope,' said Star. 'I haven't seen her in months.'

'So, she doesn't know that you've moved out?'

'Not a clue. She's got some new lame ducks that she's wrapped up in – so I haven't heard from her much lately. I might go down in a bit.' Star shrugged.

'Oh,' said Molly, who couldn't imagine a life not bookended by her mother's biweekly phone calls. Diana's verdict reverberated through every decision made, still. Noah had got the seal of approval: a relief. 'Are you working on anything new with your theatre group?'

'No.' Star's face fell. 'It's all a bit of a disaster. *The Red Shoes* got us noticed, but now Mikael has been asked to head up another company and he's said yes. We haven't got a hope in hell of organising ourselves without him.'

'That can't be true,' said Molly. But then she thought of Star's bedroom as it had been, the soup of dirty washing, used mugs and magazines, and Star's inability to retain house keys and important pieces of paper. And yet she always got by.

'And I need to lose a bit of weight,' said Star. 'Working here has made it a bit too easy to eat cassoulet every day.' She laughed and lowered her voice. 'Phillipe puts so much butter into everything.'

It was true that Star's statuesque form was more solid than before, substantial. She was no longer a slip of a thing, and her girlhood was seeping out of her like water held between cupped hands. They both knew what that meant for girls who wanted to act. For women anywhere and a certain kind of attention.

'You don't,' said Molly, staunchly. 'You look gorgeous. You don't want to get stuck here for the rest of your life.'

Star was silent, face bent towards the top of the bar as she repeatedly wiped a single spot.

'What … Sorry, I didn't mean it like that, you know,' said Molly.

'You worked here too,' said Star. 'It's not something to be ashamed of.'

'I know.' Molly slapped her hand to her forehead. 'I just meant you've got so much to offer. And you and Alice need to talk. What happened between you? She wouldn't tell me – said to ask you. I still don't understand what could be so awful that you had to move out like that.'

'I don't want to talk about it,' said Star, after a pause. 'I don't want to see any doubt on your face. I saw it on Lucas's, and it was intolerable. I thought he was my …' Star hesitated. 'I thought we meant something to each other.'

Molly paused. How to tell her?

'I need to warn you about something. Lucas and Alice have got back together,' said Molly. 'They're buying somewhere. They're *engaged*.'

'What?' Star looked up, her expression disbelieving.

'Sorry. I know it's happened really fast. I wanted to be the one that told you.' Molly coughed.

Star was silent for a beat. She frowned. 'How absolutely pathetic. They're far too young for that and they only just got back together.' Star stopped cleaning the bar and sank over it.

'Star? Star? Are you OK?' said Molly.

'I'm sorry.' Star pulled herself up, her eyes pink. 'I just can't believe it. He said he loved me. I just don't understand how it could have turned out like this.'

Molly reached across and grabbed Star's hands. 'I don't either. He's … He's a coward. You are better off without him.'

'I'm not though,' said Star. 'I'm not better off. He made me feel different, as though I really could accomplish something. I've always wanted to act, but deep inside I wasn't sure I had what it took. Spending time with Lucas made me feel as if it would happen.'

'It'll still happen,' said Molly.

Star didn't reply.

10

Riad Mousseline, Marrakesh

Friday night
Twenty-one years later

With Tommy, the music had changed. Within minutes, he had assumed control of the speaker, tossing out a dry, 'Haven't you heard this often enough, you losers?' and changing it to something unfamiliar – off-kilter beats, offset by a crunching noise. Tommy had always stayed up to date with what was happening in music, as his wider life atrophied.

More drinks had arrived, as if Mohammed and Lilith knew that the party had a new sense of direction. Different cocktails, the colour indistinguishable in the darkness. Alice thrust one into Molly's hand.

'Surely now Tom's here?' said Alice, raising her eyebrows.

'Thanks,' said Molly. 'Maybe.' She took the drink, waiting until Alice had moved on before placing it on one of the side tables. Tommy's arrival was only more reason to maintain as much clarity as she could.

She sat down and watched Tommy greet the others. Lucas clapped him on the back, while Alice leant in for a prolonged hug as if she had been longing for his arrival. But Molly knew that Tommy would eventually settle alongside her. That was the way of it. An invisible wire stretched between them. All she had to do was tug.

'I thought you weren't going to come?' she said as Tommy sat down on what Molly now thought of as her cushions, the spot she had returned to since she had arrived earlier that day. Odd how quickly one assumes habits.

'Last-minute change of plan,' said Tommy. 'I was sitting at home this morning, in my flat, and I just thought … why not? It's not often we all get together any more.'

'So, are you still …?' asked Molly quietly.

'Yup,' said Tommy. 'I'm being a very good boy.' He raked a hand through his hair.

'You look so much better,' said Molly. It was true. Tommy's skin had lost its greyish cast, his eyes glittered in the gloom, and he had filled out a little, losing that cadaverous quality.

'I think I might have cracked it this time,' said Tommy. He coughed. 'Although I shouldn't say that out loud.' He frowned. Tommy was as superstitious as Star had once been.

'But are you going to be OK around everyone?' Molly gestured at Alice, who had her head tipped back as she gulped down one of the new cocktails. Despite the group's outward sympathy for Tommy, none of them had ever thought to wonder about perhaps having a weekend where drinking opportunities didn't form the spine upon which events hung themselves. Until very recently, the very idea had never occurred to Molly herself.

'I'll be fine,' said Tommy. He leant back against the cushions; his long legs stretched out on the coffee table in front of him. 'I knew this was what it would be like. It's not like I don't know you guys.'

'I didn't think you were going to come,' Molly repeated.

'I came for you,' said Tommy, lightly. Something moved in Molly's guts. 'I got a text from Noah that said—' He was cut off by Lucas striding over.

'I'm keen to venture to the Atlas Mountains tomorrow,' said Lucas. 'If you fancy a proper change of scene? The fresh air might do you good, Tom. What do you say?'

'Don't feel like you have to,' said Alice, now at her husband's side, covered again. 'The rest of us are just going to hang around here. This weekend isn't supposed to be hard work. I might visit the Jardin Majorelle if I feel like it. Yves Saint Laurent restored it after he fell in love with Marrakesh. Or I might just lie around all day and work on my tan.'

'Sounds tempting,' said Tommy. 'I'll decide in the morning. In the meantime, what I could do with is a toilet and dumping my bag somewhere? I came straight up here to this glorious roof. This paradisal garden.' He tipped his head back, exposing his throat, the hollows beside his collarbones. His fedora fell off, onto the floor, and Alice picked it up, handing it to him.

'I can show you your room?' said Molly. 'It's the one at the end of the corridor, right, Alice?'

'Yes, that's the spare,' said Alice. There was a hollow between her eyebrows where a wrinkle would be if the muscle
hadn't been paralysed at great expense. This wasn't how the
weekend was supposed to go. Tommy's invite had been a
mere formality. It had been so many years since he had at-
tended anything.

'Wonderful,' said Tommy, standing. He was still the tallest, even taller than Lucas by a smidgen, but despite a bit
of weight gain, his body was so slender that his height only
added to his air of insubstantiality.

'Come on then,' said Molly, as brisk as she would be with
Bella or Eve, an attempt to cover her uncertainty. 'This way.'
She reached out her arm, and Tommy clutched her wrist with
his bony fingers as she led him down the curving stairs, away
from the stars and the jasmine and the music, the rising smell
of exhaust from the alleyway below. Molly felt very aware of
the points where their skin touched as they walked along the
corridor to the room at the end. It was Mousseline's most
diminutive, but still magnificent, windows shuttered against
the night, the bed turned down as if Lilith had been expecting Tommy all along.

'This place is something else, Mol,' said Tommy. 'I mean
– look at it.' He gestured to the lantern in the centre of the
room, lozenges of amber and red, the gauzy muslin twisted
over the four corners of the bed, the tufted rug. The room
smelt of the particular incense that Lilith favoured, frankin-
cense in a tureen on one of the side tables.

'It really is,' said Molly.

'I used to stay in places like this all the time. On shoots

and stuff. Amazing what you take for granted.' Molly didn't reply. 'Mind if I smoke?'

'Be my guest,' said Molly, looking at him.

Tommy cracked the shutter ajar and settled into the window seat, drawing his knees up alongside him. From his top pocket, he drew out a packet of Camel Lights, always his brand, extracted a fag and sparked it.

'Where's Noah?'

'He got held up at work,' replied Molly, looking away, up at the light, anywhere but into Tommy's eyes. She walked over to the dressing table and trailed her hand along the top of the mirror, aping nonchalance.

'Bollocks,' said Tommy. 'What's going on?' Molly didn't reply. She shrugged. 'Don't tell me then,' said Tommy. 'He sent me a very cryptic text. That's why I decided to come. Also, I see things more clearly than I have in ages. My brain is just working again – feels weird. Not sure I like it, frankly.' He looked out at the night and exhaled. He always had smoked elegantly. Molly still remembered the first time she had seen him do it. They had all gone out to one of the clubs in south London. A converted church, uplit so that its white curves glowed skull-like against the urban night, the revellers streaming towards it in their own kind of spiritual pilgrimage. She had been so intimidated by Tommy at that point: his caustic humour, his beauty, his unpredictability. It was the more approachable Noah she had befriended first.

Noah had asked Molly, Alice and Viv along to this particular night, and they had found him and Tommy in the queue outside. Tommy had been sucking on a cigarette then, exhaling upwards, so the smoke slunk up his face. As Alice instructed, Molly had dressed for inside the club and hadn't realised how long she'd have to wait, her upper arms and thighs stupid and exposed.

'Do you want one of these?' Tommy had extended his hand, which contained a white pill, stamped with the three diamond-wings of a Mitsubishi logo.

'Tommy!' Noah had said. 'Leave the poor girl alone.'

'No,' Molly had said, quickly. 'No thanks. Um.' She knew herself to be blushing, could feel the blotch of blood rising on her thighs.

'Shame,' Tommy had said, and he had popped it into his mouth, gulping it down and then smiling at her.

She hadn't spoken to him for the rest of the night, but had occasionally encountered him in various rooms of the club, hair iced by blue and pink lights. Even once, strikingly, on a podium. He was a drum-and-bass Puck, omnipresent and incorrigible.

'What feels weird particularly?' asked Molly.

'Realising that I've wasted so much time,' replied Tommy.

'Do you wish you could go backwards?' said Molly. 'Just for a night? Do things differently?'

Tommy didn't turn to look at her, but stayed looking out of the window towards the alleyway below.

'All the time,' he said. 'I'd do *everything* differently.'

'Not everything, surely.'

'No. Not everything.' He looked at her then.

'So, are you going to offer me one then?' said Molly.

'What?' said Tommy. 'Of course, you don't need to ask. This is my last remaining vice.'

'I know that's untrue.'

Molly walked over to the window seat and sat on the cushion next to Tommy, pulling her knees up too. She took a cigarette out of the packet, lit it and inhaled sharply, so that the back of her throat ached. She had given up her occasional social smoking after conceiving Bella had proven so difficult – that interminable delay that she had interpreted as some kind of cosmic punishment. Molly coughed, and Tommy laughed.

'It's been a long time,' Molly said. 'I stopped doing things that might kill me.'

'So, what's changed now?' asked Tommy, levelly.

'I've given up believing that I can control the universe through good behaviour,' replied Molly. 'Recent events have made it quite clear to me that it was a huge mistake.'

'Yes, that was always a misconception,' agreed Tommy.

'I'm just not sure what I want any more,' said Molly. 'That's the worst thing. I'm just not sure about anything. I don't recognise myself.'

'But you always were indecisive,' said Tommy, blowing a perfect circle of smoke over her head.

'This is different,' said Molly. 'It's as though everything in my life is just a bit pointless.'

'Do you think you might be depressed?'

'I mean: yes. I'm on antidepressants and they're making me feel less bleak, I suppose, but I still don't feel *motivated*. Do you know what I mean? I miss feeling as though things really matter.'

'Funny, because I'm just starting to remember that they do,' said Tommy.

'Come on,' said Molly. 'Enough of this sort of chat. There's a games room. Let's go and find it.'

'What about the others?' said Tommy.

'We won't be long,' replied Molly.

'That dress suits you,' said Tommy as he stood.

'Shut up. I look like the kind of woman who buys her clothes from catalogues,' said Molly. 'Which happens to be what I am. Come on.' She reached out her hand and pulled Tommy out of the room. 'I can't remember the last time I had you entirely to myself.'

* * *

An hour later, Molly watched Tommy angling his shot. The rumoured games room was past the bedrooms at the end of a long corridor. It had a foosball table, a dartboard, shelves lined with board games and books, and a pool table, green baize glowing. There was a stocked honesty bar in one corner, with bottles of spirits suspended in gleaming rows, but they had both ignored it. The window at the back was open and the perfumed, blue wholeness of the night drifted in from outside.

Tommy stood with the cue under his arm and squinted.

'I forgot what a shark you are,' he said, shaking his head.

'An error,' said Molly. She was no longer having to fake her enthusiasm as she had on the roof terrace. She had potted a succession of balls easily, moving around the table. It was enough to make her forget the previous week. Her father, Alan, had taught her; playing pool better than everyone else had always been her party trick, all the more surprising for her general clumsiness. 'But it's my only skill.'

'Well, that's rubbish,' countered Tommy. 'You're extremely accomplished.'

'I'm not sure about that,' said Molly, looking at the balls on the table.

'So, what's new with work?'

'I've been made literacy lead. I'm co-ordinating writers to come into the school and give talks. It's pretty cool. I mean, in some ways it is. I love watching how the children respond, but it also makes me a bit … well, regretful, I suppose.' This was what she had been unable to say to Lucas.

'That you're not the one writing?' said Tommy.

'Yeah,' replied Molly. 'The fact they're actually doing it and making it work.'

'It's not too late for you to do that, if that's what you want,' said Tommy.

'I know – so they say,' said Molly. 'But I'm not sure. I think "they" might be wrong. I seem to have forgotten how to feel things properly and I don't see how you can write anything good if you're numb.'

'You don't know until you try.'

'Tommy,' said Molly, warningly. 'It's not as though I haven't tried.' Noah had given up talking to her about it. Her husband's life was so saturated in literature, and she knew that, deep down, he thought her aspirations futile. In contrast, Tommy had always maintained a touching conviction that she had something unique to offer.

'Have you submitted anything?'

'No,' said Molly. 'Not for ages. I don't know what the point would be, Tommy, really. It's hopeless.' She could see how unhappy she must look in the mirror of his face.

'Hey – who am I?' Tommy walked over to the bookshelf and picked off a book. He flipped it open and frowned at a page, stroking his top lip with his thumb in an uncanny impersonation of Lucas. Molly started giggling, relieved at the change of subject.

'That's not fair,' she said. 'He's paying for this place.' She used her cue to gesture around the games room.

'Yeah, fair point. But I'd forgotten how vanilla that man has become. He was always a dork, but at least he had a sense of humour. Now the mask has melted into his face.'

'Harsh,' said Molly.

Tommy shrugged. 'True.' He rubbed chalk on the end of his cue again, fastidiously, still aping Lucas perfectly. Molly laughed again. Tommy walked across the room, his loping stride replaced with something tighter and more constricted. Molly yelped and bent double, giggling.

'Having fun?' Lilith appeared at the door, wearing a kimono, holding a mug of herbal tea, the bag's string flopping over the side. She had removed her make-up for the night, and her face had lost its outlines.

'Yes, thank you,' said Molly, a shudder of amusement still moving through her. 'This is my friend, Tommy.'

'Oh yes,' said Lilith. 'The fellow who turned up late. But not your husband – right?' She frowned as if she was trying to work something out.

'No, not my husband,' said Molly, glancing at Tommy. He

wasn't husband or father material, she had always known it. Perhaps he would have risen to the challenge of lack of sleep and zero free time, the brutality of parenthood, but she rather doubted it. He was altogether too delicate and otherworldly.

'A pleasure to meet you,' said Lilith. 'I'm so pleased to see the games room getting some use. Some guests aren't interested.'

'It's great,' said Tommy, himself again. 'I hope we haven't been keeping you up,' he added.

'No, it's fine. I'm used to it,' said Lilith. 'Everyone who comes wants to have a good time, and they often stay up late. That's part of the job. Also, I don't sleep much anyway – so *thé*.' She raised the mug. 'Not that it makes much difference. I don't mind hearing people having fun. It makes me feel less … alone. During *mes nuits blanches*. I like to think of Mousseline used properly. Inhabited. Anyway, I will let you two continue your fun. It seems like you are having a good time, as old friends should.'

Lilith left, and Molly looked at Tommy.

'We should probably find the others now,' she said. 'Don't you think?'

'I'm going to crash,' said Tommy. 'I've worn myself out. But thanks – that was more fun than I've had in ages.'

'It's just good to see you …' said Molly.

'Don't say it,' said Tommy.

'What?'

'"Doing so well" – I'm sorry, but it's what everyone says and it makes me sound like a toddler,' said Tommy. 'Like you're about to give me my dummy and put me down for a nap.'

'But you are!' said Molly. 'I don't care how it sounds.' She took his hands for a moment and looked at him, trying to communicate what she couldn't with words.

They parted in the corridor, and Molly climbed the steps slowly up to the roof. Lucas and Alice were talking to each other in low voices, and Molly paused at the top of the stairs, uncertain if she wanted to rejoin them or turn and head straight for bed. The thought of having to sweep away the rose petals was enough to propel her forwards.

'Molly,' said Alice. She sounded neither happy nor annoyed. It was a statement of fact.

'Where have you been? Where is he?' asked Lucas. 'Bloody maniac. I'd like to know what he's thinking just showing up at the last minute.'

'You asked him,' said Molly, indignant on Tommy's behalf. 'We've just been playing pool in the games room. You should have a look. It's great down there.'

'I did tell you,' said Lucas, looking at Alice, 'inviting him was asking for trouble.'

'But how could I not?' said Alice. 'He's one of us … This was supposed to be everyone. That's what I wanted, what *we* wanted …' She looked at Lucas and then at Molly. 'Everyone together.'

'It's going to be fine,' said Molly. She couldn't look at Lucas without recalling Tommy's impersonation, so she kept her eyes trained carefully on Alice's face. 'Maybe it might even be fun? He's doing so much better. You need to give him a chance.'

'I'm surprised to hear you say that,' remarked Alice. She

raised her eyebrows. Molly had always been unsure precisely how much Alice knew.

'What are you talking about?' said Molly.

'This weekend is important for Lucas and me,' said Alice. 'We've got this big surprise tomorrow. A bit of an announcement really. We can't have Tommy just making it all about himself. Will you babysit him, Mol? Please? Like you did tonight?'

'I'll do my best,' said Molly, sighing in relief. If Alice knew the secret baked into her marriage, like butter in a pie, she wasn't letting on.

Star

Midday

Star's stomach contracts. She is starving. It must be the beginning of lunch service now. Cal will be starting his shift at the restaurant, changing into his regulation waistcoat, tucking his pen into the top pocket, his surf-bum hair tied back.

She is certain that he remains spitting mad at her unexpected return to London, not realising that she is actually stuck on Pete's roof garden where he left her the previous evening.

Cal, sweet Cal, her unwitting jailor.

She first encountered him in the restaurant four months earlier, introduced as the new girl. At that point, she had spent six months travelling across Asia on her own, trying to forget about Lucas by distracting herself with as many new experiences as possible. It hadn't worked; the plan was to be a bit more settled in Sydney for as long as her visa would let her.

'A pleasure to meet you,' Cal had said, extending a hand.

'I'm Star.'

'Star? What kind of name is that?' he'd said, with a grin.

'An excellent one,' Star had replied. She was used to this.

'You from London?' he'd added.

'Well, Devon. Then London.'

'How long have you been in Oz?'

'Just arrived.' She had smiled, accepting that he liked the look of her. One could usually tell.

'Well, this is a great place to work,' he'd gestured around the dining room at Claws, with the lobster tank at the front full of its unwitting, navy-blue inhabitants, red leather booths and view of the Opera House's pavlova peaks. 'The tips are great and so are the staff,' he'd added, with a wink.

The following weekend, he took her on a tour of Sydney. After visiting the botanical gardens and getting ice cream, they had ended up on Bondi, stretched on the sand, drinking beer and watching the waves and the bodies in the honeyed end-of-day light.

'This is the way to live,' Cal had said. 'You'll see, you are going to have the best time in this city. Everything is better than it is in Britain.'

'I hope so,' Star had replied. 'I could do with a good time.'

'What do you mean?' he'd asked. Star's face must have betrayed her.

'Things weren't going that well in London. I, um – I decided to come away for a bit of a reset.'

'How come?'

Star had paused. 'I had some difficulties with my friends.' She swallowed, recalling the scowl that Lucas had when he was concentrating, that occasionally broke into a smile upon realising he was observed. The view from the window of the warehouse, a cross-section of London skyline, that she saw for the last time on the morning that Alice made her accusation. Then the awful final straw of what Molly had assumed. There were some things she would struggle to explain to anyone. 'I couldn't work out what I wanted to do with my life, and they all seemed so certain.'

'What? Who needs to have that stuff figured out now?' Cal had said. 'There's plenty of time for all that.' He'd drained the end of his can and sunk his head back onto the sand behind him. Star had looked at his upturned face, the slight pitting on his cheeks of historic acne. In the twilight, the evening stretching ahead of her, she'd had to agree.

In many ways, Cal was the anti-Lucas. He was short and swarthy to Lucas's burly fairness, with a Brummie lilt instead of Lucas's carefully placeless accent. And rather than the laser focus on attainment and concrete markers of success, Cal fetishised freedom. He surfed and worked in Claws and professed never to want anything else, approaching his slacker lifestyle with an earnestness that was aeons away from Lucas's relentless irony.

Star willed herself to fall for him. How convenient it would be, if she could just forget about Lucas with a rebound love affair. So, she agreed to all of Cal's invitations to hang out, hoping that she might develop feelings for him. They went to the beach, she met his friends, they arranged their shift pattern to mirror the other's. But the inconvenient truth was that he was her friend – nothing more.

As the weeks went by, she opened up more to Cal about Lucas and Alice. He was the perfect audience for her scathing riffs about *their magic circle training contracts, their conventional lives and their mystifying plan to get married at such a young age. He reliably told her what she wanted to hear – how dull they sounded, that he couldn't believe she had ever been friends with people like that, how they would come to regret the single-minded pursuit of money, what a lucky escape she'd had.*

She supposes that last night's conversation must have been a quite a shock, after all these previous discussions. It had started sparringly, their usual register, although she'd noticed that Cal seemed particularly cheerful. Looking back, she wonders if he had assumed that she had brought him outside to progress their relationship onto the next stage.

'What's this all about?' Cal had said. He sat close to her on the sunlounger, so that their thighs were almost touching. He gave off heat.

'It's hard to tell you.'

'Go on,' Cal had said, a smile in his voice.

'I . . . I'm flying back to England, tomorrow.'

'What?' Cal had spat out a mouthful of his cocktail.

'I spoke to Lucas and he wants to see me before the wedding.'

'But you hate him! And he's getting married to your friend Alice this weekend, isn't he? You must be joking. Star? Please tell me this is a wind-up, like.'

'I'm not,' Star had replied. 'I'm sorry.' She had put her hands over her eyes. 'I know it sounds awful, but Alice isn't blameless, I promise you. I haven't told you everything. And I thought you guessed how I felt about Lucas. We've spoken about him an awful lot.'

'Don't do this, Star. This Lucas bloke sounds like an idiot.

You've said it yourself.' Cal had angled himself to face her, then reached for her hands in a way he never had before, holding them loosely, his touch dry and warm. 'Stay here with me and have fun. Come on. We're just getting to know each other.'

'I know. And you're great, but I can't ...' Star had broken off, then looked at Cal in the semi-darkness. The music from inside had been blaring and she'd realised how drunk she was. She should have told him she was going while she was still sober, when she could formulate her sentences properly. Leaving it to the last minute was so typical of her. 'I'm so grateful for how well you've looked after me since I arrived here and for our friendship. It's been so much fun – really, it has – but this is what I have to do. I can't expect you to understand it.' She'd pulled her hands away.

'Don't come back here, crying to me when it all goes wrong.' Cal had stood, glanced away and then back at her one final time, before turning and stalking over to the bifold door. Star had let him go and turned to stare at the skyline, sparkling in the dark. She'd heard tears in his voice and wanted to preserve his dignity, give him time to leave.

It was ten minutes later that she'd stood to go herself. And then she realised that, in his upset, Cal had pulled the door shut, automatically locking it from within.

And here she remains. Trapped. Perhaps no more than she deserves.

II

Riad Mousseline, Marrakesh

Saturday morning
Twenty years later

There was another body in the bed. Molly woke slowly, feeling the sheet beneath her, the whisper from the window that she had left ajar the night before. Her new dress was over the chair in the corner, where she had tossed it before creeping naked under the sheets. The sunlight had that different, foreign quality to it: a clarity and strength. It poked through the shutters, forming a fretwork of diamonds on the wall.

She was turned away from the centre of the bed but could feel the weight of someone else on the mattress. A male heaviness. It hadn't been there when she had eventually drifted off, after a couple of hours of rigid wakefulness. Perhaps Noah had turned up without telling her and joined her in the night.

She blinked and turned slowly towards the sleeping form next to her. It wasn't Noah, but Tommy. He must have woken and come in during the small hours, seeking comfort. His shoulder so sharply at right angles to the sheet. The vulnerability of his face in sleep, the heaviness of his breath, these reminded her of Bella and Eve in the mornings when she crept in to see them. Here he was, this precious, troubled man. She was aghast to find him so close.

She could see the changes to his skin, the vulnerable creases next to his ears, the signs of ageing that nobody warns you about. He stirred a little, and Molly held her breath. She half hoped he might wake up, but he stayed asleep.

Molly sighed. Her breath was rank, and she rose, headed straight for the bathroom and her toothbrush, then show-ered. She was self-conscious of her morning appearance. Without the foundations of pencilled eyebrows, underwear, brushed hair, she felt amorphous and ill-defined, her outline jellyfishing. Sometimes, it seemed that she was no longer a woman at all without props but was shifting into something ungendered and in-between.

She wasn't surprised that Tommy had come in. It was just the kind of thing Tommy would do, but nobody else needed to know. She didn't want to have to answer more questions when she didn't know the answers to anything.

When she had gone to bed, she had tried to ring Noah again, but he still hadn't picked up, but this morning, as she turned on her phone in the splendour of her marble bath-room, there was a text.

'Getting the midday flight. I'll see you there this evening.' This was followed by a string of the emojis which he had re-cently started using since working on the documentary, since working with *her*. It was as if nothing was wrong between them. But Noah had always been effusive in texts, as he was in life. It was a reflex, it didn't mean that everything was OK. She didn't see how it could be. Things had changed when they hadn't been paying attention. Molly glanced out of the bathroom and looked at Tommy.

She dressed in shorts and a T-shirt. More clothes purchased for projected fun, but self-conscious-making in reality. She applied moisturiser, then make-up, approaching her complexion in segments, a close-up of her eye socket for eyeliner and concealer, a squint for blusher. She couldn't recall when her face, unremarkable, but lovely in its way, had started letting her down. It had been incremental, like the shift in her marriage. You thought you achieved some kind of stasis as an adult, a parent, only to realise that things were mutating as quickly as they ever had. That what you'd had, only months before, had been so much better than you'd ever given it credit for. She wished she had valued her beauty before she lost it, had understood that she was desirable. Perhaps then she could have been a better person.

She left the bathroom. Tommy was still fast asleep. If Noah wasn't coming until later, there wasn't any rush to wake him. Nobody needed to know. It would be just another secret between them, like the others.

* * *

Downstairs, Alice and Lucas were breakfasting. They were slick, showered, attacking bowls of thick yoghurt studded with pistachios and drizzled in honey. Their phones were laid out on the table in front of them, like pets.

'We went for a run in the souk,' said Lucas. 'To get the alcohol out.' His face still bore the violence of exercise. 'Set a pretty good pace, although we almost sent one of the carts flying.'

'The best way to start the day,' said Alice. 'Get the blood pumping. We got a few funny looks. There were all these women gardening in the city – pruning the plants.'

'We had to dodge round a couple,' said Lucas.

'Sounds good,' said Molly. She was disconcerted by their easy avowal of their usual routine, their blithe disregard of their surroundings.

Molly sat on one of the wooden chairs in the courtyard. Breakfast was conducted outside, under the voluptuous purple shade of the fig tree. The water from the pipe into the swimming pool trickled on. Mousseline's cat lay sunning himself on a terracotta tile, body elongated like a stave. The sky above was already an implacable cerulean.

'How are you feeling?' asked Alice.

'Fine!' replied Molly. 'No headache, for a change.'

'Oh yes, well, hopefully, tonight, you might unwind a bit,' said Alice.

Lilith appeared, asking Molly if she wanted black or white coffee and would she eat the yoghurt, too, or a kind of Moroccan pastry soaked in honey?

'At least you slept a little,' Lilith said. 'I can see by your face.' She reached out a hand and touched Molly's cheek, a maternal caress, her fingertips surprisingly cool.

'And you?' said Molly.

Lilith shook her head.

'No, but I'm used to it. I will doze later. After lunch. My siesta.'

Molly chose the pastry and sat, feeling the sun already on her shoulder blades, through her T-shirt. She thought momentarily of telling Alice and Lucas about Tommy, sleeping upstairs in her bed, but recalling Alice's words the previous evening, she thought better of it.

'So, what is the plan today?' she asked.

'Well. Lucas is staging his macho trip to the Atlas Mountains,' said Alice, rolling her eyes. 'I have no idea why. We're only here for the weekend, and it's supposed to be about relaxing.' Her voice had the spousal tone of affectionate complaint. She didn't mind, it said, she would prefer it even – marriages as enduring as theirs functioned on pockets of autonomy, even within a weekend.

'It's not a macho trip, I'd just like to add,' said Lucas. 'We aren't here for long, it's true, but the Atlas Mountains are supposed to be something else, and I'm itching to get out, already. Yesterday was lovely, but there's only so much lying around I can do.' Unspoken: that restless energy was why the job he did so well suited him, the ferocious accrual. His copy of *The Waste Land* was replaced with a thick doorstep of a novel that Molly hadn't heard of, but which had won a literary prize; its front cover emblazoned with a golden circular medal. 'Oh, this is a *brilliant* Portuguese author,' said Lucas, following her glance. 'You must read it.'

Lucas hadn't even studied English at university, but despite his impossibly long work hours, he read more these days than those of them that had, eschewing box sets as a waste of his time. His literary endeavours bothered Noah more than Molly. It was important for Noah to prevail in that arena, the one he had devoted his life to, whereas Molly had got to a place where she almost found books painful, rather than the refuge they had always been.

The coffee, brought in a small cup by Lilith, was thick and scented with cardamom. Molly tried to appreciate it but would have preferred something longer that she could linger over.

'Noah's turning up later,' said Molly.

'Brilliant,' said Alice, clapping her hands together. 'I'm so pleased, Mol. It didn't feel right without him, especially once Tommy arrived. What time is he going to get here?'

'About seven, I think,' answered Molly.

'And what are you going to do. Head off with Lucas or come with me? I'm planning the Yves Saint Laurent garden, the Jardin Majorelle.'

'Yeah, I'll probably just stay with you,' said Molly. 'But maybe you should take Tommy, Lucas? Keep him out of mischief?'

Lucas grimaced and then turned his attention back to his bowl of yoghurt.

'We'll see if I can drag him out of bed,' said Lucas.

'No, don't worry about that,' said Molly, quickly. 'I can do that.'

Viv and Iona turned up. They were ready for an expedition, Viv already sun-hatted, dependable legs in shorts, while Iona wore a floppy, tie-dye dress. On tour. They walked into the courtyard holding hands.

'Morning,' said Viv. 'Jeez, that was a heavy night,' she added, rubbing the back of her head sheepishly. She was the only one of them not to have a single grey hair. Alice and Molly dyed theirs without questioning it. Lucas's sandiness was gradually lightening, Noah's chestnut brown lightly frosted at his temples, while Tommy's had always been so pale that any white hairs weren't discernible.

'For that, there is coffee,' said Alice, throwing out her arms expansively.

She looked fresher than everyone else. If you didn't know her, you might think she was bare-faced, but Molly understood that her friend's complexion had been built up in layers like a fresco from a clatter of bottles and tubes. She admired the effort, so much more effective than her own.

'We have two factions,' continued Alice, smiling. 'I'm lozzing around here and then going to the YSL garden. Lucas is mounting some desperate escape to the Atlas.' She gave a hostess's smile. 'Who wants to do what?'

'The Atlas Mountains will take all day,' said Lilith, who had appeared with more cups of coffee. 'Don't you just want to relax, to enjoy Mousseline?' She looked aghast. 'It seems completely *fou* to run off.' She gestured at the courtyard, stippled with morning light. There was the sound of birdsong from the fig tree, and the fountain's trickle. 'It seems to me that it is more sensible to relax, *non*?'

'We've got tomorrow,' Lucas shrugged. 'We'll be back for the party later. And I feel very well acquainted with

Mousseline's many charms already.' He smiled widely at Lilith, indivisible from her house.

'Well. Thank you,' said Lilith, smiling coquettishly in return. 'Of course, you must do as you want, but, I have to say, the energy of my guests never ceases to surprise me.'

* * *

After breakfast, Molly went back up to her room, prepared to shake Tommy awake. But he had gone. There was still the slightest smell of him: the sour redolence of cigarettes and synthetic spearmint. Nobody would ever know.

She had an hour before they planned to leave for the garden. An entire unscheduled hour. She slipped into the corridor outside and began to browse the yellowing paperbacks. Lots of John Grishams and Dan Browns and Maeve Binchys. The odd more modern release and then some more dated treasures – Alison Lurie and Penelope Lively. She pulled out a copy of *Foreign Affairs*, its cover creased, and lifted it to her nose to sniff.

'They smell good, old books, do they not?' Lilith was heading to the roof, carrying a trug of tea-light holders and tiny candles in the crook of her elbow.

'Yes, and not like anything else.' Molly lowered the book, embarrassed. 'But I must look completely ridiculous.'

'Not at all,' said Lilith. 'A well-loved, much-read book assumes a life of its own. I love having them around. I don't suppose you'd mind helping me put these on the table upstairs?'

'Sure,' said Molly. She slid the paperback back onto the shelf, lying to herself that she would find time to read it later. She felt, more than ever, like a weekend guest in someone's house.

On the roof, Lilith arranged the small glass coffers and Molly dropped in the tea lights.

'All set for later,' said Lilith, once they had finished, surveying their handiwork.

'Great,' said Molly.

'Are you having fun yet?' asked Lilith.

'Of course!' said Molly.

'Truly?'

'To be quite honest, I'm having a difficult time for other reasons. Your riad is spectacular.' Molly paused, but Lilith didn't say anything in response and so she rattled on. 'I'm at a crossroads, personally and professionally, I suppose you could say. And I thought I'd have it all worked out by this point.' She raised her right hand, apparently to shield a slant of sunlight from her eyes, but really for something to do.

'We never have it all worked out. I know this for sure,' said Lilith. She was erect, her trug tucked into the crook of her elbow. 'And it's also OK not to know what we want immediately. Decisions take time.'

'But I've felt like this for so long!' said Molly, with a vehemence that surprised her.

'It will pass. You'll find the thread back to yourself,' said Lilith. 'If you really listen in here ...' The older woman used her free hand to bang on her chest, above what a yoga teacher would describe as a heart space. '... It's pretty reliable.'

Molly nodded, remaining on the roof after Lilith left. Once she was sure she was alone, she moved her own hands to her sternum, left on top of right, bowed her head and tried to listen. But there was nothing. She'd never been good at trusting her own intuition – indeed, every time she had, the consequences had been little short of disastrous.

Star

Star picks the skin around her thumbnail, tearing off tiny strips of flesh. She is hunched over on the sunlounger, her jaw set. The sun is high in the sky now. The seconds are ticking past and soon she will reach the point of no return. Perhaps Alice was right: Star is not to be trusted with anything. Certainly, Alice would never have got herself in this situation.

The fact that she got Alice so wrong still stings. Star knew Alice was strong-minded, but she also thought her fair, and Star has long considered herself a good judge of character. Working in hospitality for so many years while she tried to build her acting career made her practised at reading people. In a pub, you witness a tableau of humanity in a single shift: you're there for celebratory bottles of Prosecco, coercive shots of tequila, fifth pints for men with broken veins like Chantilly lace across their cheeks. You watch people plaster smiles on their faces, learn to guess the things they aren't saying to their friends. You grow up fast.

She started working in her local when she was only sixteen. A pub in the nearest hamlet, reached by climbing over a stile at the top of Moira's rambling garden, then crossing two potato fields. In the spring, the vegetable flowers were like miniature white stars, and in the winter, the ground was frozen rock solid. She lied to the owner, Ritchie, about her age, and he wasn't a man for checking. Moira hadn't approved, but she wasn't that bothered either. Her only true parenting ideal was – conveniently – the avoidance of any form of repression. The German couple had recently moved into the mill house, and Star's mother was consumed with settling them in. Star couldn't bear them. Shifts at The Wheatsheaf were a convenient way of avoiding the wife, with her desire to dig vegetables and only the most idealistic idea of what a sharing life involved, and her husband, the kind of cupboard lech to stare at a teenager with hangdog eyes.

It wasn't the best timing, with GCSEs coming up, but nobody stopped her, despite Star secretly wishing that they would. In the end, Star didn't even sit her exams. She hadn't been able to revise. Whenever she sat down to read about the open field system, or igneous rocks, or the periodic table, her attention had flitter-fluttered away, on to something else: the patch of damp on her bedroom wall, the view of Hans and Ellen rapturously picking the tiny bitter apples in the orchard outside, her upcoming shift, whatever. Star had never been able to concentrate. The only thing she'd ever genuinely enjoyed at school was drama, and after Mrs Chamberlain went on maternity leave, even that was a letdown.

She'd left soon afterwards for the city. She wanted to live and perform, which couldn't happen in a classroom. She tried to get away from her mother's ideals, which always looked like hard work. She has become pretty adept at looking after herself in the years since. Nobody else was going to. But perhaps Lucas will, if she can only return to him.

Star stands. She will try calling out one more time. She looks up at the sky – so vast, seemingly within touching distance. Hard to imagine that beyond what she can see lie stars and planets, galaxies of ice and fire. She shuts her eyes and prays.

12

Finsbury Park

Five years later

The park nearest Tommy's flat consisted of two halves. On the benches around the main entrance were clustered men, come rain or shine, drinking from bottles of spirits, barely concealed in paper bags. Rubbish bloomed out of the nearby, insufficient bins and pebbles of dog shit were bleached white by unreliable sunlight.

But after climbing an interminable hill, you reached a copse of trees surrounding a cafe, and the scene flipped to urban-bucolic, with a pond full of ducks and pedalos, a children's playground, the unused bowling green haunted by the whites and cucumber sandwiches of an earlier century.

Noah and Molly had arranged to meet Tommy for coffee. It had been months since they last saw him, and they didn't relish it now. But everyone else knew: they had to tell him.

The choice of location was tactical. It was near enough to Tommy's flat that he was less likely to succumb to his usual last-minute disavowal. And there was no alcohol served in the cafe, just bad coffee and disappointing paninis: a homage to American footballs in shape and texture. Yet the place wasn't without a kind of steamy, municipal charm. The clientele ranged from mothers to the elderly, with a smattering of the middle-aged mentally ill looking for warmth and clamour to lighten the load of their crushing loneliness. The walls were decorated with the rainbow handprints of a class of primary school children, long since grown up.

Tommy was already by the window.

'Cappuccino?' said Molly, not sitting down. 'I'll get it.'

'Yes, great,' replied Tommy.

'I'll have an Americano,' said Noah. 'Black.' Noah had recently developed a paunch, as if in sympathy with Molly. The development appalled and fascinated them both.

'Make sure you get plenty of sprinkles,' called Tommy. Molly turned round. 'Last time I came here, they missed the chocolate sprinkles,' he said, darkly. He wore a knitted hat with toggles draped over each ear and a lurid orange puffa jacket.

Molly queued for the drinks, her hand unthinkingly placed on her stomach. She glanced over at the table and caught Tommy looking at her. She flushed and looked away. So, they wouldn't have to spell it out: Tommy knew.

'Thanks,' said Tommy, as she came back with a tray. 'Good sprinkle action.'

'Sure,' said Molly. She passed Noah his muddy coffee and

placed down her hot chocolate, looking at it mistrustfully. Everything made her sick, still, despite being in the second trimester.

'You look well, Tom,' said Molly. She sat heavily. She had wanted the pregnancy for so long, and she had thrown herself into it so that every movement conveyed her new reality.

'Nonsense,' said Tommy, ripping open a sachet of sugar and letting the grains slide out onto the table in front of him. He poured the shape of a capital T in demerara. 'I look terrible. I've hardly left the house in three months since I quit work. I'm like some kind of zombie.' It was true that his complexion was of sour cream, with a patch of red scurf on his chin. 'It's not *me* that looks well, Mol. Have you got something to tell me?'

'Yes! It's finally happened.' Molly's right hand had found its way back to her stomach. 'We had started to think it wasn't going to.'

'It's so wonderful, congratulations.' Tommy looked at them both, suddenly serious. 'You are both going to be wonderful parents. I mean that.'

'Thanks, man,' said Noah. 'We wanted to let you know, but it wasn't just that. We also wanted to catch up.' Another lie. It would be far easier to let Tommy slip away. But they had allowed that to happen to Star, with such disastrous consequences. Once could be careless; it would start to look pathological if it happened a second time.

'Oh, did you. Did you really?' said Tommy. His expression had shifted from sincere to mocking – it had always been his default mode. The glimpses of who he had been were always the hardest to take.

'We brought something for you to look at,' Noah said as he glanced up at Molly. Noah reached into his rucksack and extracted the brochure. It was slippery and heavy, full of pictures of swimming pools, airy rooms, sunsets. The captions evoked personal transformation and recovery. Freedom. Freedom. Freedom.

'Thanks, mate,' said Tommy, taking the brochure but not opening it, staring at the picture on the front of a woman in a gauzy white dress standing against a backdrop of green leaves.

'South Africa,' said Noah. 'Lucas says he'll foot the bill. It's supposed to be one of the best in the world.' Tommy was silent. 'It's getting out of hand, Tommy, we all thought—'

'Do I get her if I go?' said Tommy, pointing to the female shape, his long fingers grazing the image. 'Because then I might seriously consider it.'

Noah laughed, but then stopped abruptly.

'Lucas heard about this place,' Molly was urgent. 'Apparently, one of his clients went there. Said it was amazing, totally turned his life around.'

'I see,' said Tommy. He raised the cappuccino to his mouth and took a slurp so that foam coated his top lip. He was ridiculous in his hat, his coat, but still somehow compelling, with his washed-out eyes and the peculiarly pale hair that poked out of the corner of his hat. And didn't he just know it, thought Molly.

'Well. You should consider it,' said Molly. 'Things can't go on as they are. It's time to think about the future. You've still got plenty of time left.'

Since what had happened to Star, Tommy's predilection for oblivion, always pronounced, had taken on a darker, more insistent quality. It wasn't a choice any more; it hadn't been for a while.

'Plenty of time for ... what?' asked Tommy.

'For life, having a good life.' Noah looked down at the table in front of them, took a long swig of his Americano.

'What ... like you two?' said Tommy. 'Or Lucas and Alice? *Viv?*' His voice was scathing.

'There's nothing wrong with slowing down a bit,' said Molly. Tommy looked at her. 'You need to change things, Tommy. You lost your job.'

'They didn't renew my contract. It's not a big deal. I can easily get another one. They were a bunch of tossers anyway,' said Tommy.

'I thought you liked that agency. You said they had some of the most creative campaigns in Europe.'

'Yeah. I was wrong,' said Tommy.

'Well, take it with you. Have a look. The website has more info,' encouraged Molly. 'Lucas says that the success rate is remarkable.'

'Oh. "Lucas says ..."' mocked Tommy. 'I don't give a flying fuck what Lucas says about anything.' Their old rivalry had curdled further. As the two most showily bright of the group, they had once been worthy adversaries. But now, Lucas was assuming the mantle of incipient middle age – it had always been there, lurking for him in the wings. Red trousers were possibly only months away. Once he had settled to it, his union with Alice was part of it. Together, they were formidable. Edward and Olivia completed the package.

They changed the subject. There were still other things to talk about – Noah's promotion in the department and his research. And the pregnancy – the reason they had come. Molly and Noah had been trying for years. This latest successful attempt was the last roll of the IVF dice. After discovering their infertility, Molly had assumed she was suffering divine retribution; after all, her first, terminated pregnancy had happened so easily as to have been accidental. Sometimes, she struggled to believe it had ever happened at all, that her body had been capable of something which now eluded her. In her private appointment with their IVF doctor, a well-preserved woman in her fifties with a glossy, swinging bob, Molly had been emphatic that Noah wasn't to know that she had ever successfully conceived.

'It's very unusual to conceal such information from your partner,' the doctor had said.

'It's just ... If you don't mind, I'd prefer not to get into it,' Molly had replied. 'The timing was problematic.'

'A little girl,' said Molly, now. She couldn't stop her happiness leaking into the pronouncement. It coloured everything. Behind the nausea and anxiety was a distinct sense of pulsing joy. She had wondered if it might pain Tommy to see it, but she found she couldn't help herself. Or perhaps she *wanted* to hurt him; she wasn't entirely sure. Tommy always brought out the worst in her.

'That's wonderful, Mol,' said Tommy. He became serious for a second. 'I'm so happy for you.' He met her eyes, then looked away, out towards the play area. 'Anyway, I've got some food for the ducks. Shall we?'

'The ducks?' said Noah, puzzled, but they finished their drinks and followed him out to the area near the pond. It was surrounded by a curved wire fence, behind which the ducks waddled, waiting, feathers the shimmering green-black of crude oil.

Tommy shuffled forwards and reached into his pocket where he had cold pizza crusts wrapped in a piece of kitchen roll. He quacked at the ducks, and they eyed him sceptically in return.

'Here, ducky, ducky,' he shouted, throwing down margherita crusts beneficently onto the mud beyond the fence, the ducks' area, which was covered in puffed curls of their shit.

'Do they like pizza?' asked Noah.

'Oh yeah,' said Tommy, as the ducks moved surprisingly quickly, grabbing the long crusts in their beaks, regarding him with mistrustful, orange eyes. 'I do this all the time. They don't like it as much when I get pepperoni, so I've started making sure that I always get the plain ones.'

It saddened Molly to think of Tommy in the park feeding the ducks, ordering pizzas to please them.

'We should think about heading off?' She looked at Noah.

'Yeah,' said Noah. 'We are going to Lucas and Alice's later. I'm sure you could come if you wanted.'

'Nah, it's all right. I'm seeing Emma later,' said Tommy. Emma was the girl he was seeing. Molly disapproved. The only time she'd met her, she had noted Emma's glazed expression, and Tommy had affectionately referred to her as a 'benzo head'.

Nonetheless, she was pretty, younger than they, her nails black-red, colourful trainers, a succession of hoops climbing up her right earlobe. She still worked as an account manager at the agency Tommy had recently left. There was every outward appearance of functionality and success, so who was Molly to judge?

'Well. Have fun,' said Molly. She knew that Tommy wasn't having fun. She had the same creeping sense of letting him down that she'd had with Star.

Two days before Alice and Lucas's wedding, Star had sent a surprising email, saying that she was coming home from Sydney – *because Lucas had asked her to* – with no mention of whether she planned to attend the wedding or not. Molly, who had been in the thick of last-minute preparations with Alice – a bulging to-do list of top-up sunbed sessions and sourcing bunting for the garden – hadn't known what to say in response. She had been desperate to see Star; of course, she had. But she had considered her friend's timing selfish. If Star had wanted to fight for Lucas, it had needed to happen earlier than the morning of his wedding to someone else. So, Molly had ignored the email, and then Star had died, and she wasn't able to ever speak to her again.

In the years since, it was this final betrayal that Molly hadn't been able to forget. It was after her rash accusation that Star had left London. Weeks later, Molly had emailed, apologising for her presumption. After that, they'd had a warm email correspondence, with Star filling her in on the beaches and temples she was visiting. But Molly had sensed the melancholy simmering under the stories. And then Molly hadn't replied to her final email, unsure of what to say. She had let her down, again.

She wouldn't fail Tommy in the same way – however impossible he might become. Yet, Lucas always said that you couldn't help someone if they didn't want to help themselves, and Molly knew it to be true. It didn't help that Tommy's loneliness reminded her unhelpfully of Star's. This was hard to bear witness to. Molly wanted to cocoon herself in her new-found contentment, return to the garden flat that she and Noah had recently bought after renting for so long, with its nasturtiums in the back garden and wide floorboards of pale pine, and sit on the sofa imagining the galaxy twisting in her stomach until it was time to go out.

Mostly, they had withdrawn from Tommy, as they had once withdrawn from Star. Much as Molly might have wished they hadn't. A collective subconscious shrinkage. As the years had gone by and he hadn't made the shifts the rest of them had, they'd had to. He didn't fit the shape of their lives. You couldn't have Tommy to dinner these days. He fell asleep at the cinema, embarrassed himself at the theatre, became incoherent at picnics.

It wasn't so much that he was doing anything that exceptional. They all still liked a drink, didn't they? But he didn't know where to draw the line or adjust his behaviour for the environment. Didn't take days off. Tread the delicate tightrope between industry and intemperance.

At one barbecue in Lucas and Alice's back garden, Tommy

had lit a spliff and sat under the parasol where Edward lay sleeping on an immaculate checked rug. Tommy had sworn he hadn't meant to blow smoke over the baby's tiny bud of a face, but Alice had been furious, thudding across the grass in her pumps and throwing the roll-up into the flower bed.

'You're a *loser*,' she had hissed. Lucas, turning sausages on the grill, a tea towel tossed over one shoulder, didn't even turn round.

Yes, Alice had been insatiable in her heyday. But growing up required a certain shift in sensibility, an awareness of when to cut loose and rein it in – a thermostat for hedonism.

Molly looked back at Tommy, watching the ducks, and he looked at her, raising his hand in a jaunty wave. He still looked, just about, like someone with plenty of friends and places to go, who could crack open the city. But Molly knew he spent most of his time in the flat his mother had so helpfully left him, her London *pied-à-terre*, still full of the furniture she had bought – Ercol butterfly chairs and Conran cushions which had cost a fortune but which Tommy failed to look after and were increasingly marred by scratches and blim burns. Each scar was small, but they contributed to an overall sense of decline.

'I don't think he's even going to look at it,' she said to Noah as they walked back down the hill, in the direction of where their car was parked.

'Probably not,' said Noah. 'I hate to say it, but I'm pretty sure that things are going to have to get worse before they get better.'

They were both right.

Star

1 p.m.

Star is still upright, her back to the glass door. She's been listening intently to see if she can hear the sound of Pete returning home: a door opening, car keys tossed on a side table, the clink of ice in a glass. Pete is a drinker; of this, Star is sure. It takes one to know one. But there is nothing. Pete isn't coming. Not in time. She knows this too.

An aeroplane moves across the sky and Star moans softly. In just over two hours, her own flight is supposed to be taking off. She swallows. The tissues of her throat feel as though they're sticking together. She longs for a tall glass of water.

Lucas. Lucas. Lucas. They were always an unlikely pair, she and him, but they unlocked something in the other.

She can't give up. She has to try something. As long as she is back before the ceremony starts, she stands some chance of influencing events in her favour. How she regrets all those months of inaction.

If she had known how Lucas was really feeling, she would have returned so much sooner. Why couldn't he have called a week ago?

Star walks back to the cactus at the corner of the roof garden. She steps up onto it and looks down at the view again. It's dizzying. She shuts her eyes. She hasn't eaten anything for twenty-four hours and her body feels slow, her movements lagging behind her brain's instructions. If she looks down, there is no way she will be able to do it. She must focus on what is directly in front of her. Star studies the balustrade, made from a slippery tube of toughened steel. She grips her fingers around it and takes a deep breath. She hoists herself up. It's now or never.

13

Jardin Majorelle, Marrakesh

Saturday morning
Twenty years later

The blue of the building was a synthetic shade: Majorelle blue. This vivid poster-paint pigment clashed with the swatches of mustard yellow on the adjacent walls and the more timorous iteration of the sky above.

The plants themselves were equally unsettling; alternately bulbous and angular, an alien garden. Cacti pronged up to the sky, intercut with banana trees, aloes, bamboo groves, coconut palms and pools cluttered with water lilies and terrapins.

Already, at eleven in the morning, the place was thick with tourists. Middle-aged mini-breakers and families with children lurching between the plants seeking the stretches of shade, a respite from the heightening sun.

'This place is mad,' said Molly to Alice. 'The plants are crazy.'

'Beautiful,' said Alice, who was walking a couple of steps ahead in a billowing zebra-print maxi dress. She had pushed back her hair with a headscarf; the black hexagons of her sunglasses almost entirely obscured her face. Like Lucas, Alice's style had changed as she had got older and wealthier, all whisper of velvet hairbands and rugby shirts relegated, replaced with the kind of eccentricity that denoted a certain level of effort and expense.

Molly wondered if Alice's headache had kicked in – whether memories from the previous night were rearing up: splashing naked in the plunge pool, dancing, carping about Tommy. Probably not. Alice seldom expressed the kind of morning-after regret that Molly did. She seemed proud of her exploits; they had always been the flip side of how hard she worked. After she had given up her job at the firm, Alice had remained competitive in all the other areas of her and Lucas's life together – the house, the children, herself. If life were a game, Alice had won, Molly had to concede.

Molly scanned the people ahead of them. For a second, she thought she glimpsed Star. A tall, monochromatic woman, black hair spilling down her white neck. That red mouth. She looked again. It was someone else; of course, it was. Much younger. After all, Star would be their age now, not still in her twenties. She would be lined, her skin starting to slide. This girl had Star's voluptuousness, but none of her naughtiness, you could tell just from the set of her face. What had happened to them all since Star left had been so brutal, their diminishment, and yet Star's fate had been another order of brutality altogether.

Today was the day. Twenty years ago, Alice and Lucas had got married. Star hadn't been there, although Molly had been half expecting her to turn up after the email she had sent. To burst in at the back of the church when the vicar asked if anyone knew of any lawful impediments.

Instead, as they had been drinking champagne and dancing under canvas, Star was already dead. It was unthinkable; it always had been. Molly shuddered.

She had googled Star a couple of times, as Lucas had confessed to doing. Star Braithwaite. But nothing had come up. Or rather, another Star Braithwaite had. A Texan marketeer with frosted lipstick and a cross-training addiction. It was almost worse. That there was someone out there, with her name, living a life of wholesome hobbies and marketing spiel, so unlike Star's own existence.

Molly's phone buzzed in her pocket, and she drew it out. Bella.

'Hi, Mummy,' her daughter said, still using the baby version. Perhaps they had babied her? Maybe that was the source of her overweening innocence, so precious, only latterly starting to become a concern.

'Bella, darling. How are you and Eve doing? How was last night?' Molly watched Alice dip behind a cactus that was taller than her, the startling hide of her dress flashing just out of sight. Viv and Iona were somewhere else in the garden, too. It was just her and Bella. She could almost be in their kitchen, watching her daughter read, the downward tilt of her eyelashes, that absolute focus on words, so like her father's.

'Yes, OK. All good. Astrid and I watched a film. Dad let us get burgers.'

'How's Eve?'

'She isn't awake yet,' said Bella. 'I think she and Miriam stayed up talking.'

'Dad's coming now. He's decided to.'

'I know, he's left for the airport already,' said Bella. A silence then between them. 'Is everything all right?' asked Bella. 'I mean, why didn't Dad come last night like he planned to?'

'He got held up,' said Molly.

'He just looked a bit weird this morning,' said Bella. 'A bit puffy, like he'd been crying. And he was talking on his phone to someone for ages last night. In the middle of the night. Was it you?'

Molly paused. She'd had nothing from Noah but the text.

'Yes, yes, it was me. We were discussing him coming today. Anyway ...' She didn't want Bella to clock that she was changing the subject. 'We're just in this lovely garden having a walk around. Lucas and Tommy have gone into the mountains for a drive, but we've come to see this house. It's where the fashion designer Yves Saint Laurent lived. It's all painted these amazing colours. I'll get some postcards. You could use them in one of your art projects.' Bella's art reassured Molly. Her paintings, her oil drawings, collages all had a freedom and a wildness to them that couldn't be discerned elsewhere in Bella's life. Molly didn't want her daughter to assume that following the rules was paramount.

'Thanks, Mummy,' said Bella. 'Astrid and I will probably just read this afternoon.' Molly pictured the two girls. Lovely giantesses with fine academic minds, reading on the living-room sofa. It was a familiar scene and one she suddenly ached for: the view from the window of the plum tree outside their house, about to lose the last of its leaves, the flutter and roil of their boiler's digestive issues, the noise of post flopping onto the doormat.

They said goodbye and she stood thinking, wondering what Bella had noticed, what Bella knew. She was naive, but she wasn't stupid. She must have noticed that something had happened between her parents. The gap that they had papered over. Molly wanted to explain to her daughter how hard it was being with someone for so long and knowing so much about them. But Bella hadn't even had a single love affair yet; it was unfair to disillusion her about passion's transience.

'I'm bored now.' Alice was by her side again; geometric sunglasses pushed back. 'Is it too early to start drinking?'

'Far too early,' said Molly, a trickle of sweat running down her back. So much sweat, these days, more than she could have ever believed possible.

'Lunch, then?' said Alice. 'In the cafe.'

'Definitely,' said Molly, looping arms with her old friend. 'I think we've seen enough cacti by now.'

The cafe was an extra limb to the garden, tables arranged in a courtyard. The walls were painted the warm terracotta of sun-baked earth, and sunlight sieved through leaves trained upon a trellis.

'Can I be hungry again?' asked Viv. 'We only just had breakfast.'

'We're on holiday,' said Alice, smiling around at them. 'Of

course you can. Being here is such a treat for me. Having old friends here ... and new ones.' She beamed at Iona, who gave a gracious nod. Molly found herself aching to impress Iona, or rather to be found acceptable. The conversation about Star had made her wonder what the younger woman thought of her.

Viv, in contrast to her lover, seemed excitable. Her face was flushed, and she kept laughing. Molly felt happy for her friend and jealous of that early hormonal flush. It made you do things that you normally wouldn't countenance, imbued everything with a certain magic. It had only happened to her twice. Or, if she were honest with herself, perhaps only once.

'Alice ... Mol ...' Viv held out her finger, around which was wrapped a twist of thin copper wire. 'Just now, by the fountain. Iona asked me ...'

'Oh my God!' yelled Alice standing up, leaning forward over the table to embrace Viv and then Iona. 'Congratulations. That's just so wonderful, Vivi.'

'Congrats,' said Molly.

'This is just until we get a proper ring,' said Viv, looking down at the wire.

'Well. I think this definitely calls for something fizzy,' said Alice. 'And it is my wedding anniversary.'

They attracted glances, ordering the bottle at lunchtime. The clutch of British women, old enough to be grandmothers, whooping over their alcohol. They ordered a mezze of dishes to go with it. Flatbread striped by the grill, hummus, diced and fried aubergines, tabbouleh so thick with herbs that it looked like lawnmower mulch.

Iona and Viv were beatific.

'Not for me,' said Molly to Alice, the latter poised with the bottle.

'Come on, Viv's just got engaged!' said Alice. 'You've got to.'

Molly nodded, succumbing. What was the point of holding back?

'So where will you get married?' asked Alice. She watched them intently, and Molly could see the cogs of her friend's brain working. Alice was already projecting herself into the event, what she would tell her other friends. A gay wedding! Love celebrated in all its forms – what veritable joy. Alice would arrive impeccably dressed, having bought the most expensive item on the wedding list.

'I don't know. Maybe Lambeth Register Office,' said Viv. 'It's near, and it's easy. I've always watched wedding parties outside and thought it looked like a good spot. I just never imagined it would be me.' She reached across the table for Iona.

'You and Noah got married in the one in Islington, didn't you, Mol?' asked Alice.

'Oh yes, of course,' said Viv. 'That was a great day.'

Molly nodded. She stood and pushed her chair in. 'Got to nip to the toilet,' she said, then navigated her way through the chairs, a weak strobe of sunlight flashing on her eyeballs. She was loosened by the small amount of alcohol and close to the tears she had been holding back. She had known that drinking would uncork them, never mind the recollection of her wedding day.

Noah in his blue suit and brown shoes, cleanly shaven and expectant. Nothing notably terrible had happened to them. They had two healthy children; they were both well themselves. They had enough money, just about. But happy ever after turned out to be complicated. She'd stopped writing. They were never going to afford to move out of the flat. The girls were going to leave. And everything was just going to be the same, same, same. Or get incrementally worse.

Molly sat on the closed toilet seat in the cubicle, took out her phone, and scrolled through pictures. The ones from Noah's phone that she had forwarded to herself. He didn't know she had them. She hadn't wanted to look since she'd found out. But now, suddenly, she couldn't fathom the minutes she hadn't.

She flicked. Blonde plaits. Freckles. Plush skin. A forthright gaze. Despite her comparative youth, the woman looked sensible. The kind who could change a tyre, rewire a plug, navigate motorway junctions with ease – a more practical type than Molly herself. Molly could picture her striding around the set of *Shakespeare's Compulsions*, a lanyard around her neck. She imagined Noah holding her and started to cry.

The toilet door opened. A waft of sound from the cafe. Life. People out there – her friends included – were enjoying the afternoon.

'Molly. Are you all right?' It was Alice. 'I can hear you in there, you know.'

'Yeah. I'm just …'

'You looked a bit off. What's going on, Molly? Come out.'

Molly opened the door.

'You've been crying. Come here, you idiot.'

Molly found herself pulled up against Alice, pressed against the black-and-white stripes of her dress, the thwack of her perfume. She relaxed into the hug.

'You need to tell me what's going on, Mol,' Alice said, pulling back to scrutinise Molly. 'Enough is enough. I've gone along with this, but it's getting to the point where—'

'Noah – he's ... He's been sleeping with someone else,' said Molly, looking down at the phone. It contained the evidence. Those pictures. What was her name? Greta. 'The production assistant on his documentary. I found out, and we had a huge argument, which is why he didn't come yesterday.'

'Shit,' said Alice, looking at her. 'I can't believe it. Really? *Noah?*'

'Yes,' said Molly. 'But it's not as straightforward as you think.'

Alice frowned slightly. 'How come?'

'It's just ... I haven't wanted to go near Noah in so long. I mean, years, if I'm being honest. I didn't want him to touch me. I knew I was rejecting him, but I didn't seem able to address it, and now he's ...' She started to cry again and looked at herself in the mirror. Twin snail tracks of snot ran down to her mouth.

'Don't be so hard on yourself,' said Alice, meeting her reflected gaze. 'You have supported Noah for a long time. You've had a good relationship. No matter what was happening between you, you don't deserve this.'

'But ...' Molly paused. She thought of all those times that she had shucked Noah's hands away, shrugged a shoulder, twisted her calf, turned out the light as she heard his hopeful tread on the basement stairs. It wasn't as simple as it looked from the outside.

'Can I see?' asked Alice, pulling away.

Molly tapped in her passcode and handed her friend the phone. Another woman came into the toilet then. In the middle of her life, like them, but evidently not British. She wore her age less self-consciously. She passed them, smiling, and ducked into a toilet cubicle.

Alice stood scrolling through the photographs. If she were able to frown, she would have, but instead, her forehead puckered slightly, a transposed line at the edge of her hairline wriggling in compensation.

'Young,' she said, finally. 'Blonde.' A pronouncement as if she were bird-spotting and had just come across a greater-crested thrush.

'Yes, these pictures were just on his phone, so I sent them to myself,' said Molly, sadly. 'She's Danish. I think she looks kind of *nice*? Clean. If I were her mum, I'd probably feel like I'd done a good job. I *could* be her mum.' She started to cry again, tears leaking out of the corners of her eyes.

Alice didn't reply but turned to face her reflection in the mirror. Her glassy skin, her lips with that tiny synthetic moue; Alice met her own reflection with an expression of challenge in her eyes. There was a flush, and the other woman came out and moved towards the sink to wash her hands.

'You look as if you are having a party. You and your friends,' the woman said.

'It's my wedding anniversary today,' replied Alice. 'And our friend just got engaged. We had a double reason to celebrate.' She flashed the woman her dazzling, closed smile, brooking no further enquiry.

'Congratulations,' said the stranger, looking at Molly's flushed, miserable face. She had a French accent, like Lilith, and a little silk scarf was knotted jauntily at her throat, covering the ropes of her neck. 'You are in – how do you say it? The prime of life. Enjoy!' She banged out of the toilet, leaving Molly and Alice alone.

'So, what do you want, Mol?' asked Alice, thoughtfully. 'Is this a deal-breaker?'

'The issue is that I don't know *what* I want any more,' said Molly. 'That's the problem. What should I do? You always seem so certain.'

'Well, right now, you're going to splash your face, apply this ...' Alice waved a lipstick, 'and have another glass of champagne. And then we'll go from there.'

Star

Star opens her eyes. She is lying on the ground next to the cactus, which has fallen over, earth spilling out of its pot. Her right shin is grazed and blood oozes out. She can feel cactus prickles caught in her ribs, and her beloved satin dress, which has come so far with her, is ripped at the hem.

It was a comedy pratfall. She hoisted herself onto the balustrade, sitting for a second, preparing to swing her legs over, but then her hem caught on the cactus and she lost her balance, falling backwards onto the decking, but hitting the spiky plant and the side of the pot as she fell, bringing them with her.

Every part of her body aches. Star shuts her eyes. She starts to cry again, sobs pulsing through her body.

She is so stupid. It's just another mistake – there have been so many of them, stacked on top of each other, a Jenga tower of idiocy.

Instead of trying to climb to the lower flat, she should probably

163

just throw herself off the top of this building. Then it would all be over: the pointy pain that has sat in the pit of her stomach for so long. She would probably be doing everyone a favour. Alice would be delighted. And Lucas – well, she'd be saving him from making a terrible decision. His phone call begging her to come back was almost cetainly down to last-minute nerves and he will have lived to regret it. Right now, he's probably dreading Star turning up and complicating everything.

And now it's 2 p.m., anyway, almost the point of no return. Star should be checking in her rucksack and gently moving through security, ready to spritz her wrist with perfume samples and buy multipacks of cigarette cartons in duty-free. She ought to be scanning the departures board, girding herself for hours on an aeroplane, instead of flat on her back, on this terrace.

'No,' Star whispers aloud, to herself. 'No, I can't bear it.' She balls her fists and puts them over her eyes.

14

London

Five-and-a-half years later

The bedrooms were in the basement of their flat. The Baby's had a subterranean, soupy air, a greenish glow from the ivy encroaching its window, which looked out onto their garden; overgrown grass, some pots of salty geraniums which had cheerfully weathered their neglect, a forlorn square of cracked patio tiles.

They pretended this back room was where The Baby slept, but, in truth, she was in their bed, wedged in the crook of Molly's arm, as she dozed, practically upright.

The Baby's room – Bella still seemed a ludicrous appellation for such a small, squidgy thing – was for changing nappies and soothing themselves. The immaculate nursing chair, with its high arms for resting The Baby's tiny skull on, the pink cot with a mobile of stars hanging above it, an unthreatening cosmos in a state of suspension; this was the sanitised version of parenthood, designed to comfort when all was confusing.

'You look beautiful with your hair down like that,' said Noah. He had just come back from his run and had rushed downstairs to find 'his girls', as he had grown fond of saying. Molly was standing, swaying, with Bella on one shoulder and a square of muslin on the other. The position she so often assumed these days.

'Oh. Thanks,' said Molly, looking out of the window again. She wasn't annoyed Noah had gone on a run – she'd told him to – but she was irritated by the compliment, as if how she looked should be of any significance at all any more. 'I think she must be teething again,' she added. Bella's cheeks had high spots of colour on them, and Molly had spent the entirety of the time Noah had been out trying to soothe her tiny daughter. A breast milk tie-dye covered her top.

'Do you want to give her to me?' said Noah. His T-shirt was wicked with sweat, and he looked euphoric from the movement. It seemed so easy for Noah to access pleasure.

'I think she's about to go off,' said Molly. 'Have a shower, go on.'

Noah emerged again ten minutes later.

'She's down,' Molly said triumphantly. 'Thankfully.'

'Coffee?' said Noah.

'Yes. Please.' She was emphatic. She sat at the chair and examined her hands. 'Do you think it's normal? That she cries this much?'

'Yes,' replied Noah. 'All babies cry. It's how they communicate, isn't it? You told me that. God, I don't know.'

'But she cries *all* the time,' said Molly. 'I just wish I knew what to do to make her happy.'

Noah handed her a coffee. She took a sip. He had stirred sugar into it. He did this without her asking when he noticed she seemed particularly upset, a little treat – one of those silent communications that develop over the course of a long-term relationship.

'I think it's normal,' he added slowly. 'Nobody said this was going to be easy.'

'Nobody said it was going to be this hard either,' said Molly. She was still wearing that special nursing vest she had bought, which had an opening under each breast so she could discreetly feed in public. It had been worn so often in the preceding months that the fabric was starting to sag and pill, but she knew that Noah found the concept erotic. Breast access. That was fashion design her learned husband could get on board with.

It hadn't been an easy labour. Molly had torn when the forceps were deployed, a jagged lightning bolt to her perineum. All those weeks of massaging it redundant in a few frightened heartbeats. She'd had a special pillow to sit upon afterwards at home, like a miniature life-ring, perched among the first-baby flowers and cards with a dazed expression, as Noah brought her cups of tea, all sugared.

The stitches had taken weeks to heal properly. They had become infected, and Molly had needed strong antibiotics.

'I just feel disgusting,' she had whimpered in bed. 'I won't ever be the same.' She herself had been born by caesarean, neatly plucked from Diana's abdomen. She had wanted something different for her baby, for herself. How was she to have known?

A part of her was angry that Noah's body had been left whole. Hers has been proven mutable and unfixed, breaking and remaking itself. It made her resent his untroubled form and the sheer linearity of his desires. His appetites, which insisted upon themselves.

'What time are they arriving?' he asked.

Their friends were coming to meet their baby. Molly had wanted to do it en masse. 'Gets it out of the way,' she had said. Yet now, the thought of everyone descending on their living room was almost more than she could bear. She wouldn't be able to guarantee that Bella wouldn't scream, and she knew she looked terrible, puffy and grey, a diadem of tiny new hairs fuzzing her hairline.

'Half an hour,' she said, looking at her watch. 'I'm going to shower, and there's cake. Hopefully, they won't stay for too long.'

* * *

Alice and Lucas bore expensive macaroons in a pistachio-coloured box. They walked in behind Edward and Olivia, immaculately dressed in matching Aran knits. Privately, Molly thought that Alice and Lucas's children had a slightly froggy cast to them through a combination of Lucas's huge eyes and Alice's wide mouth. However, there was no arguing that they were cute and compliant. Viv brought a teddy bear, the Harrod's label woven in gold on its right paw. Even

Tommy came with a bottle of corner-shop Prosecco and, bizarrely, a bunch of bananas.

'She is gorgeous,' breathed Alice. 'She looks just like you, Noah.' It was true that the jaunty angle of Bella's ears on her skull, the determined set of her chin, owed everything to her father.

'Apparently, most babies look like their dads, to begin with,' said Lucas. 'So that we don't eat them ... or something.' Everyone laughed.

They ate the macaroons, which had a soapy sweetness; they looked far better than they tasted. Edward and Olivia both touched Bella's betighted feet. Tommy ate a banana with satisfaction ('I needed some potassium.'), guzzled more than his fair share of the Prosecco and then asked if there was anything else to drink.

'It's mid-afternoon, Tom,' said Molly gently. Only in Tommy could she find any succour. Alice, further on in motherhood, was impenetrable to her. Her hair straightened, toenails painted, her children able to sit and communicate. Molly was still adrift, and the only person who could relate to that was Tommy. Star could have done, once, but Star was no longer there and never would be again. Every time she remembered this, Molly wanted to vomit. That Star would never meet Bella, her new and forever focal point, seemed impossible. She had learnt to push away what had happened, it was the only way to get on with her life, but something about childbirth had brought it all back.

'I know,' said Tommy and hiccuped. 'But it's a celebration!' He waved his glass, looked at everyone.

'Come and help me get everyone some water,' said Molly. They went to the kitchen together.

'She's so *beautiful*, Molly,' said Tommy. 'I mean that. So perfect.' He had deteriorated since the meeting in the park, when they had offered the brochure, and it was now clear that Tommy was someone with a problem. It wasn't that his clothes were dirty or that he was otherwise visibly unkempt – no specific detail gave it away – but his whole was subtly diminished, and there was a wrongness to his movements; a clumsiness had replaced his genetic grace.

'Tommy.' Molly had to work hard not to let herself cry. 'You know—'

'I'm so happy for you both,' he said. He reached out his arms for her. 'Truly. Hug me then.'

Molly looked at him, assessing, and then stepped into his open arms.

'I think I'm a terrible mother,' she whispered into his neck. 'I'm doing it all wrong.'

'That's impossible,' said Tommy. 'You are an amazing mother, I'm certain of that.' He released her, filled a pint glass with water, and gulped it down. Molly watched his Adam's apple move in his throat.

In the years to come, on drizzy, neverending Tuesday afternoons after Eve had also arrived and Molly was shut inside counting down the minutes to bath time, she was occasionally to return to this exchange. By then, she learned that hoping to be an amazing mother was an unrealistic goal. That being consistently good enough was ambitious in itself.

15

Riad Mousseline, Marrakesh

Saturday afternoon
Fifteen years later

They arrived back at Mousseline, grateful for her shadowy, scented embrace. The water babbled on incessantly in the central courtyard, and the house cat toasted himself in a splotch of sun. Molly and Alice went to the latter's room and splayed on the clean cotton like teenagers. Mohammed had brought them up mint tea, which they poured, a stream of jade from a silver teapot. The air-conditioning unit clicked into life in the corner. Sweaty when they entered, both women were stippled with goosebumps within minutes of being inside.

The others had headed up to the roof for more sunbathing, but Alice had insisted that she and Molly needed to talk.

'I knew something was up,' Alice prefaced. 'I mean, I know his career has suddenly taken off, but there had to be a reason that he wasn't here last night.' Alice placed a hand on Molly's arm. Shellac, the colour of salmon sashimi, marzipanned on top of her fingernails.

Molly didn't answer immediately. Noah would be arriving in an hour or so. Now she had the prospect of having him there and having to negotiate what happened next with everyone watching.

'Don't tell the others,' said Molly. 'I don't want to over-shadow Viv and Iona. Or ruin your weekend. This is just something Noah and I need to sort out.'

'I don't understand how any of this is your fault, though?' said Alice. 'You aren't to blame. It's classic. Man gets a new job and fucks younger woman. It's a tale as old as time, surely?'

'I don't think it's that straightforward,' said Molly. 'Things haven't been right between us – for years. He tried so hard to make it better, but I couldn't be ... It was almost like I couldn't be bothered, even though I knew it was destroying us.'

'Was it just the sex?' asked Alice, lowering her voice on the last word. She had retracted her hand and smoothed it through her hair, fluffing out the blonde tips reflexively.

'No. I don't know. There was always so much to do, all the time. I just felt angry that it was just another area where I had to put in all the effort to make it better. As if I was the one that always had to do the work. I didn't see why I had to make myself feel a certain way if I just didn't, so pushing him away was almost like a punishment.'

'Hmm.' Alice regarded her friend. 'Did you just not fancy

him any more? I mean, you've been together a long time. Things definitely change.' Alice looked away.

'What about you and Lucas?' said Molly. But as she asked, she dreaded the response. She knew that Alice wouldn't have shied away from the labour required. Kegel exercises. Internet courses in marital psychotherapy. Supplements. Not to mention the ongoing maintenance of her physical self. After all, these days, perimenopause was no longer a life change but a commodifiable, curable hormone deficiency.

'Oh, God. Do you really want to know? Well, it's my job, really. Keeping it going. Keeping me going.' She gestured at her taut forehead. 'And yet, still ... things change, Molly.'

'Right?' said Molly, cutting in. She was relieved to talk after so long of keeping the thoughts to herself. 'I just couldn't be bothered. I love him, but whenever he came near, I just felt this deep sense of exhaustion, as if I had walked across a desert for days. I just wanted him to leave me alone. Perhaps forever.' Alice regarded her.

'So maybe this is a good solution,' said Alice. 'Perhaps you could just let it run on. Appreciate Noah for the good stuff and the girls and turn a blind eye. I'm not saying it would be easy, but separation wouldn't be either, trust me.' Alice stood. She never sat still for long.

'So, is this normal then?' asked Molly. 'This is how it is. If you want to stay together for so long, you have to either accept that the physical side of things ends or that one of you will stray.'

'Maybe,' replied Alice.

'I do love him,' said Molly. 'But almost like I love my

parents or the children, he's so dear to me, almost too dear.'

'How did you find out?' asked Alice, stalking to the bathroom and, out of sight, sitting down on the toilet and starting to urinate. She had always worn her lack of inhibition like a badge of honour, her frank physicality a contrast to her prim exterior.

'His phone, of course,' answered Molly, raising her voice slightly so that Alice could hear. 'I wasn't even prying. I was just ordering something to eat. He had the app downloaded, and I didn't. A message from her flashed up, and I asked him who it was. He just blushed. You know Noah, he can't hide anything. And I knew, straight away.'

'I'm sorry,' said Alice, coming to the sink, where she was visible, and starting to wash her hands. 'There you were fancying something to eat, and you got a whole lot more besides.'

'Right,' said Molly.

'How long ago was this?' asked Alice.

'I have no idea how long it's been going on for. But since filming, I suppose – so a year? She's a production assistant on the show. I only found out last Thursday on the night the show aired,' said Molly. 'We've been arguing ever since.'

'I'm so sorry.' Alice cocked her head to one side, regarding her reflection, and then turned towards Molly. 'I truly am.'

'I went mad. I attacked him.' Molly hung her head. 'But the worst thing is that I'm not sure how I feel about it. I don't know what I think about anything these days. I'm tired. I love Noah, and I want him to be happy, but I can't bear that he's done this; it makes me feel so foolish.'

Alice sucked the air in between her teeth.

'I do get what you're saying. I honestly don't know if I'd even ask him to stop seeing her. This Greta, I mean,' continued Molly. 'He's been happier in the last year than he was before. Our life has been easier. He's not as miserable.'

'Sometimes it pays to be pragmatic,' said Alice. 'I'm not saying that you give up, rather that you just accommodate, for a while.' She stood and lifted her kaftan over her head. 'Sorry – you don't mind?' she asked.

'No,' said Molly.

'Just getting ready for the pool,' said Alice. She wore the bikini under the kaftan, the burgundy of a heavy Pinot Noir, already ready. Her muscles were compacted from relentless exercise. The only sign of motherhood was her belly button, a cavernous tell. Alice started to apply a body oil that contained minute fragments of shimmer in swooped movements over her skin, trapped flecks that stuck to her limbs in a dull sparkle.

'I haven't given up,' said Molly, but the words sounded defensive. As if she spoke them to herself. 'I just wish I could feel passionate about something again. I miss that feeling. I used to care so much – about writing and Noah and London and teaching and bloody Gertrude Stein, for God's sake. I had all these enthusiasms. But it's just kind of fallen away. Nothing feels that important nowadays.'

'It will again,' said Alice. 'I'm sure of it. This quagmire you're in will pass, I know it.'

'I certainly hope so,' said Molly.

'Let me get you ready later,' said Alice. 'Like we used to. For tonight.' Days in the Shoreditch flat when they would do each other's make-up and share clothes, Star there as well. Star who could apply make-up better than any of them – a perfect feline flick in eyeliner, blotted red lipstick in an immaculate curve, fever spots of blusher.

'What's the point?' said Molly. 'I am not sure I can be bothered.'

Alice wrapped a bath towel around her torso. She sat down next to Molly on the bed and scrutinised her, a problem to be solved.

'And where does Tommy fit into all this?' she asked, looking at Molly.

'Tommy?' Molly had never told Alice: Tommy was the secret that only Star had known. And what happened between them had ended forever after Star's death.

'Your face lit up when he arrived. Your face always lights up when Tommy turns up,' said Alice. 'Even when he is utterly inconsiderate. You know, years ago, before you got together with Noah, I used to think that it was Tommy that you liked.'

Molly laughed nervously. Trust Alice; she was so sharp, she could cut herself.

'I don't know what you're saying. I always liked him as a friend, and I suppose I'm pleased to see him doing better. We are friends, and I'm just so hopeful that he might finally be on an upward tick.'

'Right.' Alice sounded unconvinced. 'Monogamy is pretty unnatural, as far as I can tell. We're all screwed.'

Molly didn't reply, but stood herself and drifted over to the dressing table, lined with Alice's unguents. There was an army of bottles and tubes, the artillery of eyeliners and lipsticks in an unzipped pouch. 'So many creams,' she said, picking up a moisturiser with a pump dispenser and reading the label.

'Yeah.' Alice scowled. 'Making sure I don't look actually frightening is a full-time job. The moisturising – look at my heels.' She lifted a foot. 'No matter what I do, they are so cracked. It's revolting.'

'You look great,' offered Molly.

'Sure.' Alice was dismissive. 'It just takes too much effort though …' Her face fell. 'I'm fighting a losing battle. But I can't stop, because who am I then? And I've started on injecting all this stuff.' She gestured at her forehead. 'I could see my father peeking out of my face in the mirror and I needed to put a stop to it. I want a different next half from my parents; it's like they just succumbed to old age. I'm not going to give up without a fight.' She jutted her chin.

'They've always seemed pretty content,' said Molly.

'I don't care about contentment,' said Alice. 'That sounds so staid. I want adventure.'

'You're a loon,' said Molly. She looked at Alice, still so hopeful. For what, Molly wasn't sure. 'But I know what you mean.'

Star

3 p.m.

Star finally rolls onto her side and then pushes herself up. With her knees pulled close to her chest, she begins rocking back and forth. There is a keening sound that she has just realised is coming from her. She must look quite mad. The sun is starting to dip ever so slightly in the sky. The day is on the wane; her flight leaves in an hour. This time yesterday afternoon, Star was on her last shift at the restaurant. A lunchtime one, it finished at six – leaving her enough time to go home and pack her few possessions, then to get dressed for Pete's party.

Star hadn't meant to dress up; it wasn't supposed to be that sort of a night, she was only planning to show her face. But she had thrummed with excitement at the thought of going home to see Lucas and had decided to wear her favourite slip dress, made of cement-coloured satin. She had found it long ago at Portobello Market and bundled it into the bottom of her rucksack when she went travelling, primarily for its lightness but also because she knows it flatters her.

Star has her insecurities, but her body has never been one of them. She always enjoys any chance to show it off. It was something she had in common with Alice, but she knows that not all women are like this. Take Molly, for example. Star was constantly astonished at how much Molly hated herself – bemoaning her thighs, the tops of her arms, even her faint eyebrows, as if they were items she had bought in a shop and might conceivably hope to return.

Star imagines that this is what lay behind Molly's big deception, the one Star uncovered just before she came travelling: a deep disbelief that any man could really want her. That Molly is so unaware of her own appeal makes Star feel sad.

When Star lost Lucas and Alice, she lost Molly too. Of course, Molly promised that things wouldn't change between them, but they had, as Star had known they would. Molly had begged Star to tell her what Alice had done, but Star had staunchly refused. She couldn't bear to see the same hesitation on Molly's face that she had seen on Lucas's.

She met Molly first when they were both waitressing at Petit Soleil. Star loved that place. After so long working in pubs, struggling to get her acting off the ground, working at Petit represented a certain career development. It was the first proper waitressing gig she'd had, entirely different from Claws' sunny diner vibes. The owner, Phillipe, had a reverence for the entire enterprise and so the dining room was living theatre. The blue flame licking up from a plate of crêpes Suzette. The sommelier who intoned the wine list. The starched tablecloths and blackboard with a curvy, chalk-drawn script of specials; all were imbued with the sense of drama and ceremony that Star adored.

She had been there for two years, juggling shifts with her theatre company, when Molly joined.

'We've got a new girl for the summer,' Phillipe said one afternoon. 'A recent graduate.'

To begin with, Star was wary. She was busy. She didn't need new friends. Growing up the way she had, with so many people around, she was careful about whom she let into her life. And she was suspicious about a university graduate, someone who might pity her lack of qualifications. She met Molly's smiles with practised nonchalance.

But one afternoon, Molly – a diffident and yet clumsy waitress – spilt a dish of molten dauphinoise on Star's arm in the middle of a busy shift.

'What the—' Star rushed through to the kitchen and ran her forearm under the cold tap.

'I'm so sorry,' Molly followed her into the kitchen. 'It was an accident. Are you OK?' She looked close to tears.

'That bloody hurt,' said Star, examining the scald: a blotch of pink on her white skin.

'I'm such an idiot.' Molly cringed.

Star softened. 'I'll live.'

'I'm so bad at this.'

'Oh … well, it's not as easy as it looks,' Star offered.

After that, they were friends and took their breaks together, half-glasses of wine in the alleyway at the back of the restaurant. Star found Molly so different from her knowing theatre friends. Molly spoke with her arms folded, frequently reddening. She had a certain awkwardness but an attendant – and refreshing – lack of cynicism. Molly was never patronising, rather she sought Star's approval.

One night after a shift, Molly suggested that Star meet her friends. Molly was planning to leave Petit Soleil shortly to take up her work experience at a newspaper, her summer job was coming to an end.

'We've got to stay in touch after I go. You should come and meet the others,' Molly said.

Star herself had been surprised at how much the prospect of Molly's departure bothered her. She had been fine at Petit before Molly arrived, but realised she was going to miss Molly's gentle insight, the way she listened.

They had walked together, heading south towards Old Street, with its filthy clubs and kebab houses and lethal roundabout, railings garlanded with flowers left in the memory of cyclists crushed along the side of haulage trucks.

The flat Molly took her to was in a former warehouse at the bottom of Kingsland Road. The downstairs of the building was given over to a Vietnamese restaurant, packed with customers shoulder-to-shoulder on shared tables under strip lights, spooning noodles into their mouths. Star followed Molly up four flights of stairs, the air heavy with the scent of lemongrass and peanut oil, until they reached a scuffed white door which Molly unlocked.

'I don't live here myself, but I've got a key,' Molly explained. 'I spend so much time here that Alice said it made sense.'

The door swung back to reveal a large open-plan kitchen-sitting room, dark wooden floorboards reflecting splashes of light, pillars and expansive windows facing the glittering spindle of Canary Wharf.

Star saw Tommy first, startling with his dandelion-clock hair and navy eyes, his thin body imbued with precisely the poise that Molly lacked.

'Who's this, Mol?' he asked.

'I'm Star,' Star said, speaking for herself.

'Tommy,' he replied. 'Come in and sit down. We've opened wine. Tuesday wine! Noah and Alice are playing chess, pretentious idiots. Viv and Lucas are still at work as usual, but they'll be here in a bit.'

Alice smiled at Star, briefly revealing the gap between her teeth, before flicking her eyes back to the chessboard. She had aggressively good posture, and Star was struck by the self-assuredness she exuded, like a pheromone, so different from Molly. Her clothes were on the cusp of sloaniness, but she had painted her mouth the explicit red of a cherry tomato.

'I'll get us a drink,' said Molly, reaching for glasses in the cupboard at the sink. Star sat down.

So, it began.

Alice won the match, and Noah laughed it off. He was a good sport, but Star could tell he minded. He had an appealing warmth and was almost handsome, but he was too teddy-bearish for Star to find attractive, his skin and hair an interchangeable nut brown.

Star wasn't shy; she was used to strangers. She had anticipated Molly's friends to be much like Molly herself. Well-educated and well-meaning but sweetly naive, still living the lives their parents expected them to. She hadn't expected Alice and Tommy's *confidence. She wasn't quite sure whether to take them as seriously as they seemed to take themselves.*

They asked about Petit Soleil, and Star riffed on the sanctified cheeseboard, Phillipe, the oversized tins of snails in the larder. Their laughter, which came after a pause, felt like a reward.

'How long have you worked there for?' asked Alice.

'Two years,' Star answered. She sensed their collective puzzlement. 'I'm in a theatre group too,' she added, 'but this helps to pay the bills.'

'Is that what you really want to do?' said Alice. 'Theatre?'

'Yes,' Star said. 'I love it.'

'Incredible,' said Alice, with a sip of her wine, but Star could tell she didn't think so. Alice was the sort who respected concrete markers of success, it was clear. She was devoid of artistic yearnings. 'I'm about to do a law conversion.' Alice wrinkled her nose. 'Boring, but what else are you going to do with an English degree?'

'There are a few other things, Al,' said Molly.

'And the rest of you?' Star had leant back in her chair, taken a slug of wine. She hadn't got the measure of them, but she could tell that they were the kind of people to define themselves through what they did.

'I've just got a job at an ad agency,' said Tommy. 'Mol is about to start work experience at a newspaper, which of course you know ... Noah will do a PhD, mystifyingly, because I always got higher marks than he did.'

'Oi.' Noah fake-punched Tommy in the shoulder.

'Viv is going into the civil service,' continued Alice. 'And Lucas is going to make partner one day at his firm. Which is why he still isn't home yet.' Star noticed the plaintive note in Alice's voice.

As if on summons, the door swung open, revealing a tall man with strawberry-blond hair, dressed in a suit and holding a briefcase. His cufflinks gleamed as he set it down on the floor and straightened up. The collar of his shirt cut precise triangles by his throat. An unexpected burble of laughter lodged in Star's throat; he was so absurd, even among all the premature grown-ups. He could be someone's father, freshly pressed from the past. She felt the conflagration of bitten-down mockery on her tongue. Just imagine what her theatre friends would make of him. Or her mother's comrades, with their distrust of anyone who set out to make money for its own sake.

'Hello, I'm Lucas,' he said, proffering a hand.

'I thought as much,' said Star. 'Nice to meet you, Lucas.' Their hands met, and Lucas raised his eyebrows above the top rim of his glasses in the manner that she would later grow to love.

Now she's lost him, forever, through her tardiness – a characteristic he always teased her for.

From her position on the balcony's decking, Star stops rocking. She rests her forehead on her knees.

16

Riad Mousseline, Marrakesh

Saturday night
Twenty years later

'This one, I think,' said Alice, laying out a dress. A kind of bastardised *cheongsam* with a high neck, made of blue silk in a merciless cobalt reminiscent of the walls at the Jardin Majorelle. It was both beautiful and impractical, like so many of the clothes that Alice bought, from high-end websites, arriving wrapped in tissue paper, and encased in the black cardboard boxes that Molly had seen in her house. Single items that would pay the rent for entire families. The inner label was an artwork in itself, a chunky orange square that Molly could imagine scratching against her atlas bone.

'Too short,' said Molly, thinking of the outfit she had already chosen for that evening. A sleeveless dress she had spotted in one of her catalogues. Navy, this time. Billowy. Flattering but not eye-catching, it was generous to her maternal midsection. She didn't want people to think she had thought about it, exactly. As she aged, she felt that a certain cultivated insouciance was more youthful than anything else.

'You've always had great legs. You've been hiding them for at least a decade. Think of that girl,' said Alice.

'I'm not trying to win him back,' said Molly. 'I made that clear. We aren't sixteen. Besides ... I'm not sure that I want him to fancy me. That was half the problem.'

'It's not about him fancying you,' Alice shrugged. 'It's about you fancying yourself. That's what it's always about.'

'Oh ... all right,' Molly said.

Alice made her up. Lucas was lying under a turf of bubbles in the giant tub in the bathroom. When she had come into their room, the door had been open, and Molly had caught a glimpse of him reclined, with a glass of wine to one side, the drone of some football punditry from his phone. Molly looked at his emergent foot, the flex of his arm; it was so surprising to see Lucas relaxing. Alice shut the bathroom door firmly.

'Bloody Liverpool. Right. Shall we?' She sat Molly at her dressing table and pulled out a roll of make-up. It contained dozens of lipstick colours and pots of eyeshadow, an artist's palette of blush in shades of coral and rose.

'Base.' Alice squirted from a little tube. 'BB cream.' She smoothed it over Molly's skin, rubbing it up her cheekbones in tiny movements. 'And concealer.'

Molly felt herself unclench, her body sagging in the face of the tiny darting movements over her skin. A bit like the ASMR videos that Bella and Eve enjoyed watching, the sounds of Alice snapping and unscrewing, the anticipation of her being so close, about to touch Molly, more delicious than when she actually did. Wasn't that true of so much in life? Anticipation trumped reality. That was certainly true of this weekend.

'There,' said Alice, after a while. 'Look.'

Molly opened her eyes and regarded her reflection in the mirror. As the years had gone by, she had stopped bothering much with make-up, aside from her few trustworthy favourites. It felt dishonest, and she had lost the urge to transform herself. But there it was: that capacity to look different. Her skin was smoother and browner, silicone-slick, her eyes lined in kohl, the lids onyx. Her hair had been waved in the way that Alice sometimes wore hers, done with straighteners. Neat little flapper curves that petered out at the bottom.

'You look fantastic,' said Alice, turning her head on one side to admire her handiwork.

'Shit. You do,' said Lucas, who had emerged from the bathroom with a towel around his waist. He whistled. 'There's life in the old dog yet.'

'Cheers, Lucas,' said Molly. 'I love being called an old dog.'

Lucas smiled. 'Seriously, Mol. You look terrific,' he said.

'Take the dress,' urged Alice. 'Just try it. Who knows? You might like it.'

'You holding up?' Lucas asked-, dropping a hand onto his wife's shoulder.

'Yup,' said Alice. 'I'm OK. I suppose that I'm just not sure tonight is going to turn out how I'd hoped it was going to, you know?'

'I'm sure it will,' Lucas said. 'It's going to be exactly what you hoped for, my darling.' There was an archness to his tone. 'Did you speak to Edward and Ollie in the end?' he added.

Molly watched them.

'I couldn't get Olivia – I hope she's settled down. But I spoke to Edward, and he was fine. Said they were going to get a pizza and watch a film.'

'Fabulous,' said Lucas. He padded back into the bathroom, just in his shirt and boxer shorts. Those calves, so familiar to Molly, so infused with personality that she saw them as capable, know-it-all, their arrogance masking the terminal insecurity of a boy sent away from home at the age of seven. 'I hear Noah is turning up for tonight, after all?' he called out to Molly.

'That's right,' said Molly, standing, clutching the dress and walking towards the door.

In the corridor, outside, she hesitated for a second and then headed to the games room instead of immediately back up to the bedroom. She laid Alice's dress over one of the bar stools like a pliant friend, and then racked up the pool balls, the 8-ball in the centre, their glossy, firm contours reassuring. Molly chalked a cue and broke the triangle with a crack, the balls skittering across the green. Then she methodically potted every ball, as she had long ago learnt, with no other purpose than to recall how it felt.

Star

Star is back on the sunlounger. Her sunlounger. She has claimed it forever with the spots of blood dotted across the bland Corporate Oatmeal cushions.

She has to try to calm herself, before deciding what to do next. That's what Lucas would tell her to do. Perhaps, even if she doesn't turn up tomorrow morning, he won't go through with the wedding? Maybe he'll wait for her and all will be well. All manner of things on heaven and earth.

Star tries to believe this, but fails to. She can't stop the negative chorus in her head, the voices telling her how stupid she has been and what a terrible mess she has made of everything.

Alice would never get herself in to a situation like this, would never abandon her own goals – no, Alice is out for number one. Star sensed as much on the first night that they met. But she warmed to Alice nonetheless. It was hard not to. Alice is charming. Alice is

189

fun. She has oodles of energy and precision and drive. Nothing gets in the way of what she wants. There is nothing better than being Alice's friend when your needs are aligned. When they aren't, the problems start, as Star discovered.

Still, in the beginning, it was enchanting. On a night out, they were unstoppable: Siamese twin of freewheeling energy, able to keep going long after Molly had peeled away, their shared voraciousness chiming in the other.

When Molly and Noah got together and decided to rent their own place, Star was thrilled to be offered Noah's room in the Shoreditch flat. By that point, she was spending much of her time – between her shifts and rehearsals – there, anyway. It had begun to feel like home.

She gave up her bedsit without a backwards glance. From spending years doing anything to preserve her freedom, she thrust herself into their lives, and what a relief it was. She had been surrounded by people for so long, but apart. Yet Molly and her friends assuaged Star's loneliness.

She adored the flat itself, with its cooking smells floating up from the restaurant downstairs, the distant oceanic swoosh of traffic on the Kingsland Road, the view from her bedroom window onto the abandoned railway bridge, overgrown with brambles.

More importantly, cohabiting with Lucas and Alice, watching them from the inside of their lives, being there when they woke, with morning breath and sleepy dust still spangled at the corners of their eyes, was an education. Despite the fact his mother Bibi was from Chile, or perhaps because of it, Lucas had been schooled in a kind of uber-Englishness, one familiar to Alice but bewildering, almost laughable, to Star. He and Alice followed an etiquette she had never been taught, one of thank-you letters and soup spoons and never saying what you really thought. The door of the fridge jangled with weird condiments she had never encountered – Gentleman's Relish in a circular white pot, caper berries, marmalade so sour and thick with peel that Star couldn't fathom eating it for pleasure.

Her new flatmates weren't cool in the way that Star had always defined it, but they helped her realise what a hollow aspiration that was. Instead, they had certainty about their place in their world, the futures they were going to have. Star found it a comfort to watch such entitlement at close quarters.

If she's completely honest with herself, Star knew how Alice felt about Lucas from the very beginning. It was written all over her face. But they both claimed their brief relationship was ancient history and, besides, Star had never once intended to fall for Lucas herself.

17

London

Twenty years later

From dislike to love, then back again, within the scope of a single afternoon: that was what marriage was like for Molly.

In the love ledger were conversations with Bella and Eve in the kitchen, Noah looking at their daughters and listening intently to every word. The girls' earnestness, the manner they sat on the kitchen counter, calves dangling, their gales of laughter. The incessant chirrup of their phones. The way they demanded that Molly try bubble tea, or listen to a new singer, or apply pore strips to her nose. Even how they stormed down to their basement bedroom at every perceived infraction, filling the house with movement and energy.

More love was to be found in their family cat Marcel, slinking in from the garden, sleeping with abandon in the middle of the living-room rug, his body still elegant despite his advanced age.

The home that they'd lived in for so many years, every creak and framed print familiar. The herbs in planters on the kitchen windowsill that Noah snipped over one of his elaborate risottos. The wallpaper in the toilet downstairs, leopards marching, cheering on every visit.

Her partner. His breath as he slept, like a metronome to their lives together. The way he brought the outside air in with him when he arrived back from the university on his bike with his left trouser leg rolled up, ready to talk at full speed about whatever had happened that day, the university always a ready source of intrigue and factionalism.

But these moments of appreciation for what she had, what they had built, were undercut with dislike – the seeming immutability of their allotted tasks. Cleaning out the dishwasher filter of mulch – why was that hers? The tedium of trying to police Eve's phone use when she wasn't entirely sure what the point was. Watching her daughter's swimming galas with the other mothers with their emergent grey roots and competitive love, projecting their dreams of exceptionality onto their daughters, in the chemical, verruca fug of an overheated municipal pool. The broken floorboard at the top of the stairs that they needed to do something about but never quite got around to. The way that Noah reached for her – supposedly without expectation, for they had discussed this, but always in hope, in the knowledge that any encounter between them would be profoundly satisfying for him.

Molly see-sawed, aware of the good, grateful for the love, but also bored and tired. She was lucky, so why did she feel so sad?

Obviously, her age was partly to do with it. She was a snake shedding her skin, moving into a new version of herself. Just as Eve was, but that wasn't the whole answer, she knew it, and despite what he said, Noah did too. He wanted the best for her, she knew this. He always had.

Then the night she found out. They had been gathered as a family to watch the grand unveiling of Noah's show, squeezed together on the sofa, with Bella sitting on the carpet at their feet. Molly had made popcorn, tossed with salt and sugar. She took a large sip of wine as the opening credits played out over a drone shot of London in all her pomp: the giant tit of St Paul's, the ribbon of the Thames, the phallic bulge of the Gherkin, before honing in on the bullseye of the Globe.

'It's exciting!' Molly had reached for Noah's hand. Did it make her monstrous that, along with genuine pride, she was jealous of this development in Noah's career? She rather thought it did, and so masked the splinter of envy with excessive enthusiasm that fooled neither of them.

'I know,' Noah had replied. Then he was on screen, looking as creased and academic as he did at home. 'Jesus. I didn't realise my hair stuck out like that. Does it look like that?' A note of wonder in seeing himself.

'Uh-huh,' Eve had said, for once not double-screening. 'But don't worry, Dad, it's the mad professor look. You've got it off to a T.'

Noah had been on screen talking about how Shakespeare chafed against the casting practices of the day, specifically in *Antony and Cleopatra*, using the famous beauty to complain that someone might 'boy' her greatness.

'I'm just going to order a pizza,' Molly had said, reaching for Noah's phone, where it lay beside her. 'You've got the delivery app, haven't you?'

'Hang on,' said Noah, snatching back his phone.

But it had been too late. As Molly had picked up the device, a text had flashed up from someone saved in Noah's phone only as G.

Looking good, Professor, XXXX, it said. And Molly knew.

18

Riad Mousseline, Marrakesh

Saturday night
One week later

Back in her room, Molly stepped into the *cheongsam*. She struggled with the zip at the back and stood in front of the mirror, regarding herself. The dress revealed about three inches of white thigh. Her knees, which in sunshine had assumed a certain ponderous quality in her forties, like puzzled faces, were perfectly respectable in Mousseline's treacly light. Fine. She would make Alice happy.

The party was starting in an hour. Noah was due at any moment, and she anticipated the heft and smell, the shape of him in space. So familiar to her. She knew exactly how to slot in against him.

She checked her phone. At Mousseline, she had gradually lost the itch to look at it so frequently, to dissolve into that virtual world. A text from Noah: *Just landed. With you soon.*

X – sent an hour ago. It seemed he would arrive just as the party began, always in the nick of time.

Molly rummaged in her bag. She had brought a notebook with her on the weekend; she always took one with her when she went anywhere, automatically, just as she maintained one on her bedside table at home. For ages, they had mainly gone unfilled, but Alice was right: there *was* still time for something new. Molly pulled out the plain black Moleskine and stroked the leather. She moved to the desk in the room, sat down and started to write, a fragment about a father teaching his daughter how to play pub sports. She was initially self-conscious, waiting for the familiar wash of pointlessness. To her surprise, it didn't come. The task didn't feel laborious, but absorbing, slotting together satisfyingly like the clack of billiard balls hitting one another.

An hour disappeared, with no thought. She'd done it, stepped back to the place beyond time which had eluded her for so long, since Star's death and motherhood had obscured the way.

Thrumming with her efforts, Molly decided to go up to the roof terrace. She wondered again what Alice had meant about the night holding a 'big surprise'. Alice's life was so full of treats, larded on to the days, that it was hard to imagine the thing that might titillate or enthral.

She left her room and ascended the narrow steps. The colour was leaching from the sky, and the night was closing in. Mohammed was moving around, lighting tea lights in glass jars, turning the terrace back into a temporary wonderland, but nobody else was there yet. Molly felt the breeze on the parts of her legs which were usually covered, smelt the hit of jasmine and orange blossom, undercut with the rasp of nearby desert. She noticed Mohammed look over at her, taking note of her transformation. He went back to his tasks. The central table was set up with glasses, bottles of wine and terracotta bowls containing filo squares piled on top of each other. In usual circumstances, she would feel self-conscious. Mutton. But she had a gloaming sense of her own power, one that she hadn't felt for so long. The night was a pivot; she knew it in her gut.

She moved towards the edge of the terrace, looking out over the city. Then, as if noticing someone across a room that you were at first unaware of, she saw the moon in the sky. A complete disc. She remembered what Star had always said about nights with full moons, sending everyone a little strange. Lunar craziness. Her hand trailed the insufficient railing. Children weren't admitted at Mousseline, she knew, and certainly, this roof terrace wouldn't be safe. She could just imagine trying to constrain a four-year-old Eve up there. Bella had always been a still child, but her sister was in constant motion, looking to push against any boundaries, both real and imagined.

It would be easy to tip over the edge onto the courtyard below. Splat. Like a bag of flour, she would split and spread over the dust. The projected violence of it nauseated her. She could never do such a thing, but the vertigo itch pulsed within: gravity's magnetism.

Molly stood and stared, then placed her palms on her heart, as she had before.

It was a few minutes later that she felt hands snaking around her waist. A body pressed up against her own, fleetingly imprinted before retreating, the suggestion of lips at the curve of her neck.

'Noah,' she turned. 'Oh.' She had recognised her error as soon as the words were out of her mouth. The smell wasn't right. Noah had a certain biscuity savouriness to his base aroma, whereas this was something sweeter, lighter, cut with tobacco. 'Piss off, Tommy.' She trembled on the spot.

For a second, their faces were inches from each other, and then they kissed, briefly, softly. Then again, more deeply. As they had many times before.

Molly was curious whether it would feel the same, had spent years wondering on those nights where she preferred to turn away from Noah and check her phone, questioning if it was motherhood, increasing age, or her choice of life partner which had lobotomised desire. The answer was both that it did … and it didn't. The connection was still there, but fainter – overlaid with all the time since, softened by the altered bodies they now inhabited, neutralised by the choices they had made. Molly noticed the taste of cigarettes on Tommy's tongue. She half-opened her eyes. Close up, his face looked ludicrous, glued to hers.

Molly pulled away. They weren't star-crossed lovers; they were laughable.

'I just saw this gorgeous woman standing up here on her own,' said Tommy, shrugging. 'And then I realised that I knew her. I knew her really well. Once.' He wiped his mouth, and the gesture made Molly even more convinced of their ridiculousness. She had lost herself. Or remembered herself. It had been the writing. Alice's dress.

'Alice insisted on giving me what Eve would call a "glow-up",' she said, smoothing her hands over her hips.

'It's remarkable,' said Tommy.

'Noah is going to get here any minute,' said Molly. She glanced over at Mohammed, who was turned away, but the twist of whose sinews betrayed that he was listening intently, that he knew what had happened between them. 'Besides, you never knew me *that* well.' The last words a hiss.

'Sorry,' said Tommy. He didn't sound it. He had changed into a suit. One that must have been left from his advertising days, it looked expensive but subtly outdated, the lapels too large, the finish a little shiny. It hung loose on his skinny frame. 'You just looked so ... different, again. And I ... Sorry. That was out of order. It must be this place. It's so long since I got out of London.'

'Let's sit down.' Molly motioned at the cushions. 'How was the trip?'

'Oh. Beautiful,' replied Tommy. 'Stunning scenery. And so relaxing having Lucas boss me around all day. It was a bit like being a kid again. I just sat back in the car and let him educate me. Lucas was Daddy, and we were on a day trip.'

'Right,' said Molly. 'Sounds horrifying.'

'You haven't heard about the dead goat yet,' said Tommy.

'Dead goat?' said Molly. 'Only you, Tom.'

'It was nothing to do with me,' said Tommy, holding up his hands. 'We came across it on the footpath. It stank.' He stopped talking. He looked off into the distance. 'I vomited.'

'Sounds traumatic,' said Molly.

'Yeah, it was a bit. The mountains were amazing, though. I've been stuck in my corner of London for so long now. I just have the same routes. To the corner shop. The ducks.'

'You're not still feeding those bloody ducks?' said Molly. 'Tommy.'

There was silence then, between them, until Molly broke it.

'Things aren't good with me and Noah right now.'

'I'm sorry,' said Tommy. He jiggled his right knee up and down.

'But still, I shouldn't have done that,' said Molly.

'You know …' Tommy cleared his throat.

'Tommy, don't.' The compromises of her marriage were beyond his comprehension.

'I came here to tell you something,' said Tommy.

'Well don't, please.'

'I can't stop myself. I'm sober, pretty much for the first time since Star died, and it seems like maybe things aren't as perfect between you and Noah as I'd always thought. I came here to be honest with you. I love you and I, well, I always have. I just didn't realise it. From the first time I saw you looking self-conscious in a seminar.'

'No. Tom.' Molly groaned and leant forward, with her head in her hands. 'Please stop.'

'So, you don't feel the same way?'

Molly looked up. 'I did. Once. But you didn't want me then, Tommy, not really. And now it's much too late.'

Star

5 p.m.

From far below, Star can hear a boat sounding its horn in the harbour. She lies with her eyes closed. All is lost. If only she could float out of her body and away. She is so tired.

Star thought she knew despair eighteen months ago, but her current predicament takes it to a whole new level.

She has lost Lucas for a second time. The first almost killed her. She is pretty sure she can't endure it again.

On paper, she and Lucas were chalk and cheese. She, flaky, theatrical, prone to reading her horoscope and losing her keys; he, steadier, more conventionally ambitious and academic, with a habit of reading biographies of English kings and listening to the Test match on a portable radio, in the scant hours that he wasn't working or drinking. But, from the beginning, there was an ease between them, a mutual regard.

When Lucas asked about her acting, he seemed genuinely

interested in the answers. She told him about the tradition of site-specific theatre that Lockjaw, the company she had joined around the same time as starting in Petit Soleil, espoused; how they used location to highlight the themes of whatever they planned to stage.

'So, an abandoned bank vault might be perfect for putting on Marlowe's Doctor Faustus,*' she explained one afternoon at the kitchen table in the warehouse flat, sucking on a teaspoon she had dipped into a jar of peanut butter.*

'How so?' Lucas's eyes had lit up, the green in the hazel always seemed more pronounced when he was curious about a subject, which was often.

'Well, the play is about the lengths someone might go to for knowledge and power,' said Star, looking at Lucas and then dipping the spoon in again. 'You should know about that with your rabid pursuit of Mammon.'

'Steady on,' said Lucas, but he smiled, then paused. 'It sounds good, the site-specific bit.'

'A change from Henry V *at the Royal Court, definitely,' replied Star, smiling. That was what Lucas's mother, Bibi, had taken him to see the last time she had been in 'town'.*

'I'm not just pursuing money, you know,' said Lucas, returning to their other subject.

'I don't care if you are,' said Star. She had watched many playful arguments between Lucas and Molly about how far personal ambition should be allowed to determine a life. Molly's self-effacement hid strong convictions — she disapproved of Lucas's and Alice's decision to try to earn as much as they could, believing that they should put their talents towards something that would

better serve society, as she intended to. Choose, perhaps, to become the kind of lawyers who don't become rich.

Star could see Molly's point, but her friend's earnest morality sometimes reminded her a little too much of her own mother's political views. In Star's book, everyone had to make their own decisions on how to live.

From the first night Star had met him, something about Lucas made her feel steady in a way that was unfamiliar. She hadn't grown up with her father, and Lucas's precocious maturity appealed. One night, shortly after she had moved into the flat, she came home to find Lucas chopping onions for a Bolognese, a tea towel slung over his right shoulder and the radio on in the background.

'Well, well, look at this,' said Star, shrugging off her jacket. 'Are you making me dinner?'

'I am, as it happens,' Lucas replied. 'You and Alice. She's going to be late back.' He turned back towards the stove and Star watched him from behind, his shoulders broad, shirtsleeves rolled up. Something twisted inside her and she knew, in that instant, that she liked him. It had been just beyond her eyeline, but the realisation hove into view.

As the months passed, she grew to rely on Lucas's measured judgements, his informed opinions. Her friendship with Alice was different – more combustible from the start, but also sisterly. As soon as she moved into the flat, she and Alice pooled their possessions. They were constantly in and out of each other's rooms, looking for cotton buds, tampons and clothes. That is why the accusation that Alice later made was so particularly painful – it perverted the very essence of their bond. Unlike Lucas, Star could tell that Alice wasn't genuinely interested in her acting. Alice didn't have creative yearnings; art was for consuming, with a view to knowing the right things, rather than making.

It was six months after moving in that she suggested Lucas come to Devon to meet Moira. Star told herself it was accidental that she'd chosen a weekend that Alice was occupied visiting her own parents, but deep down she knew that she wanted Lucas to herself.

Star hadn't been back to Devon for months, but she knew her mother would be happy to see her. Moira always was, something that Star took for granted, she now realises. And after so long in the city, she longed for the savage green of the valley, the stream and the pair of wood pigeons in the garden which cooed and shat and weighed down the branches of the ancient apple tree. The view of Moira in her fisherman's smock trundling around with her cutting basket, wisps of hennaed hair escaping from her ponytail.

Moira collected them from the station in her dented black-and-burgundy 2CV.

'Star!' she exclaimed on the platform, holding Star, but with her eyes roving onto Lucas. Star knew her mother to be a novelty merchant with an insatiable lust for new people. She saw Lucas through her mother's eyes – a button-down shirt over dark jeans, loafers. 'This must be …?' Moira asked. Star hadn't told her she was bringing anyone.

'My flatmate, Lucas,' said Star. Lucas extended a hand, the kind of man who knows himself to be good with mothers. In the car on the way to the mill house, he talked smoothly about their train journey, the weather, the unfolding countryside, the recent election of Tony Blair.

'What do you do yourself, Lucas?' asked Moira, her hands

gripping the steering wheel at ten to three. A terrible, terrifying driver, Moira had always compensated by holding on extremely hard.

'I'm afraid that I've sold my soul,' replied Lucas pleasantly. 'I'm a lawyer for an American bank in the City.'

'I see,' Moira replied. Star had met her mother's eyes in the rear-view mirror, sensing her recalibration.

'But it's not the long-term plan,' said Lucas, as he always did. 'I'm going to do it for five years to get a foot on the property ladder and do something more meaningful.'

'Very sensible,' said Moira. 'Make sure you don't get sucked in!' She laughed.

After that, Star had expected her mother to cool on Lucas, but she hadn't accounted for Lucas's endearing competence. Within an hour of being at the mill, he had fed the chickens, chopped a bag of carrots for soup, listened to Hans (Ellen had long since moved out) reading one of his awful poems, complimented Moira on her vegetable patch and glued a broken plate.

'What a lovely boy,' Moira had said, as Star rooted in the damp laundry cupboard for extra bedding, and Lucas chatted downstairs to the others.

'Yes,' Star had replied. 'He's a good friend.'

'A friend?' Moira had asked as they moved to put sheets on the bed in the spare room. Someone else had obviously been sleeping in it, and Star saw the long squiggle of a pubic hair on the sheet they peeled away. She knew that her room was immediately requisitioned when she had moved out; it had been hard enough to keep it to herself growing up.

'Yes,' she replied.

'I've got a spare lilo he can sleep on,' Moira had said.

'Great.'

'Sounds like a big job he's got,' Moira had added. Star knew that in her mother's book, her own hand-to-mouth waitressing and acting ambitions were preferable.

'He's a good person,' Star had answered curtly, as she struggled to pull a pillowcase over a pillow.

'He must be – you haven't brought anyone home before,' said Moira.

* * *

It was dusk when Star and Lucas went for a walk in the valley, down a path which led to a wishing well. As a child, Star had often gone there alone, to escape the house's new guests and throw in coins she had found in pockets, fervently wishing to one day meet her father instead of other people's.

'What is this place?' Lucas said, as they emerged into the clearing surrounded by a spectral circle of silver birch. The well's tiled roof was covered with pincushions of moss, a bucket attached to a piece of wound rope, suspended above the gaping hole.

'A wishing well, silly,' said Star, skipping over to the edge of it. 'You throw in some money and make a wish. Don't they have these in Surrey?'

'But who built it?' said Lucas, perplexed. He pushed his glasses up his nose, out of place in the lush pagan place.

'Who knows? Who cares?' replied Star. 'Have you got any change?'

Lucas patted his pockets and pulled out a 50p pence. 'Here you go.'

'Thanks.' Star shut her eyes. She dropped the coin down into the darkness. There was a pause of seconds before they heard a faint plop from far below. Star opened her eyes. 'All done.'

'What did you wish for?' asked Lucas.

'I can't tell you! It definitely won't happen if I do,' said Star, but she met his eyes, hoping that he might intuit. She didn't know how Lucas felt about her, this not-knowing was the problem. Did friends come and meet mothers for the weekend?

Later that night, she and Lucas talked in the darkness of her childhood bedroom. Without being able to see his face, Star was surprised at how free-ranging their conversation became.

'I think Lockjaw should work on a fairy tale,' she told Lucas. It was something that had been nagging at her for a while, but she was worried that her director, Mikael, might think it childish. 'I think we could do something really gothic and magical, especially if we staged it outside.'

'That's a great idea,' Lucas said, after a pause. 'Why don't you suggest it?'

'Maybe I will,' said Star. 'I suppose I'm worried it'll get shot down.'

'That won't happen,' said Lucas, confidently. 'You've got an instinct. I can tell.'

* * *

Back in London, Lockjaw started work on their latest production. After the weekend in Devon and her conversation with Lucas,

Star had suggested that they retell Hans Christian Andersen's fable, The Red Shoes. *Something about the story of Karen had stuck with Star ever since Moira had read it to her as a little girl.*

'Karen is adopted,' Star had said to the assembled members of Lockjaw, at one of their team meetings at the Lucid Theatre. 'She is given a pair of red shoes which she loves so much that she wears them to church, despite such vanity being a sin. Afterwards, as a divine punishment, the shoes start dancing of their own accord and Karen can't take them off. She can't stop moving, day or night, and eventually becomes so desperate that she begs an executioner to cut off her feet. After that, Karen has crutches and feet made of wood. She never dances again.'

Star had looked out at the group, catching an eyebrow raise from Thelma, another actor who she often vied with for the main roles.

'Sounds like a bit of a bummer,' said Thelma, to a ripple of amusement.

'I don't think it's a bad thought,' the director, Mikael, had said. 'I know that story and it has it all. Vanity, sin, spirituality. But we retell it.'

'That's right,' said Star. 'From a feminist perspective. Karen's vanity is her undoing, isn't it always for women?'

'I think this could be good,' said Mikael. 'I will start thinking about a script. And you should play Karen, Star.'

'Really?' Star couldn't believe it. She flashed an expression of triumph at Thelma. Mikael had listened to her idea, it was going to become a play, she couldn't wait to tell Lucas the news.

'You'll have to come and watch it when we're ready,' said Star, after she had, enjoying what she saw in Lucas's eyes. Her friends

had never seen one of her productions before. She'd wanted to wait until she knew what they were working on was brilliant. She was going to make this brilliant.

'I'll be there,' said Lucas.

19

London

Two years earlier

Molly had never set out to keep her involvement with Tommy to herself. Indeed, when it began, she hoped for the precise opposite.

She had been surprised, but pleased, by his offer to accompany her home one night. Nobody ever came to the flat she shared in Seven Sisters with Jenn, and she often ran from the last Tube with her key pointing out of her fist, an insufficient blade.

'So, this is where you live,' said Tommy, looking up at the new-build block on the end of a Victorian street, its bricks wicked by the cantaloupe-glow of a street light. Inside, the third-floor flat was hermetically sealed; its double-glazed windows had a safety mechanism which meant you could only open the panels of UPVC a chink, even on such a mild midsummer night like the one they found themselves in.

'Yes,' said Molly. She was almost falling-down drunk, teetering on the edge of blackout, her limbs melty and loose, her thoughts atomised and indistinct. A relief: if sober, she would have been too nervous about having Tommy there, so close, looking at her like that. She would have been too aware of her belly, her thighs, the fact she hadn't shaved her calves. She stepped towards her doorway. 'This is me!' She spun round clumsily and wobbled off centre. Tommy stepped forward to stop her from falling, but then continued holding her.

'Molly?' said Tommy.

'Yeah?' She giggled from the near fall, his proximity. He leant down and kissed her. She was stock-still for a moment before reciprocating. As they moved, a motion sensor clicked on the light above the doorway as if to spotlight their swoon. The kiss, one that neither of them would ever forget as long as they lived, propelled them up to her room.

'Are you absolutely certain you want to do this?' Tommy had said. Molly had nodded and lifted her arms. She had seldom been more certain about anything. For the first time in her life, and despite her drunkenness, she was suffused with a desire that overrode her self-consciousness.

'Are you?' she said, and he had answered by pulling her T-shirt over her head.

Your life can change in minutes – another of the night's understandings.

Tommy didn't stay over, but he promised to call her the following day, kissing her again, tenderly, before loping away towards the night bus.

Molly woke full of hope and the sense of having been altered forever. Lying on the sofa watching breakfast TV was unfathomably exciting. She was warmer than usual to Jenn, although she didn't mention what had happened. Later, she was glad she hadn't. As the sun moved lower in the sky, anticipation leached out of her. It wasn't going to be like that.

The next time she saw him was at the warehouse flat. He was as he always was, only once catching her glance in a way that made her skin prickle. Molly left soon afterwards, trying to keep her tears banked down until she was out of eyeshot. She sensed Tommy walking behind her as she headed for the bus stop.

'Mol. Wait!' he called.

'What?'

'I'm sorry I didn't ring you … I'm just all over the place right now,' said Tommy, looking at the bus, which pulled up. 'Is that yours?'

'I can wait,' said Molly.

'With my mum …' Tommy came to a halt. 'She has been diagnosed with lymphoma,' he said, finally, sticking his hands in his pockets. He had a distant expression on his face, and Molly imagined him entering a room, approaching a beloved face that turned to him, like a sunflower tilting towards the sun.

Still.

'I'm sorry,' said Molly. They had met Tommy's mother, Celeste, once when she had bought them all a roast lunch as a treat one Sunday in a pub on the corner of Hampstead Heath. Celeste, who split her time between the countryside and her London flat, had the kind of assured glamour Molly knew that her own mother aspired to: heeled boots, white-blonde hair cut into a precise bob, beringed fingers with long nails painted a delicate, seashell pink. She shared her son's habit of pausing before laughing, of widening her eyes as someone spoke. Molly had found her fascinating, in what she revealed about the provenance of Tommy's charm, but also intimidating. It was impossible to believe that such a sleek creature could be doing anything as inconvenient as becoming gravely ill.

'Once things are clearer – you know?' he said, looking up at her.

'OK,' said Molly, looking away. Disease was a trump card.

Yet despite what he said, it happened again. Another night out, another offer to accompany her home, and the same set of events followed, down to the reneged promise to call.

Then, again. This time, he arrived on a Saturday afternoon, when she was home alone, working on a short story. Those were the days when she was sure that publication was imminent if she just worked hard enough. She let him in, and he asked her what she was doing, asked her if he could read the story and then did so with absolute concentration.

'This is good,' he said.

Molly glowed. She knew Tommy wouldn't say that unless he meant it. This time, sober, she leant towards him and touched his forearm, submitting to the impulse that she hadn't previously comprehended.

'What is this?' she said afterwards.

'What do you mean?' said Tommy.

Molly wriggled away from him and stood up, heading to the bathroom and locking herself in to cry in front of the mirror, watching her face crumple like screwed paper.

'I'm sorry,' said Tommy, following her there. 'Everything will be different soon. Once we know what's happening with Mum.'

Molly nodded, hating herself, but unable to articulate her actual needs. Perhaps this refracted warmth, like moonlight, was enough?

The concealment assumed a life of its own.

Molly knew it had to stop after that night with Noah on the bridge. She met Tommy in her lunch break, in the square flanked by bars that they usually drank in: a dusty precinct of grass surrounded by black railings, different in daylight with none of the glowering nocturnal enchantment.

Tommy was unmanned by the daylight, his hair too pale for credibility, his skinniness always a surprise. And yet. Still. She watched him get out of the black cab which had pulled up to the gate, the motor still rumbling. The way he moved his limbs was so distinctive, ineffably him. It spoke to some part of her, and she knew that it always would.

He looked for her, found her and smiled.

They hadn't told the others that they were meeting. She had asked him to meet her alone.

They sat on the ground, surrounded by clusters of people that didn't know them. She wasn't afraid that somebody they knew might see them together. Tommy wouldn't touch her in public. He never had. Whatever it was between them didn't encompass such a commitment. The touching happened behind closed doors, and it made her stomach lurch even to consider it. But Tommy didn't want a girlfriend or to hold hands or go to Ikea and buy bath mats. That was the problem. She wanted a relationship with every fibre of her being. She was tired of schlepping around the city on her own, bored of the hangovers and the morning markets, the free-floating loneliness. She wanted to wear somebody's jumper.

'All right?' he said now, stretching out his long body, keeping the can of Diet Coke he held upright.

'Yes,' said Molly. She leant forwards and shredded a piece of grass. 'I just thought we should talk.' Tommy looked away. He thought she was going to ask him to make some kind of commitment, and it riled her. 'I've been thinking that perhaps we should talk about telling everyone about us,' she said, her voice deliberately steady.

'Wha—' Tommy looked up swiftly, his face twisted. 'Oh. You got me.' He smiled in relief.

'Don't worry, Tom. I'm not oblivious,' said Molly. 'I know you don't want this to be—'

'It's not that,' he said, almost a whisper. 'It's just …'

'I'm so sorry about your mum,' said Molly. She had tears in her eyes. 'But I can't do it any more. The nobody knowing bit, I mean. I don't know what we are doing. I don't understand why we have to keep it a secret.'

Tommy was silent. He scratched his arm. A French bull-dog was on the other side of the square, and he narrowed his eyes, looking at it.

'Odd-looking animal,' he said, taking another sip.

'Tommy,' said Molly.

'Sorry,' said Tommy. 'Um … I don't know what to say, Molly. I love what happens with us.' He lowered his voice. 'But, um, it doesn't need to be given a label, does it? Boyfriend-girlfriend? I can't do that at the moment.' He put down his can. He didn't meet her eyes, but he plucked a piece of grass and tickled her calf with it. A succession of fairy twirls on her skin.

'Something happened between Noah and me at the weekend,' said Molly, getting the words out before she could conclude that they were unsayable. 'We were together at the flat. We ate and then … there was a storm. I don't know. It was romantic, I suppose. He seems to like me. I mean, really like me.'

'I like you,' said Tommy softly. He frowned, the piece of grass sagged in his hand, those light-toned eyebrows knitting together.

'I didn't mean it to happen,' said Molly. 'You were all out, and … it's not something I planned. But since this isn't anything, I wanted to ask if you mind? I know you've been friends forever.'

'That's fine,' said Tommy, still avoiding eye contact. 'I can't stop you doing whatever you want to do, Molly; you know that.'

'But how do you feel about it?' asked Molly. 'Do you mind if I start something with Noah? He seems to want a … well, he's not trying to keep it a secret for a start.' There had been a text from him that morning. Daylight plans; what she had been craving for so long, but she knew that she was also saying the words to see if they might make Tommy act differently. 'I'm going to meet him after work tonight.'

'Does he know?' asked Tommy. 'About …' He made an ampersand in the air.

'No. I mean, nobody does. And I'd rather not tell him,' said Molly. 'If you don't mind. I don't know if it will turn out to be anything, but I'd kind of like to give it a try.'

'I see,' said Tommy. He was sitting upright now; his knees pulled up in front of him.

'So, this,' Molly copied his air gesture angrily. 'It has to end. To be honest, I'm kind of annoyed with myself that I let it happen like this. I know you've been having an awful time, but I still don't think you've been very respectful towards me.' She was resolute behind her glasses, trying not to cry.

'Molly. You know it has been, um, difficult for me,' Tommy frowned and watched the dog in the distance. The square had started to fill up, with people who defined themselves as creative through their clothes; outfits that lurched from irony to sincerity in one fell sweep.

'I'm so sorry about Celeste,' said Molly. 'I really am. But I can't keep going on like this. And I like Noah – *I do*. But I don't want things to be weird. I know how close you are.'

'Oh – right,' said Tommy. 'We're close.' By that point, the truth was that a wedge had already emerged between the two men. It happened before Molly, a slight turning apart, refuge found in others in the group. A watering-down of their friendship's intensity. Noah found Lucas's aspirations more appealing than Tommy ever would; Tommy turned towards

Star's unconformity. A realisation that other realities existed outside the parameters of their relationship.

But Celeste's illness had made Tommy remote from all of his friends. None of the rest of them had looked at death up close yet. They had no idea. Molly assumed this was why he liked to get mashed so much: to forget.

'But do you think maybe we should just never mention that this happened between us?' said Molly. Her bicycle helmet lay on the grass next to her feet; her bicycle splayed behind her. 'It's only going to complicate stuff if Noah knows.'

'Don't you think it will be odd if you don't?' said Tommy. 'Imagine if you guys end up married or something.' He snorted at the suggestion.

'I think if we just move on, it will be as if it never happened,' said Molly. She had folded her arms.

'Oh, I don't believe that,' said Tommy. 'I'm never going to be able to pretend that it never happened.'

Molly sat silent, looking at him. She was wearing a pair of culottes that looked like clown trousers. A faded T-shirt. The kind of cheerful garments designed for comfort rather than sex appeal. She had deliberately not made any effort that morning. She wasn't trying to impress. But then Tommy leant over the grass and moved his face towards hers, a move he had never made in public, landing his lips on Molly's. Molly responded. Tommy gently pushed her onto the grass, and they carried on. The kissing had always been easy between them, fluid. Like a conversation that you didn't want to end.

There was a burst of laughter from someone sitting slightly away from them, and they sat up. Molly rubbed her mouth, looked around for whoever had made the sound. Tommy watched her with a certain feline satisfaction.

'I bet Noah doesn't kiss you like *that*,' he said.

'For Christ's sake. It's only happened once,' said Molly. But it was true. It had been entirely different. Good, but different. Noah had thrown himself into it with an enthusiasm that she recognised as characteristic, but Tommy always held something back.

'But you know immediately, I reckon,' said Tommy. 'It's instantaneous. The knowing. How *it* will be.'

'It was very nice with Noah, thanks,' replied Molly. The shock of the public kiss was still working across her on a molecular level, a rainbow washing through her. She hated Tommy, just then, for the casual display of his power that he wielded over her through some biological, pheromonal quirk.

'I know Noah well. And you ... pretty well,' said Tommy, smirking. 'And I'm not sure a relationship between you is such a great idea.'

'Well, *thanks*. But I don't think you get to be the judge,' said Molly, recovering now.

'Noah is a great guy. Upbeat. But he's very literal,' continued Tommy. 'For example, he spends a lot of time thinking about books, but it's all about the mechanics for him, the actual use of language, rather than the emotions. I don't think you're like that and I mean that as a compliment.'

'Literal?' said Molly. 'If that means he doesn't mind going out with me where we might be seen, I'll take it.'

Tommy shrugged, and Molly clambered to stand.

'I'm going to go now, Tommy,' said Molly. 'You are

messing with my head, as usual. I don't want drama. And I don't know if this thing with Noah will work out, anyway. I just thought you should know, although it's a courtesy that you almost certainly wouldn't have extended to me.' She put her helmet on her head and snapped it under her chin, reaching over for her bike and wheeling it across the grass.

Tommy sprang up with that balletic grace of his, throwing his empty drink can into the bin from some distance. He followed her to the edge of the square. They stood on the pavement, looking at each other.

'Excuse me. D'you, mind if I just get past?' It was a man with a shaved head, the French bulldog that Tommy had been watching earlier tucked into the crook of his arm.

'Sure, sorry,' said Molly, shifting her bike and standing to the side. 'I've got to get back to the office,' she said.

'OK,' said Tommy. He leant forwards, this time for a respectable farewell peck on the cheek, but it brought back the memory of what had just happened. The air between them seemed sluiced with warmth. Auras, Star might have said. Molly had no truck with that kind of thing, but she couldn't deny that some invisible reaction happened between them. 'I should be heading back to work, myself. We are pitching for a butter brand later.' He looked at his watch. 'Shit. I have got to get moving. I'm presenting it.'

It felt like the end of something as she got on her bike and cycled away. She had no idea. Like most of us, if she'd known what the future was going to bring, she would have fallen to her knees.

Star

Star sits on the curved metal balustrade, looking out at the night sweeping over the city. She holds her breath, daring herself to maintain her balance. Although what does it matter now if she falls?

She has travelled further in the last nine months than she ever had before in her life. But everywhere she went, one thing remained constant. Men entitled to their desire.

In Bangkok, they buzzed past her on mopeds, a swarm.

'Julia Roberts.' 'Sexy lady.' 'Nice legs.' 'Marry me.'

Sometimes they drove too close so that Star could feel a breeze of motion against her skin. She wondered if they would carry on across her back if they knocked her down, leaving tyre marks on her skin. She would return to the hostel and lie on the bed, underneath the fan that sliced through the warm air, examining the bites on her limbs, the colour her arms were very slowly turning, like yoghurt with honey stirred through it.

They spoke with their eyes on the beach at Phra Nang, as she strolled in a bikini and sarong. Fishermen by their craft, looking with lust and disdain as their fingers teased out tangles in the fine mesh of their nets.

Other tourists, too, sitting with their girlfriends. Appraising eyes everywhere.

At the full moon party, they were primarily European, many English. The look was the same, transcending language. You have something for me. Hand it over.

Star became heartily sick of the presumption. There was only one man she wanted to look at her like that, and he was with someone else. And yet she carried the collective gaze as proof of something. Even though her heart had been torn into a thousand stained little pieces, her surface hadn't changed. Given that it was all she had, this was something.

She looked at her face in the electric strip light of a hostel bathroom, the night air around her as succulent as one of the mangoes she ate in her breakfast salads. The same lips, arched eyebrows, innately knowing expression. She didn't look like someone who had no idea what they were doing and who had jacked in her life.

After opening herself up to Lucas and Alice, Star had been completely unmoored by what had happened. The puff had been knocked out of her. And then Mikael had abandoned Lockjaw, focused only on his own success. After that, it had been hard not to disintegrate.

While she travelled, she searched hard for someone else to fall in love with. There were many candidates. Richard, the Essex boy with whom she sat companionably on the beach as the sun rose, the fizz of chemicals dwindling in her bloodstream. Dieter, from Germany, with his broad, industrious shoulders. Pilar, from Spain, with boyish hips, a monobrow and a mane of black hair.

They were plausible friends and lovers, but none sustained Star's interest. She missed her real friends. She missed Lucas. Molly. Even Alice. The traitor. Even her.

She corresponded by email with Molly, who filled her in on what was happening in her absence. Molly had told her that Lucas and Alice were decorating the cottage on Columbia Road. A doll's house. 'Just a two-up, two-down.' As if that minimised it, as if homeownership were insignificant. Star couldn't bear it. She knew that Alice would be making this urban cottage homely, buying cushions and pastry brushes. She could just imagine Lucas's books on a shelf, the radio running with the sound of the cricket, the ironing board constantly extended waiting for their work clothes to be pressed, orange-black marmalade chilling in the fridge. Together they would be building a home using a shared blueprint that they had learnt as children.

Star moans. The city sparkles beneath, oblivious.

20

Riad Mousseline, Marrakesh

Saturday night
Twenty years later

The cork popped damply, and foam sputum bubbled out of the top of the bottle and splashed onto terracotta.

'Quick. Catch it!' shouted Alice, looking around for someone. She wore a shimmering column of gold sequins, her hair slicked back, her lips the purplish-red of raw sirloin.

Lucas stepped forward and caught drops of the liquid neatly in a glass. Viv and Iona cheered. Molly hadn't moved from her position on the banquette. After her muted response to his declaration, Tommy had disappeared. She was still in shock. She reached her fingers to her lips, certain that something about her appearance might reveal her betrayal. Noah was on his way, this was a defining point if they wanted to save their marriage, and yet here she was, compounding the damage.

As Molly had sat, heavy with guilt and disbelief, Lilith had brought up a selection of tapas, and laid them out on the tables on the roof: salads jewelled with pomegranate seeds, tiny cubes of cheese, more filo squares, falafel. A feast. As well as the champagne, there were more cocktails, the margaritas they had had when they first arrived, in tall glasses full of ice.

The others had started to arrive. Now, Alice came up to Molly and thrust a drink into her hand. 'You need to unwind tonight like you did at lunch,' she said, pointedly. 'We'll have no more of that puritanism.' No matter that Molly's drink at lunch had made her cry.

Alice was at her loudest, passing around the food, making sure that everyone had a drink, changing the song multiple times. This one. No, this one. That's it. No. If you didn't know her better, you might have almost thought that she was nervous, thought Molly, there was a freneticism to her extroversion that wasn't usually there.

'Nobody is allowed to go to bed until they've danced,' said Alice. 'And gone skinny-dipping and eaten all this incredible food. Let's try to break dawn. You know, like we used to.'

'What about your alleged surprise?' said Molly, spearing an olive with a cocktail stick and popping it into her mouth.

'Oh. You'll see,' replied Alice. 'Later. But now. Eat. Drink … Make merry. I want tonight to be special.'

Molly was on her second cocktail when Noah appeared at the top of the narrow staircase. She didn't realise that he had arrived for a moment and then saw him looking at everyone, discombobulated; his hair ruffled up. He wore a T-shirt, jeans and those bright Birkenstocks he had bought last summer that made her wince. She saw him looking for her and his face softening with relief when he found her, then recalibrating in recognition of everything that had happened in the previous week.

'Noah,' said Molly. 'You're here.' It had only been a day and a night since they had been together, but he seemed changed, older – the rivets along his forehead a little deeper than she recalled.

'Noah.' Alice rushed towards him and hugged him. 'We've been waiting for you. The TV star! Haven't we, everyone? We knew the party couldn't start properly until you arrived. A drink?'

'I think I'd just like to have a quick shower?' said Noah. 'If that's OK?'

'Molly, show him where to go. But be quick,' said Alice, winking.

Molly rose.

'How was the flight?' she asked as she led Noah down the narrow stairs. 'The room is this way. You're going to be amazed when you see it. Lucas put his hand in his wallet for this one.'

'Look at that,' said Noah, on the terrace outside the bed-room, taking in the view over the courtyard below, a cross between a garden and a room. 'I can't believe that I was in London just a few hours ago. This is like a different world. The taxi took me around the edge of the souk. It's crazy. All the colours and the stalls.'

'Yeah, it's remarkable,' said Molly. She was barefoot, and she could sense Noah assessing the *cheongsam*.

'You look nice,' he said. 'Pretty.'

'Oh, this? Alice's,' said Molly, looking down at the dress, as if she hadn't noticed it before. 'I feel a bit of an idiot, to be quite honest. Here,' she added, opening the door to their room. The bed had been made again and freshly scattered with rose petals. She wished that Lilith would stop doing that. From being that girl who ached for romance, she now considered it a cheap con. Alice had been right all those years ago: sex on its own was more honest. It had nothing to do with love. She loved Noah – it would be so much easier if she didn't – the exact nature and expression of the love was the problem.

The room was fragrant and cool. But she wanted to feel authentic night air and, irritated, moved over to the air-conditioning unit to dial it down.

'This place is ... epic,' Noah offered. Since working on the documentary, he had started to incorporate slang that made Bella and Eve laugh, and Molly shudder. He shouldered off his rucksack and looked around. It was worse than being there with a stranger, Molly reflected. What could they say to each other? Every conversational avenue had been exhausted, aside from the ones that neither of them was sure they wanted to venture down.

'I'm glad you decided to come,' she said. 'It's good to see you.'

'I'm so sorry,' said Noah, sinking back onto the white cotton of the bedspread, his shoes hanging over the end of the bed. 'About Greta. I didn't mean for it to happen. It was ... an accident.'

'An accident?' Molly was arch, despite herself.

'Honestly. I was lonely, Molly. I was working such long hours on the show. And I was so tired of feeling undesirable.' Noah twisted his face towards her. He had that puppy-dog expression that she had always particularly hated on him.

'I ... I don't know what to say to that,' said Molly. 'You weren't alone; I've always been right here.'

'You haven't, though, have you?' said Noah. 'I mean, you've been in front of me, literally, but your mind has been somewhere else. For a long time. It's all about the family, but not about *us*.'

Molly was silent. What he said was true. And even as he spoke, she could sense the deep lassitude that something in him engendered in her. Cocktail-tired, she wanted to climb onto the bed next to him, lie down and sleep, perhaps forever. She didn't want to kiss him or go through the same motions that he seemed to find endlessly enthralling but that were now mere mechanics to her.

'Let's not do this now,' she said. 'Alice will be waiting for us. Have a quick shower. We've spent all week talking and we can do it again later.'

She sat on the bed and waited while Noah was in the bathroom. She glanced over at the notepad on the desk. It looked welcoming and, remembering the ease of before, Molly surprised herself at wanting to go back to her own words. She picked up her biro and opened the page.

'Are you writing?' Noah was in the bathroom doorway; a toothbrush lodged in his left cheek.

'Yeah, I just did a bit earlier,' said Molly. 'Something about being away seems to be helping.'

'Great,' said Noah, moving back into the bathroom and spitting out his toothpaste.

'You don't mean that,' said Molly.

'What are you talking about?' said Noah.

'You think it's pointless,' replied Molly. 'I know you do. And that has been stopping me, I think. But I've realised that I have to try. That's it's not about doing it for anyone else.'

'I've never meant to give you that impression,' said Noah, although he didn't contradict her. It *was* futile, in a sense. But wasn't everything, every last human endeavour? Until it wasn't.

Molly placed down her pen, but she had the clear understanding, one she hadn't had in so long, that she would return.

Noah began to change, with his back to her, pulling on the striped special-occasion shirt he'd had for years, slightly creased from being rolled up in his bag, and a pair of black jeans. She could still admire his shape, that torso, every freckle and scar long ago charted. He had agonised over that tattoo on his upper arm and only got it when he was forty. A thread of script: *There is nothing either good or bad but thinking makes it so . . .'*

'I can't believe that Tommy came,' Noah said.

'I know,' said Molly. 'Alice wasn't happy.'

'Is he still on the straight and narrow?'

'He seems to be,' replied Molly and Noah frowned.

'Long may it last,' said Noah. As he regarded himself in the mirror, his phone started to pulse with a tinkling sound, a repetitive digital peal of shattering glass. It lay on the bedside table next to Molly, and she looked over.

Greta. Greta. Greta. The name was insistent. The mobile was embodied with the girl, from so far away, assuming a fleeting femininity. Molly had only seen those few pictures of Greta, but her youth was a sneer reflected in the iPhone's glossy contours and unyielding screen.

'I think your girlfriend is calling you,' she said.

Noah was silent, but he didn't move to pick up the phone, just looked down at the floor, regarding his bare feet.

'Pick up,' said Molly. 'She'll be wondering where you are. Does she have any idea that you're in Marrakesh? With me? Or did you tell her that things were over between us?' Noah didn't respond. 'Come on, Noah, old thing. Don't leave her hanging. That's too cruel.' Still, her husband didn't move. He stayed rooted on the spot.

'I'm not speaking to her now,' he said, finally. 'We need to talk first.'

'For you to decide if you're going to stay with me?' said Molly.

'Maybe,' said Noah, eventually, holding her gaze. Molly regarded him. She narrowed her eyes. Noah disliked change, but once he decided to alter something, he was immovable.

'Do you love her?'

'I ... I ... don't think so,' said Noah. 'But she seems to like me, Molly. It feels nice.' Molly looked down.

'Let's go back up,' she said. 'Alice will be looking for us.'

'Does she have any idea?' said Noah. 'Alice?' It was Molly's turn to be silent. 'You told her?' Molly nodded.

'It just kind of happened,' she said. 'I didn't mean it to. You don't know what it's been like, trying to act like everything is just fine.'

'I hope you told her all the facts then,' said Noah. 'The fact that you couldn't stand me near you.'

Molly stood as if to leave. There was a soft knock on the door, and she moved to open it. There stood Lilith. She had dressed in a chiffon blouse with an immense, almost obscene, pussy-bow that hung down over smart trousers, heeled boots – ever the Parisienne.

'It's time for the toast,' she said, looking frankly from Molly to Noah, not shielding her curiosity. 'Up on the roof. Alice was asking for you.'

* * *

They climbed the stairs. Molly led the way, and she could feel Noah's presence behind her. There was a comforting familiarity to it after the previous day. As they emerged, it became clear that night had fallen comprehensively since their absence – so many stars, dusted above their heads, so different from London's milky orange sky.

'Wow,' said Noah, looking up and then around. Every crevice of the terrace contained a twinkling light: the tea lights that Lilith and Molly had set out earlier. Music was playing. A soft spiralling beat. That smell again, Mousseline's distinctive perfume of charred flesh and jasmine.

'You're back.' Alice was upon them immediately. 'It's time.' She pressed a flute glass into each of their hands, and

Lucas came at them with the bottle angled forward like a glass bayonet. He moved around the group, topping everyone up and then placing it back on the table.

'I just wanted to say a few words,' he said, slipping easily into corporate mode. 'Before we get stuck into all the food and some more drinks.' He gestured at the table loaded with appetisers and then towards Lilith, who was standing slightly to one side of everyone else. 'I wanted to thank our marvellous host, Lilith Maillas. She has been so hospitable and furnished us with everything we could need for a wonderful stay.' There was a ripple of appreciation from the group. 'Thank you, Lilith.' Lucas bowed in Lilith's direction, and the older woman nodded graciously. 'It's just such a treat for Alice and me. To have all our friends here, after so many years.' He cleared his throat.

Molly bowed her head. He wouldn't mention Star, despite the fact that this was the anniversary of her death, just as much as it was the anniversary of his and Alice's wedding. It had been safer for Lucas to try to deny Star's existence, Molly knew, but she was actually grateful. Any tribute made to Star never did her justice. Molly loved words, but they didn't work to describe Star. You needed images, colours. Star dancing in *The Red Shoes*, a knockout in her scarlet trainers, every twist and twirl like the answer to a question. Molly had been awed by her that night, the clarity of her voice and the sinuous way she moved. And yet so soon afterwards, it all fell apart and Molly failed her.

Lucas raised his glass. He continued. 'I know that Alice feels so lucky to have such wonderful, loyal friends – as do I.

And that's what Alice has been to me for so long: a wonderful friend. Still, I have to admit that when I first saw her, all those years ago, I thought she was the best-looking girl I'd ever seen. And she has barely aged a day since.' The ultimate compliment.

'Hear, hear!' shouted Tommy, cupping his hands around his mouth.

'Shush,' said Molly, unable to stop herself. Tommy looked over, and she put her finger to her lips but smiled behind it, trying to soften the caution. Since the unsatisfactory kiss and his declaration of love, something in him had loosened, she saw, with dismay.

'We hope you've been enjoying yourselves at Mousseline,' continued Lucas. 'We wanted to get you all together somewhere nice. This is slightly unconventional on our wedding anniversary, but Alice and I have got a bit of an announcement. We wanted our nearest and dearest to hear it first ...'

Everyone fell silent – even Tommy.

Star

8 p.m.

Eventually, with difficulty, Star talks herself down from the edge of the roof garden's barrier. She can't end her life. Yet the despair is crushing. Without Lucas, how will she ever go back to London? She longs for the place, but without him, it will be too painful to ever return.

She enjoys being a waitress, but only if she can act as well and she can't see how that is going to happen in Sydney.

From the minute she could walk, Star danced and twirled, performing for the mill-house's occupants: in those days, that was just Moira and another couple renting the master bedroom. As Star grew, she acted and sang in all the school productions, told everyone who asked that she was going to live up to her name. Her ambition rationalised some of her more difficult characteristics – the height that saw her as tall as Moira by the time she was thirteen, her deep voice, dire concentration span and insatiable

235

requirement for attention. If she succeeded as an actress, these qualities became admirable.

Star also understood early that her particular type of prettiness relied on a certain showgirl pale-skin and nipped-waist glamour, so she was drawn, instinctively, to clothes and make-up from an earlier era.

By the time she met Molly and the others, Star had been working for years. She had an agent and had done the merry-go-round of auditions, scoring some roles. A small part in a long-running police drama as a teenage tearaway. A dancing role in a West End musical. And, best of all, the role of Marianne in Sense and Sensibility for a production at the Kilburn Theatre. There, she realised that her real love was live theatre. Joining Lockjaw felt like coming home. As one of the youngest but most dynamic site-specific theatre groups in the UK, the company already had a pedigree. That didn't mean that Star was going to earn much – there was no chance of giving up her shifts at Petit Soleil – but it meant there was a future.

Not for a minute could she have imagined that Lockjaw's success with The Red Shoes was going to tear it apart, but Mikael, the director, was offered a role elsewhere. He had been involved with one of the other principal actors who also left, and Lockjaw dissolved, overnight.

Living in the room she'd found after moving out from the flat she shared with Alice and Lucas, Star found herself facing open auditions again. Older, more disappointed, less sure that her dreams were going to come true, strands of white appearing in the boot-polish black of her hair. After a few months, she took the *decision to go travelling, telling herself that it would only enrich her acting once she returned.*

Now, on the roof terrace, she doubts that she ever will.

21

London

Ten months earlier

The signs of difference had been there when Molly thought to look back for them. An ache in her breasts, as if permanently premenstrual, a deep tiredness that saw her fall asleep on the sofa. A taste in her mouth, a waft of something metallic and ancient. Odder still: a rising possibility, full dreams, a sense of smell so acute that the tube became a panoply of other people's shower gel and toast toppings.

She and Noah were living on the rented upper floors of a narrow Victorian terrace in Holloway, with draughts and doors that didn't close properly, but a charming view of London rooftops, wet slate and chimney stacks stretching as far as the eye could see. Their place was near where Tommy was living, in his mother's flat. Too near.

It wasn't until her period was three weeks late that she

thought to do a test. When she had the result, peeing on a stick in the bathroom of their flat, the only person she could think of who wouldn't judge her was Star.

Lucas and Alice were engaged in an aggressive establishment of their domestic lives, an underpinning of their future. Star offered her something that the others didn't: friendship without conditions.

Later that day, she waited for Star, and then they walked, arm in arm.

'Talk to me,' said Star. She was wearing a vintage pinafore, with a checked blouse underneath, her curls pinned back with a barrette, like a child evacuee. Molly noticed some silver threads against her temples. Star's life might not be moving on, but her body was, inexorably.

'I'm pregnant,' said Molly, once they had rounded the corner from the restaurant. Tossing out the words before she could think about them too hard.

'Oh,' said Star. 'Shit. Wow. I mean, congratulations? Or, no – not congratulations.' She paused, looking at the expression on Molly's face. 'Have you told Noah?'

'I don't know if I'm going to,' said Molly. Star stopped walking and turned to look at Molly.

'Are you serious?'

'I am,' replied Molly.

'So, this wasn't planned?'

'No,' said Molly.

'But I thought you and Noah were ...'

'We are.' Molly enjoyed every aspect of her new-found domestic life. She and Noah were starting to institute their rituals precisely as she had always hoped. Fish and chips in the park. Runs on a Sunday morning, then reading the papers in bed. Preferred bottles of wine, cleaning products, varieties of yoghurt. Sketching out the particulars of the life they planned to lead. And they both wanted babies. They had discussed it, and Molly thrilled at Noah's enthusiasm for the idea. Not all men were like that, she knew. Their unborn children hovered over the relationship, implicit in every activity they undertook together. Chubby and gummily perfect, little hands and feet starfishing just out of sight. But they were a long way off that point. Noah had to finish his PhD. She wanted to progress with her teaching, maybe even try for a deputy headship.

This pregnancy was not part of the plan and not only because it had come too soon. After the conversation in Hoxton Square, she had been so confident that she had severed the connection with Tommy forever. If only that had proven to be the case. Instead, the aberration between them had continued occasionally, haltingly.

She blamed Tommy. He provoked something in her that she would have preferred not to know about herself: a capacity for betrayal. She liked to think of herself as a conscientious person, but Tommy seemed determined to prove that this view of herself was a mere construct. After the Greek holiday, he had popped round to return one of Noah's books when Noah was out. *The Satanic Verses*. He had talked about the writing for a long time, as if he were trying to prove something. Then they had come together, awkward afterwards. As if it had been an out-of-body experience. Intermingled with

Molly's shame was a seam of rich excitement. For the first time in her life, she felt powerful.

She didn't know how to explain any of this. But she knew that Star would be the last to judge.

'I am not necessarily sure this pregnancy is Noah's,' she said quietly.

'OK.' Star looked at her, squinted her eyes slightly and patted her hair. 'Let's sit down.' She gestured to a wall running outside a pebble-dashed terraced house, one of the rows of streets behind the main road where Petit Soleil was situated. 'Here?'

'It was a mistake. I don't know what I'm doing. I didn't think I was this kind of person.' Molly sat down slowly, as if in a daze. They hoisted themselves up, backs grazing the bush behind them. Star squinted into the distance.

'What kind of person *did* you think you were?' said Star. She looked interested, and Molly flinched. 'Sorry, Mol. I just mean that we all make mistakes.' Molly noticed that Star's fingernails were long and slightly dirty, crimson vestiges of a long-ago manicure eclipsing the nail crescents.

'I know that,' said Molly. 'But this kind of betrayal, so early on – it's not how I saw this relationship. This is supposed to be it.'

'What now? Who is the other person?'

'I'd rather not say.'

'OK. Keep your secrets,' Star said. 'You surprise me, Molly.' She shook her head, smiling. 'You do. But that's a good thing.'

'I surprise myself,' said Molly. 'I don't know what I'm

doing. Noah makes me so happy, but there is something about this other person that I just … He makes me behave in strange ways. It's only with him. And so, the point is that I can't be certain. And I can't deal with this.' She paused. 'Will you come with me, Star?'

Star nodded, not asking Molly if she was sure if she knew she was doing the right thing. Molly had known she wouldn't.

* * *

A week later, Star went with Molly to the hospital. And afterwards, she took Molly back to the top-floor flat and set her up on the sofa in front of the television, placed a cushion under her head and made her a cup of tea so thick with sugar and tannins that it looked like soup.

'There you go, sweetheart,' said Star. 'You're going to be just fine.'

'My stomach hurts,' said Molly. Usually, if she felt this bad, she would have called Diana. But this was something that could never, ever, be discussed with Diana. She had taken a tablet but nothing else. Such a simple thing to cause such a seismic reaction in her body, to change the course of two lives. Three. Four. Six if you counted her parents too.

'That's why I've got these,' said Star, holding out two neon-pink tablets in her palm. Her voice was soft. 'It's over now, and you don't need to think about it again.' Molly smiled at her gratefully. Star had dressed soberly for the occasion, in the smartest clothes she had – a teal skirt suit and a cream blouse with a scalloped collar, T-bar heels.

'Thank you so much for coming. It meant everything to me,' she said. Noah had no idea and assumed she was at work. Perhaps it had been his – but they still had plenty of time for those babies they had promised each other.

'Of course,' said Star. She puffed up another cushion at the end of the sofa. 'Do you want something to eat?'

'No. This tea is fine.'

'I'm going to have to leave soon. I'm starting my shift at four.'

'OK,' said Molly. Inside her, she could feel a rupture and then a flood. There was an ocean within seeking release. 'Star? What's happening with Lockjaw?'

'Kaput.' Star drew a finger across her throat, like a mafioso making a threat. She widened her eyes and grinned, but Molly saw the pain.

'I'm so sorry,' said Molly.

'It's OK. I've still got Petit.'

'You need more than that.'

'Ultimately, yes. But I happen to enjoy my work there. I do important things with cornichons,' said Star.

'*The Red Shoes* was so incredible,' said Molly. 'It just doesn't seem fair.'

Star puffed out her cheeks and then let the air out slowly. 'I hate to break it to you, kid, but life isn't fair.'

'You are talented; you know you are. Don't lose your self-belief,' said Molly.

'And you?' said Star. 'What about your writing?'

'It's hard,' replied Molly. 'I'm not saying it's easy. But you …' *You don't have anything else.* The words hovered behind the ones she spoke. Easier to bottom-drawer creative ambitions if respectably occupied with other things. 'How's the new flat?' asked Molly, changing the subject.

'It's terrible,' said Star. 'Honestly, Molly, I don't have the energy to try to get to know them all. Just the thought of it makes me feel exhausted. London is getting so expensive. Just surviving here takes all my energy. Nobody is going to lend me a spare flat like Tommy's mother has.'

At the mention of Tommy's name, Molly looked away. Star caught her doing it.

'Shit. Wait a minute. It's not Tommy, is it? You ...' Star's expression cleared as the realisation sank in, clouds parting to let in a shaft of sunlight. 'Huh. That actually makes perfect sense.'

Molly didn't make eye contact again, but she could feel the flush spreading out across her cheeks and down her neck. A stain.

'Shit,' repeated Star. She sank onto the chair that was perpendicular to the sofa. 'Tommy, eh?' She shook her head. 'I can see why you had to keep this one to yourself.' Star shook her head.

'Don't tell anyone, will you?' said Molly. 'It's just this ... thing. It's been going on since before I even got together with Noah. He made me feel different about myself. I tried to stop it entirely, but then he came over to drop off some of Noah's books, and it happened. It's like a kind of sickness. I need never to see him again, but he's so available, just round the corner, always keen to pop over. Noah has no idea.'

Star was looking at her. 'The lives of others,' she said,

smiling. 'Here I am, feeling like the only fuck-up and you're cheating on your boyfriend with his best friend. It actually makes me feel sane, for once, which is magical. Thank you.' She laughed in disbelief.

'Glad to be of service,' said Molly. She could feel warmth soaking into the sanitary pad she was wearing. Whatever had begun within her was now concluding. 'I am thrilled my predicament is cheering you up.' She looked at Star again properly. Her friend's face was more animated than it had been in months, as if the revelation was a profound relief on some level for her.

Pat. Pat. Pat. A succession of pebbles hit the upstairs window of their flat.

'What the . . .?' said Molly, reluctant to stand, to admit the reality of what was going on inside her body. She wanted to stay as still as possible.

'I'll look,' said Star, standing and walking to the window. 'Oh my. It's him. It's Tommy.'

Molly stood then, too, and looked down into their road. She and Noah lived on one of those characteristic London streets, the mood of which changed utterly from one end to the other. At the eastern tip, there was a Tube, a pound shop, a particularly grubby Tesco Metro with vacuum-packed joints of meat wreathed in security tags. Towards the west, it became almost bucolic, the front doors painted in blush pinks and petrol blues, hollyhocks in the front gardens, homeowners' bikes stored in vast metal boxes. Tommy was standing directly outside their front gate, hand curled back past his head, about to fire another piece of gravel. He wore a stripy T-shirt with the silhouette of a ganja leaf on it, his pale hair cropped close to his head. He looked like a dosser. Molly thought of Noah heading off on his bike, all checked shirts and cords and his carefully packed lunch box. There was no contest. What had she ever been thinking?

Star leant forward and cracked open the window. 'Why are you behaving like a small child?' she said, repinning her fringe. Star flirted with everyone; Molly had to remind herself. She could practically flirt with furniture. It wasn't like Tommy was hers, in any way. And yet, it bothered her. It did.

'I was just walking past,' called up Tommy. 'I saw the lamp was on, and I wondered if Molly was home from work for some reason?'

'I am,' said Molly, standing at the window and looking down. 'Not feeling that well. But there is a doorbell, you know.'

'I don't like doorbells,' said Tommy. 'Too loud. Aren't you going to ask me up?' Which was how the three of them came to sit together in the living room, drinking more sugary tea, while Molly bled heavily. The secret meant she could hardly look at him even as she could feel his gaze regularly graze her face.

'Aren't you supposed to be working today?' asked Molly.

'Yeah,' replied Tommy. 'A heavy night last night, and I was feeling a bit fragile. The client I'm working on the project for will understand. He was out as well.'

'What it must be like – to go clubbing with your client,' said Star.

'It's better than lunch,' said Tommy, grinning.

'Excuse me,' said Molly. 'I'm just going to the loo.' She stood, feeling as fragile and full as a watermelon, stepping out of the room. She went to the toilet, gathered herself, and slowly returned, pausing outside the door.

'If you like her, you need to tell her,' Star was saying. 'Really like her, that is.'

'What are you talking about?' Tommy replied.

'Molly. That's why you're here, isn't it? If you like her – love her even – you need to do the decent thing and be honest. Or you're going to lose her.' Tommy was silent. Molly tried to guess what his expression would be. Tommy wasn't one for sincere emotion; everything was a joke. 'Molly wants to know where she stands. It's fair enough. Noah gives her that. But now is your chance. If you feel for her, tell her, mate. I know you've had a lot on your plate with your mum, but still – if you like her, you've got to do it. But don't come round to their flat playing games and confusing her, OK?'

Molly cleared her throat and pushed the door. Star was erect on the sofa. Tommy was looking out of the window.

'Sorry, you two. I think I'm going to have to have a nap. I'm not feeling right,' said Molly. She was shocked about what she had encountered in the toilet, the crimson ineffability of it.

* * *

A month later, on a Saturday when Noah was at a football match with Lucas, Tommy called round. Molly welcomed him in, reluctantly.

'Tea?'

'Go on.'

'Sugar?'

'Three.'

Molly rolled her eyes, clicked the kettle and made the hot drink, aware of Tommy watching her. He had chosen to call at a time when he knew that Noah wasn't going to be there.

'Here you go,' said Molly, placing two cups down on the table. 'I can't be long. I've got a bit of lesson planning to do and I'm planning to pop to the shops.'

'I went to see Star in her new flat,' said Tommy, picking up his mug and wrapping his long fingers around the side of it.

'Yeah. What did you think?' Molly asked. She hadn't liked the place in Tottenham. Another warehouse, but far less cosy than the one they were all familiar with, with an unwieldy number of tenants and a sound system permanently erected in the living room.

'It's big, I suppose,' said Tommy. 'Not sure it's going to be that easy to sleep.'

'Yeah,' replied Molly, glancing around her small kitchen, grateful for the privacy of it, for growing up.

'Hey, Molly. I wanted to ask you something. You know *it* broke before,' said Tommy and Molly was astonished to see a blush working across his pallid cheeks. 'You didn't get pregnant, did you?'

'What makes you say that?' said Molly, gripping her own mug, suddenly more interested in its contents.

'Oh nothing, it's just – you'd tell me, wouldn't you?' said Tommy. She had never seen him so serious.

'Why – are you suddenly ready for fatherhood?' said Molly. Tommy winced. 'That's what I thought. It's my body, Tom.' Tommy looked nonplussed and Molly found herself suddenly furious. 'If you must know, yes. I was pregnant. I wasn't sure whose it was and I dealt with it,' she hissed. 'While you were pissing around doing whatever it is you do. And that's it. Whatever this has been – it's over. You need to go.'

Molly didn't make eye contact as he stood up. Instead, she looked out of the window, at the tree in a nearby garden moving in the wind, its leaves rippling like silk. The front door slammed, with a bang.

Molly waited for half an hour, burning with injustice, and then decided to visit Star. She took the bus, the whirr inside her intensifying. Outside, she pressed the buzzer for the building, more of an industrial estate than a residential block.

Star answered and then came to let her in.

Molly was surprised at how dishevelled Star – normally more fastidious about her appearance than other aspects of her life – looked, her black hair greasy and her signature red lipstick absent. They walked to Star's flat in silence along a corridor, the floor of which was unpolished cement.

'You want some cornflakes? I was just about to have some,' Star said once they were inside her flat, extending a hand of hospitality, a roll-up wedged between her fingers.

'No. I had lunch already.' Molly momentarily paused before she launched into what she had come to say. 'You told him, didn't you?'

'What?' Star yawned and raised her eyebrows, which had

been plucked into skinny crescents. She put down the corn-flake packet which she had just picked up.

'Tommy. About the …' Molly looked around the room, as though one of Star's many new flatmates might have been listening, but there was nobody else there but them. 'Abortion.'

'What? Of course not. I would *never* do that,' said Star. 'What kind of a friend do you think I am?' Star reached for Molly's arm, her eyes wide with dismay.

'Nobody else knew but you.' Even as she said the words, Molly sensed they didn't constitute a coherent argument in themselves.

'It wasn't me. Perhaps he just guessed? It's been a bit of a dangerous game you've been playing, Mol.'

'I can't trust you,' said Molly, stung at the admonishment and retreating into her assumption.

'What? Listen, Molly, I've had all sorts of my own stuff to deal with lately. Even if I had the inclination to run around spilling your secrets, there's no way I would have had the time. It's your business.' Star's voice was tired.

* * *

Two weeks later, Molly called in to Petit Soleil to apologise. She should have at least listened to Star's version of events. Perhaps she *had* jumped to conclusions.

'Where's Star?' she asked Phillipe, who was behind the bar polishing a wine glass, with his habitually mournful expression.

'She's gone,' said Phillipe, with a lugubrious shrug. 'She went travelling. Round-the-world ticket – Thailand, Cambodia, Australia. She didn't tell you?'

'No,' said Molly, pausing stock-still. 'I can't believe it.' She hoisted herself onto a bar stool and rested her head in her hands.

'She's not been having such an easy time,' said Phillipe. 'I think she's been quite lonely since she moved out from the place with your other friends.' He peered at Molly and she sensed the judgement that lay behind his words. 'And the acting – it hasn't been going so well since Lockjaw broke up. I offered her more shifts, but she didn't want that, I think it felt like a defeat.'

'I can't believe she's actually gone,' said Molly, lifting her head. Without Star in it, the restaurant seemed drabber than it had before. The rivets of wax that glued the unlit candles into the wine bottles were suddenly grotesque, the walls more scuffed – and how had she failed to notice the smell of grease?

'She'll be back,' said Phillipe, returning to polish the wine glass he was holding and turning his back.

His statement seemed believable. Neither of them was to know that Star was gone, that the most recent encounters with her, experienced in full expectation of so many more to come, were their last. But in this, they were like so many of us, casually interacting with people we'll never again see. Perhaps our dogged focus on 'firsts' in our intimate relationships – babies' words, days at school, eyes meeting across crowded rooms – is because we can't ever know the 'lasts' until we look back. They're grenades, lodged in our days, but we'd all do well to bear them in mind.

Star

On the dark roof terrace, Star stands, shakily, and starts to move her feet, ignoring the pain from the cut on her calf. One, two, heel turn, back. She lifts her arms above her head, tracing the steps she performed at the climax of The Red Shoes, *just before Karen loses her beloved shoes – and her feet – forever.*

It was always Star's favourite bit of the production, the moment that she could throw herself into the movement. And on the night that Lucas and the others came to watch, every twist of her body was an exultation.

It was one of those magical performances where it all comes together. The actors performed in the beam of a car's headlights, which had been driven to the edge of the glade in the forest as if the entire show was impromptu. Star wore a red tracksuit and bright red trainers, with crimson leg warmers and a whistle, a raver's accessories contrasting with the classical elegance of the dance itself.

Star couldn't see the faces of the audience, standing near the trees at the edge. But she knew that Lucas, Molly, Viv, Tommy and Alice were out there somewhere in the clearing. She danced for her friends, keen to prove herself to be not just good at something – but the best. It was important on this occasion, the first they saw her perform, that she excelled. She might not have what they did, those clear-cut life trajectories arcing in front of them, but she had something else of value, and she wanted to impress it upon them. Freedom. She was free. Remembering it now, she weakly steps through a circumscribed version on the balcony, tears pouring down her cheeks.

She is free no longer. The dance only serves to highlight her imprisonment. She drops her arms and hangs her head. She is as stymied as Karen with her wooden prostheses.

Star stops dancing and comes to kneel. The steps have made her dizzy, and she moves to lie down on her side. She's not sure if she will be able to get up again. She can feel the sleep that eluded her during the night, tugging at her. Oblivion beckons.

After the performance that the others came to watch, they all went to the pub together, Star still in her bright Karen-clothes.

'You were amazing! Wasn't she amazing?' Molly had been wide-eyed. 'You never told me you were that good. Star by name, Star by nature.'

'Thanks, Mol.' Star had reached over to hug Molly.

'You were,' said Alice, nodding, a slightly perplexed look on her face. 'It was such a good production, and I didn't realise that you could do all that ...'

'Yes,' said Star, smiling, flushed.

'It was remarkable,' said Lucas. He didn't smile; he seemed curiously serious. Star looked at him.

'Really?' she asked. Lucas's opinion mattered the most. It was for him that she had taken flight.

'Truly,' he said.

Later that night, things changed between them. On the underground platform, Lucas pulled Star back before she stepped into the carriage behind the others, so the doors closed in front of her face.

'Let's get the next train,' he said. 'Catch them up.'

On the balcony, Star remembers, and she shuts her eyes.

'You were amazing,' Lucas said. 'Everything about you is just so ... alive.' He had leant down and kissed her, on the platform, behind the yellow line, pressing her against the tiles on the wall. Star had responded eagerly. She liked him, she really did. And it wasn't her fault that Alice did too. Lucas didn't kiss in a lawyerly fashion – he threw himself into it, in a manner she couldn't possibly have predicted, but that confirmed something about Lucas that she had long suspected. Behind his exterior, he was someone else entirely.

Finally, they broke apart.

'Wow,' said Star. 'You're ... That was ...' She laughed. Lucas had pulled her towards him, wrapping her in the sides of his open coat. 'But what about Alice?' Star had whispered into his chest. 'She likes you. She'll be furious.'

'Don't talk about that now,' said Lucas. He looked up towards the train that was arriving, his grey eyes inscrutable.

'Look at me,' said Star. Lucas looked down.

'It's you I like,' he said. 'Come on,' he tugged her hand. 'We should catch up with the others.'

'But are we going to tell her?' Star said.

'Not yet. Let's just take things slowly,' said Lucas. 'We don't have to tell anyone.'

On the balcony, Star presses her fingers to her lips.

22

Riad Mousseline, Marrakesh

Saturday night
Twenty years later

Lucas had frozen. His corporate ease appeared to have deserted him, and his mouth opened and closed several times, guppy-like.

'Oi, Lucas,' said Tommy. 'Get on with it, mate.'

Lucas looked at him and then scanned the faces of everyone else. Still, he said not a word. Lucas, who since they had all first met him, had always known exactly what to say.

'Let me take over,' said Alice, making eye contact with Lucas. 'I'll do this bit.'

She moved forward, stood next to her husband, and touched him lightly on the arm. They looked, as ever, right together. The deep cerise of his shirt offset her burnished dress. Expensive watches, haircuts, carefully maintained muscles and teeth; that indefinable nimbus of wealth. As good as middle age got.

'Come on,' heckled Tommy.

Lucas frowned, and Noah shook his head, but Molly could see that her husband wasn't truly annoyed, actually welcomed Tommy's insurrection. She was so familiar with Noah's expressions; she could discern the slight deepening in his left cheek dimple that denoted amusement.

'OK, *OK*,' said Alice. She took a deep breath and brought her hands together. Molly had never known Alice need to build herself up for something.' Well, this is a little unconventional, which isn't like us, as you probably all appreciate.' Tommy laughed bitterly, and Alice glared at him. 'Lucas and I had a reason for bringing you to Morocco. Obviously, we wanted to spend time together. As you get older, you tend to appreciate the people who have been there since the beginning. But we also wanted to make a little *announcement* to all our friends together in a nice environment ... Sorry, do you mind just lowering the music a bit?' She turned to Lilith, who observed, just like everyone else. The playlist had kicked on to Portishead, so redolent of everyone huddled on the floor in student bedrooms. 'We wanted to do this away from Edward and Olivia. Just us. Our relationship grew up out of the friendship we all shared and it seemed appropriate that we should tell you all first. The thing is ... um ... Lucas and I have decided to separate. Well, divorce, I should say. We're in the latter stages; the decree nisi is not far off.' Alice paused. She looked at Lucas. She didn't have tears in her eyes, but there was something vulnerable in the angle of her head.

'Shit,' said Tommy, not laughing this time. 'I didn't think you were going to say that. I thought you were going to tell us you were buying another house.' He looked crestfallen.

'We decided we've got enough of those,' said Alice, with a thin smile. 'We wanted to try to make this something positive. It's an ending for us as a unit, but we wanted to show you that we still consider our wider friendship group important. Essential, even. That's why we wanted you to be here.'

Lucas moved forwards once more, reinvigorated by his wife's address. 'We aren't unhappy. We will always love each other and our family. But we've come to realise – how best to put it – that we weren't *excited* about our future together any more. We didn't want to dishonour what had gone before. That love brought us so much. And Ed and Ollie are almost fully baked. We will always be united for them, but we want something separate for ourselves. We'll still stay nearby each other in London. We'll probably still go on holiday together. But we want to be ambitious about the scope of our capacity for happiness in the years ahead. Rather than settling.' He shut his mouth and looked at Alice for approval. They were obviously her words, not his.

As Lucas said them, Molly watched his mouth move. Lucas was an excellent public speaker and, after his blip, he was applying the usual rules to what he was saying. Projecting. Pausing. Looking around the room for a reaction. Gesticulating with his thumb and forefinger at right angles, like a media-trained politician. But then his voice broke.

'Sometimes,' Lucas said, looking down at the tiles, still

warm from all the sunlight they had absorbed throughout the day. 'Sometimes people change. And there's nothing you can do about it. The things we choose, and hold on to, don't always work out.' He looked up again and then turned to Alice. These sounded like his own words, meant for her.

Molly looked at Noah, trying to gauge his reaction. Had he known this was coming? He looked back at her and raised his eyebrows. No. A surprise then, for all of them. Few of those at this stage in proceedings. The heady dopamine hit of schadenfreude pleasurably obliterated their problems for a few moments.

There was a silence then as the group assimilated the new information. The music stilled; the only background noise was the city's sound below, the horns and buzz, the beat of the drums. It wouldn't be long before the evening call to prayer. They shifted, unsure of where to place themselves, how to process it. Lucas and Alice were their pivot. They were Mum and Dad, Mr and Mrs, the Lord and Lady of the house.

'I'm sure you must have thought long and hard about this,' said Viv, eventually. Iona was watchful at her right. 'We're your friends. We'll support you in whatever you both do next. You must know that. And I agree with what you said about being ambitious for happiness. Not settling.' She reflexively looked at her hand, joined to Iona's.

'I just can't believe it, though,' said Molly. 'Sorry ...' She covered her eyes with her hands. 'But ... you two.' Lucas and Alice needed to be together. They were their foundational stones.

'It's OK,' said Alice, brightly, moving away from where

she had been speaking and walking towards Molly with open arms, her sequins dazzling. She was crying too, tears sliding over all that carefully applied make-up. 'We've thought about it for a long time. We want different things and we just wanted to tell you all at once.'

'We heard about divorce parties. And we thought maybe we'd do one together as a way of informing you all,' said Lucas. 'To demonstrate our enduring commitment to each other and our friends.' He blinked. The spiel was out, disgorged. He had practised the words, as he would for any corporate address. Too late, perhaps, he sensed the discrepancy between delivery and content.

'Very progressive,' murmured Noah.

'Well, I think that's very modern,' said Lilith. But her expression was disappointed, her gaze looking out across the rooftops as if she could glimpse something that nobody else could see. This clearly wasn't the party she had planned. Lilith wanted Mousseline to be a place for celebration and joy. *Très sage.* She moved towards the stairs as if annoyed at being snared in the group's intimacy. Molly caught her shaking her head, barely perceptibly, as she progressed down them.

'And now,' said Alice. 'We party!' For their group, that meant alcohol, even with Tommy in attendance; more cocktails, beer, wine, a sticky bottle of neon limoncello that had appeared from somewhere. Seeking that blurry softening they knew so well, the flush and relief, they fell on their favourite drug with even more alacrity than usual. Over the years, they had forsaken the others, but alcohol was the most enduring. It was everywhere, even here. It gave their lives texture and pace. A price worth paying, even as the hangovers got incrementally worse.

The music restarted. Lucas and Alice courteously circled their friends as if it were a conventional anniversary gathering. If you hadn't heard their announcement, you wouldn't have known that anything was wrong or different. Molly waited half an hour before she went to Alice. She took her friend's lightly muscled arm and pulled her towards the stairs.

'We need to talk,' she said. 'Why didn't you tell me? After everything we talked about. What on earth is going on?' Alice smiled and allowed herself to be pulled in response towards the narrow stairs. The two women slipped away together.

'Our room or yours?' asked Alice, who still hadn't answered the question. She was already drunk, Molly could tell. She hadn't slurred her words, but was walking in that precise way she had on the brink of complete inebriation.

'Yours,' said Molly. 'It's the honeymoon suite after all.'

They walked into Mousseline's largest bedroom. The four-poster bed was identical to the one in Molly and Noah's room, but there was also a large seating area, chairs inlaid with the same mother-of-pearl flowers blooming against dark wood. It smelt of orange-blossom water as if Alice had spilt the bottle she had bought in the souk. Lucas's and Alice's things were ranged across the furniture: dresses slinking across the bed, sliders discarded in the middle of the carpet, airport-bought books on the side tables, a heap of jewellery on the dressing table. It looked like a room inhabited by an affluent couple whose effects and lives were carelessly mingled and who were debating where to go for dinner or whether to buy a specific expensive souvenir. Not those amid a break-up.

Alice headed straight for the bed and flopped onto it. She lifted her head.

'I imagined it would feel different to that,' she said. 'I thought if we framed it like this, I might feel in control.'

'Al. I'm so sorry,' said Molly. 'Why didn't you give me any idea? After I spoke to you about Noah and everything? I didn't have a clue.' Alice didn't reply, and Molly moved over to the bed as well. She sat next to her friend and stroked that modish hair. But from this position, Molly could see some roots at the hairline, fragility poking through. Molly moved her hand down to rub Alice's back, her xylophone ribs, the dip at the side of her stomach. 'I'm sorry,' she said.

'Don't pity me,' said Alice, rearing up into a seated position. 'Please.' Her face was blotchy, a squiggle of eye make-up moving down the centre of each cheek. 'I can't handle it.' Alice started to cry again, taking great gulps of air as if struggling for oxygen.

'I just want you to know that I'm here for you,' said Molly. Alice was silent, but her face contorted. 'I had no idea,' continued Molly. 'I'm not trying to make you feel worse.'

'It's been a mistake,' said Alice quietly. 'The whole thing.'

'That's not true,' said Molly, shocked. 'You've got two beautiful kids. You've been together a long time.'

'I've tried so hard,' said Alice. 'To make it work. I've done everything I could. It had to work after what happened.' She motioned at her slick face, her candyfloss hair, the gold dress. 'For Olivia and Edward.' She coughed out her children's names, the terms of an insurance policy. With such an organised mother, Olivia and Edward had never lacked anything. As babies, they were swaddled as Gina Ford instructed, fed home-made fish pie pureed to glue, flipped over onto their stomachs for tummy time.

'Do they know?' asked Molly.

'We told them last week,' said Alice. 'Lucas has bought a place round the corner. It's all worked out. One advantage of all the cash.'

'How did they take it?'

'Oh, you know,' said Alice. 'It was awful. Olivia ran out and wouldn't listen. She wouldn't pick up her phone. We were worried she was going to hurt herself.'

'What happened?' said Molly.

'We rang around her friends and managed to locate her. She was OK.'

'No. I mean between you. There was no sign of this. You always seemed so ... happy.' But that wasn't the right word. Invulnerable, Molly wanted to say. Shored up in wealth and convention and varnished with ski holidays, private schools and fixed-rate bonds. Secure. Grown-up. Done.

'It turns out that, um ... well ... I don't know if I told you at the time, but one of Edward's friends had an accident about a year ago. At a party. A nasty fall. He had to be airlifted to the Royal London. There were drugs involved.'

'You didn't tell me,' Molly said quietly.

'It brought it all back.' Alice looked away from Molly, towards the open window, which someone had come in to unlatch while they were all upstairs, as if it were implicated in what she had to say. The night breathed beyond it. 'How me and Luc got together and Star's death. You know, at the time, I never really let myself think about it. Or properly grieve, or forgive myself. I was so keen on Lucas then. You know I was. And when we'd fallen out, it was because I felt like Star was taking something that was *mine*. I suppose I thought she and I would make it up one day, but then she went so far away and then ... well, *it* happened. I couldn't ever talk to her again and I had to pretend that it didn't matter. Then this thing happened to Eddie's friend and I started thinking about her. Star. I became obsessed. I remembered how close we'd been. I'd denied it for so long. Got out all of our old photographs. We were so young, weren't we, Mol? So young.'

'Yeah,' said Molly simply. 'We were. Young and stupid and selfish. I let her down too.'

'You just think there's so much time and then suddenly, overnight, there isn't. And everything's different.' Alice leant into Molly then.

'Hush,' said Molly. 'Try not to cry.' It was what Diana had always said to her when she'd got upset as a teenager. *Try not to cry. Try not to cry.* That plea from mothers everywhere: don't hurt me with your suffering, for I can't bear it.

'I even tracked down Star's mum. She's still alive. Still in the house in Devon, would you believe?' Alice looked up.

'Did she know who you were?'

'Oh yes,' said Alice. 'Her mum – Moira – she's not really what Star described.'

'What did you do?'

'I went to see her. Drove down to Devon. This boy

– Frankie – was still in a coma, and Ed was so distraught, he was barely coping. I felt as if I could somehow help him if I faced up to the past. I tried to make amends for that person I'd been. Crazy magical thinking.'

'And what happened?' asked Molly.

'We drank tea. Moira's really something – she just welcomed me in. We both cried a bit. We talked about Star. She knew all about us, you know. Lucas. You. It seems like Star had told her mum a lot more than she had ever let on. She looks like Star, even though she's almost eighty now. Her hair is white, but she somehow had Star's ...' Alice shook her hands. 'Charisma, I suppose.'

'I still don't understand what all this has to do with you and Lucas,' said Molly. She was still picturing Star's smile on someone else's face. Slow-moving, but stretching into a dazzle. She longed to see it one more time.

'Well. Um. I'm not exactly sure either. All I know is that that's when I realised how far we'd grown apart. The boy – Frankie – he's OK. Thank God. But ...' Alice finally turned her face from the window and looked at Molly straight on. Her eyes glittered, encircled by black. 'It just brought back a lot of stuff that I'd buried, about how we'd got together. It was almost like we'd been too busy with work and the children to ever really consider it. But suddenly there was no choice, and we realised that we didn't want to spend the time we have left doing the same things.'

'I know what you mean,' said Molly.

'I am not that person, the one who chose him. Who prioritised him,' said Alice. 'I mean – obviously, I'm not. But for so long, I could understand her, her motivations, and now I just feel like I can't. She was me, and then one day she wasn't.'

Star

Midnight

It's dark now on the balcony, the private dark of cupboards and closed mouths. Star shivers on the sunlounger. She thinks of other sunloungers she has seen, in happier circumstances – like Kefalonia. Before her recent travels, that holiday had been Star's most exotic. The island was so hot and blue and brown, the dizzying drive down to pebbled beaches, the sea so clear that Star could see her feet resting on the stones, the breeze which smelt of indefinable herbal green. The food – garlicky tzatziki, meatballs in warm tomato sauce, rings of calamari. Countless pints of lager in icy glasses.

It couldn't have been a more ideal holiday. And yet, now Star can see it was the beginning of the end.

She and Alice shared a room. They smoked and sunbathed on its balcony together, tried on their bikinis, shared a razor. Star hadn't mentioned to Alice what had been happening with Lucas in London, which had mutated in the weeks since the Tube platform kiss, but which they had kept to themselves. She had been performing every night in The Red Shoes; *he had been as busy at work as he usually was. In some corner of her brain, she assumed the holiday would force matters to a head. And so it did.*

On the last night, as they were getting ready to head out to dinner with the others, Alice had asked Star to help zip up her dress at the back. They had already drunk cans of Mythos and Star was pleasantly giddy, anticipating the meal in the taverna on the seafront, coloured lanterns strung above its terrace, the sense of Lucas looking at her.

'Do you think Lucas will like this outfit?' Alice asked, conversationally, as she fluffed her hair out. Her eyes met Star's in the mirror.

'Do you care if he does?' said Star, snorting, as if the idea of Lucas being at all attractive was laughable.

'I do actually. Don't tell anyone, but I've realised I miss him,' Alice giggled. 'I think maybe we should give it another go. But – sssshhhhh! – I haven't told him yet.'

'Oh.' Star searched for an answer. Alice had finally articulated what Star had seen for herself on the first night she had met them all: Alice was still hung up on Lucas.

'What?' Alice turned and looked at Star. There was a challenge to her expression, then an understanding.

'Something has been happening between Lucas and me. In London after the production and a few times since and then again, here, the other night,' Star admitted. 'I didn't tell you because I didn't know if it was – is – going to come to anything. I haven't known what it is myself.'

'I don't understand,' said Alice.

'I'm sorry. I had no idea you still liked him.'

'But he's my ex and you're my flatmates,' Alice said. 'How could you?'

'We didn't set out to hurt you.'

'We?'

'It's not like that.'

And it wasn't. But only because Alice ensured it couldn't be. That night, at a taverna near the dock, she had behaved as if nothing had happened, only once shooting Star a smile that was so warm, Star had been confused. Later, that night, as the group returned from their dinner, the three of them fell into step behind the others.

'So, Lucas, I hear you're sleeping with Star,' said Alice, coolly. She looked particularly preppy, a navy jumper slung around her shoulders under her butterscotch hair, brushed out like a sixth-former's.

'What?' said Lucas. He stopped walking and flashed an alarmed glance at Star.

'Yes, Star told me. I had no idea. I just wanted to say congrats.' Star looked at Lucas. 'It would have been nice if you'd had the courtesy to let me know, instead of sneaking around behind my back, but, still … well done you. I'm sure you'll have beautiful babies – although you don't actually want children, Starry, do you? Have you mentioned that to Lucas, yet? He wants a football team.'

'Alice,' hissed Star. 'Stop now.' She looked longingly at Molly's retreating back, ahead on the path to the hotel.

'I'm sorry. I suppose it's just hard for me to take it in.' Alice laughed. It wasn't a pleasant sound. 'Lucas? Got anything to say?'

'Well,' Lucas's voice was tight. 'It's true that something has happened, but we're taking it slowly, figuring it out.' Star's heart contracted.

'But you're together?' Alice asked.

'Yes. I mean, sort of,' said Lucas. 'It's early days.'

'Come on,' called Tommy. 'Nightcap by the pool.'

'Sure,' said Lucas, lengthening his stride to catch the others.

For the rest of the evening, Star longed for Lucas to grab her hand, to pull her aside, but he didn't. To compensate, she drank quickly and horsed around with Tommy, jumping into the pool, covering her confusion with high jinks. It was only later, in bed, that she replayed Lucas's words. His hesitation hurt, but still, it was a tentative commitment. Wasn't it?

23

Biddenden, Kent

Sixteen months later

The wedding was convention itself. A church set in the rump of a Kent village. Ushers. Fascinators. Flimsy programmes. Pachelbel's Canon in D. Lumpen bridesmaids in pale pink. A dress the exact shape and colour of a home-made meringue, baked egg white faithfully rendered in expensive slip satin.

A red-faced, nervous groom, alcohol still rootling around his veins. A vicious mother-of-the-bride. A sky of milkiest blue, cloud threatening to predominate.

A cellist. A priest.

A wedding breakfast in a marquee, the unmistakable smell of canvas, squashed grass, skin. Touching, yet cringeworthy, speeches. A disco. Dancing, feet sliding and stamping over a temporary floor, trying to grip on to something. A moment. Love. Intimations of a fresh start.

Molly watched Alice sink into the role of bride, surrendering to it with relief.

Molly was maid of honour, of course. Viv, the other bridesmaid.

The church, like one you'd find on the front of a biscuit tin, was in Alice's home village of Biddenden. The marquee in her parents' garden obscured the greenhouse, full of sweet peas and her father's tomatoes.

It was perfect. Even Tommy looked smart in a dove-grey suit and polished conker brogues.

Nobody knew until the following morning. That while they had all been eating salmon en croute, drinking too much and dancing, Star was already dead.

Alice and Lucas were already on their way to Italy when the news emerged. A headline in a newspaper. Followed by many more. Star precisely the kind of striking girl that sold copies, her face staring out of newsstands. A photograph her mother must have given them. Abundant hair, that cryptic smile, the precise wings of her eyeliner.

'British Girl Dies in Tragic Fall.' The headlines all variations on that theme. A modern Sydney condo owned by a local entrepreneur, with sky-high glass windows, a balcony. Twenty storeys: not a chance.

Alcohol in her blood. Weed. Nobody knew how many others had been at the flat. She had been passing through, working in a bar. But records revealed that she had bought a ticket home and was set to arrive on the wedding day itself. Molly longed for this alternative possibility, the drama she had dreaded, of Star arriving to disrupt the wedding. At least then her friend would have lived.

It had been Molly who had told Alice on the phone, ringing the Tuscan hotel she and Lucas were staying in.

'You'd better sit down,' she said.

'What?' said Alice. 'Molly? Is everything OK? We were just about to go on a wine tasting. It's absolute *bliss* here. You know, I was worried – Lucas booked – but he's done a good job. It's a palazzo, basically.'

'Alice. Stop. It's Star. She ...' Molly broke off into a sob. 'She had an accident in Sydney. She's dead. She's *died*, Alice.'

'You're joking.' Alice's voice was flat.

'I'm not. Alice, this has really happened. I spoke to her mother, Moira. They are flying her body home.' That statuesque body was whizzing through the air in the hold of an aeroplane, across the salt brown and blue expanse that had separated them. She must be so cold, so lonely, that girl who had radiated warmth.

'God. I'm sorry.' Alice let out a strange mew, and there was the muffled thump of the handset falling.

'Alice. Alice?' Molly called. There was an extended silence and then a rustling sound.

'Sorry. Sorry. I just don't understand ...' Alice recovered the receiver.

'Well, you need to,' said Molly.

'I just need to think,' Alice said. 'To try to take it in. What happened?'

'She fell from the roof garden of a tower block on the Sydney harbourside. The authorities don't know what happened – whether there was anyone else with her or if she meant to commit suicide, or even if she tripped.'

'Surely not,' said Alice. 'How could she have *tripped?*'

'What does it matter?' said Molly. 'She's gone. We let her go and then this happened.'

'We can't blame ourselves,' said Alice. Her voice was expressionless; the spasm of emotion had moved through her. 'She chose to move out. She *chose* to go away. Those decisions weren't ours. This is a terrible tragedy.'

'But ...' said Molly. She wanted to accuse Alice, but she had failed Star herself. It was her own paranoid assumption about the abortion which had appeared to push Star to go travelling. 'She was our friend and I think we could have been there for her,' she said, at last.

'Molly,' said Alice. 'Should Lucas and I come home?'

'I don't see what good it will do,' replied Molly. 'It can't bring her back.'

Star

4 a.m.

Star awakes. She must have finally fallen asleep, all cried out. It's dark around her, but this time she knows exactly where she is: still in Pete's roof garden. The despair is so thick, she struggles to catch a breath.

She thinks of Alice at her parents' house, almost a bride. Life isn't fair. Some people get so much, doing the right thing doesn't guarantee anything. That Alice will be marrying Lucas is proof of that.

The week after they returned from Kefalonia, Star had wanted the three of them to properly continue the conversation that had been started while they were away. But both Lucas and Alice returned to dramas at their firms, sinking into big cases which saw Lucas sleeping at the office and Alice working fourteen-hour days. While Star herself came back to find that her director, Mikael, was defecting from Lockjaw to another, more prestigious, site-specific theatre company. Star was personally betrayed by the news. Her efforts as Karen had merely been Mikael's springboard.

It wasn't until Saturday that the flatmates had finally sat around the kitchen table, where Star had first met them both. 'We need to talk,' Alice said. She'd had violet smudges under her eyes, her hair was pulled back with a scrunchie and she wore an over-sized sweatshirt with the name of her law firm written on the back. It was mid-afternoon, well before the rush of evening trade downstairs, but the air was pungent with coriander and garlic.

'We do,' Star replied. 'I never meant to hurt you. I'm sure Lucas didn't either.' She flashed a smile at Lucas. She hadn't told him about Lockjaw yet; she longed for his sympathy, for him to take her hand and soothe her.

'We can get on to that,' Alice said, raising a hand. 'There's something else I wanted to raise first and there's no easy way of saying it.' She'd paused. 'Things have been going missing from my room. Cash. My mum's earrings. My iPod. It started before the holiday, and I didn't know if I imagined it, but this week – well, I realised that I wasn't.'

'What are you saying?' Lucas had frowned, palms turned upwards on the kitchen table. His Greek tan clashed with his strawberry-blonde hair.

'I don't know. What am I saying, Star?' Alice looked at Star. Star's mouth hung open. This she hadn't expected.

'Are you accusing me?' The concept was so ludicrous that Star had laughed. She and Alice had pooled possessions once Star had moved into the flat. Alice often rummaged through Star's make-up and borrowed her hairgrips. Star hadn't minded. It had felt like intimacy.

'This is serious,' Alice said. 'I know that money can be tight for you, Starry, but I never had you down as a thief.'

'That's because I'm not one.' Star had shaken as she pushed her chair back and stood. She didn't get angry often, had long learnt that it didn't help anyone, but this was nothing less than an assault. 'You're just saying this because of what happened in Greece.'

'Come on, you told me how you used to shoplift in Devon,' Alice continued. 'Is it such a surprise that when my things go missing I—'

'That was when I was a kid,' Star shouted. 'I would never, ever steal from you.' She'd looked at Lucas, imploring him to take her side, to stand with her.

'Come on, Alice,' Lucas said. 'You know Star wouldn't do that.' He'd nodded at Star reassuringly, but she'd made out a slight hesitation on his face and he'd remained seated. He still hadn't committed to her properly, and in that moment, she saw that he wasn't going to. That this could be his get-out-of-jail-free card, just as Alice intended.

'Really?' Alice said. 'Well, how do you explain this?' She stood and moved to the peg on the back of the kitchen door, from which hung Star's beloved denim jacket, slipping her hand into the top pocket and pulling out a slim grey cartridge attached to a white tangle of earphones.

'I didn't put that there!' Star was indignant. She hadn't been able to believe that Alice would stoop so low. Yes, she had coveted the device, but she would never have stolen it.

'What, you're saying that I did? To frame you? As if I've got the time, Star. I've hardly been here all week. I could do without this, to be honest. I'm not going to call the police or anything, but

*I think perhaps you should consider finding a new place to live?
It's a trust issue.'*

*Star had turned to Lucas but was repelled by the confusion on
his face.*

'Don't you believe me?' Star asked him.

'Did you take it?' he said, face solemn.

*'Of course not! How could you ever ask such a thing?' Star
screamed. Lucas paused and, in that split second of vacillation,
she'd lost him.*

*'I don't know who to believe,' Lucas said. 'I'm going out for a
walk to think.' He slipped out of the flat, leaving Star and Alice
alone.*

'How could you?' Star was crying by then.

'How could you?' Alice replied, unyielding.

'I'm not a thief,' Star said.

*'You are,' Alice replied. Star realised that she wasn't talking
about the iPod; she was talking about Lucas himself.*

*'You don't need to do this,' Star said. 'Let's talk about it. I know
you like him too.'*

*'You're going to be fine,' Alice said. 'You're so adaptable. You've
got your whole life ahead of you.'*

*Star has avoided this memory for so long. It's too painful. She
should have stayed in the flat and stood her ground, but – profoundly hurt by Alice's accusation – she hadn't. Instead, glaring
at Alice, she'd grabbed a roll of bin bags from the kitchen drawer
and rushed into her bedroom, hurling her possessions into several
of them. Her clothes and jewellery and books. If Lucas wasn't
prepared to defend her, to bring their relationship out into the
light of day, it could never work, could it?*

Now, in the solitude of the roof garden, it's this decision that haunts her. If only she had stayed.

24

Riad Mousseline, Marrakesh

Saturday night
Twenty years later

Nobody saw them leave. Sounds drifted down from the roof terrace – Tommy's barking laugh, a ripple of synth – but Mousseline's inner courtyard was empty, the only movement the trickling of the fountain, which never seemed to stop.

'All Arab gardens need running water,' Lilith had told the group when they had first arrived. 'It's imperative. It symbolises the lake in Paradise.'

There was no sign of Lilith anywhere, but Mousseline's front door wasn't locked, either. They stepped through the door within a door, into the street outside. It was unlit by street lights and seemingly empty, but it felt alive. How long ago it seemed since Molly had been knocked down by the moped and briefly surrendered to the dust.

'Where would we go?' Molly had asked when they were still upstairs in the suite.

'Somewhere that's not here,' Alice had said. She'd gathered herself and tidied her errant make-up, the vulnerability she had briefly shown folded away. 'Back to the Jemaa el-Fna? Let's see what's going on. Have a bit of an adventure. Let the rest of them do the same old things. Let's do something different.'

'I'm not sure we are dressed for it,' Molly had replied, looking down at her silky dress, then at Alice's Oscar-statuette column of gold. Inside Mousseline, middle-aged glamour had been acceptable, necessary even, for the game they were playing: that pretence that they were all still at the apex of desirability, that their lives could be riven apart by attraction. But outside her walls, it was a joke. They would be confronted once more with that uncertainty of how the world would judge them now that it no longer wanted to fuck them. As a group, they could time-travel back to their previous selves, especially after a few drinks, but faced with the scrutiny of others, they were stitched into the present.

'I've got shawls,' Alice had said, going over to the wardrobe and pulling out a pair of pashminas. She'd draped one over Molly's shoulder, fine-grade turquoise alpaca, which clashed with the darker blue of the dress. Molly drew it around her torso but felt the bareness of her legs afresh. Exposure. 'Come on,' Alice had prompted, as if reading her mind. 'I just need to get out of here. I thought that I was going to feel OK with the whole thing. The divorce party was for Lucas, really; you know how he always likes to do what he thinks is current, the latest thing. He is so concerned about what everyone thinks.' She gave a bitter cough of a laugh. The shawl that she wrapped across her own shoulders was off-white with a border in myxomatosis pink.

'You don't think we should tell them?' said Molly as they ducked out into the road, both looking at their phones.

'Send a text,' replied Alice, shrugging. 'I can't be bothered. We won't be long.'

But something stopped Molly from texting Noah. She told herself that they were just popping out, that he would know she was with Alice. But, really, she wanted to be the one going somewhere he had no idea about, just as he had regularly disappeared off to an undisclosed part of London over the past year. He'd told her that Greta lived in Deptford, an unknown area for Molly, who mostly stayed in her corner of London, shuttling between home and the school she worked in.

'Oh, look. A missed call from Olivia,' said Alice, holding up her screen.

'Do you want to call her back?' asked Molly.

'I'd better,' said Alice. She pressed the phone to her ear and looked past Molly as she waited. 'She's not picking up.' Alice's forehead puckered, her attempt at a frown.

'I'm sure she's fine,' said Molly. 'I've had about six calls from Bella today.'

'Yeah,' said Alice. 'She's probably already gone to bed. She's just been a bit fragile since we've told her about the split.'

'I'm not surprised,' said Molly, thinking of Bella's questions earlier in the day.

Alice and Molly looped arms as they often had before, but silently. So many words had been exchanged, already, between them. It was a comfort just to feel the animal warmth of the other, to move in silence. Molly wanted to analyse what Alice had told her, about separating from Lucas, about Star and her mother, but she knew that any reach for understanding would have to wait until later, when she was alone.

The Jemaa el-Fna was still teeming. People were sitting eating at all those trestle tables that they'd witnessed being laid out earlier in the afternoon – plates of meat; tiny blackened chops, chunks of thigh, long moulded spears of mince. The moon hung low.

Molly and Alice felt male eyes on them. A glance up and down and then away. They were too old for the looks to linger. There had been a time when they had competed for male attention, as all young women do, whether they choose to or not, but now they were united against it. They had been caressed and tongued and fingered and penetrated and ultimately impregnated: there were no mysteries left for them in lust. Once, it had been the ultimate aphrodisiac – the sense of someone wanting you more than they wanted anyone else. Now Molly knew it for what it was: a card trick.

In the centre of the square, another crowd circled two young men. One was playing the drums, and the other was singing, ululating. The sound rose into the night like the smoke from the nearby grills. Above, a rash of stars against the blue-black.

'Come on,' said Alice. 'Let's go there.' She pulled Molly by the interlinked arm, and they joined the crowd. There were some other tourists, younger and less dressed up than they, but the group was also full of locals. Mostly young men, in T-shirts with logos and stonewashed denim; many of them clapping in time with the performers.

'Let's dance,' said Alice. She dropped her arm from Molly's and started to sway, raising her arms above her head, the pashmina stretched out between them like a banner, slinking her sequinned hips. Molly hung back, embarrassed. She wasn't drunk enough for this. Typical Alice. How many times had she led the charge onto a dance floor?

They had been invisible by virtue of their age, but now the crowd was looking at them with polite, faintly amused interest. The performers noticed too and gestured for Alice to come closer, to dance next to them in the centre of the crowd. Alice acquiesced, shimmying closer to the eye of the storm. Her natural habitat. Her dress caught the light, and – from a distance – she looked quite beautiful once more, rejuvenated by obscurity, her princess hair rippling as she moved.

Molly smiled and started clapping in time with the rest of the crowd. But she felt annoyed, caught in Alice's slipstream. She brought her hands together, but her thoughts drifted. Molly had searched for Greta online. The day after she had found out. Greta Vester. A production assistant on Noah's show. She had found her social media, her LinkedIn, an interview she had given to a website about the new programme. Molly had gone through all the pages she could find on her. Greta was Danish. She pictured Noah in Copenhagen, wobbling behind his paramour on a bicycle, eating rollmops, jumping into a frigid sea. Desire still took you places, after all. It built things, moved people across continents, changed the course of lives. What would life look like without that animating force?

Greta wasn't a beautiful girl exactly, but she had an appealing air of implacability, dusted across her face like her copious freckles. This wasn't a young woman who would shape her predilections to what she thought a man wanted. Molly wished she had realised that had been an option when she was younger. Perhaps she wouldn't have even chosen a man. There had been women she found attractive, but it had been so much easier to stay within the confines of what was expected. To want the future that she understood she ought to. Yet Lucas and Alice's announcement had made her realise that she wasn't the only one to found her life choices upon misapprehensions – perhaps that's all anyone ever did?

'Mol ...' Alice was reaching out her arm, swaying. 'Come and join me.'

'Shit,' said Molly, under her breath. There was little she wanted to do less than perform with Alice in front of a crowd of strangers. She paused. The singer gave a particularly commanding ululation, indubitably an injunction. She stepped forwards to her friend's outstretched hand and started to move. The whoops of the crowd redoubled, the odd snatch of incredulous laughter. They danced.

25

Guildford and London

Twenty-six years earlier

Molly's father, Alan, adored her. She could do no wrong, and every time she entered a room, his face transfigured. With her dancer's poise, Diana never quite forgave her daughter the usurpation.

Molly worshipped him back. Alan was a self-polished gem of a man, a natural-born performer with a fine tenor voice and a deeply ingrained capacity for enjoyment. From babyhood, he sang to her and whirled her around. As a toddler, he tossed her in the air like a bag of sugar.

If Molly fell out with a friend or felt annoyed with her teacher, it was Alan to whom she would talk. Diana was always at one remove, with a distaste for life's procedural details, whereas Alan hungered for them. He listened. He would question her school friend Kelly's judgement with just the right degree of outrage. If things seemed really bad, he would make them fried egg sandwiches as solace, moving around their pine-cabineted kitchen and shooting her occasional smiles.

The family lived in a semi on Guildford's outer fringes. Externally, it had the jauntiness of a holiday-park chalet, with its sloping roof and timber cladding, but inside was beige perfection: acres of carpet, striped daily by Diana's vacuum cleaner. Despite the bland safety of their surroundings, Alan hailed from murkier waters. He had left school in Newquay summarily at sixteen to work as a mechanic. His accent retained a clotted burr, and a blown-out tattoo of a mermaid trod water on his right shoulder blade. Yet, he had made something of himself, with the garage he owned, a Rover franchise, where he went daily in a shirt and tie. Other men got car grease on them now, not Alan. Instead, he stood on the forecourt, next to the motors, gleaming with wax, surveying his empire.

He occasionally sold a car or two to keep his hand in, although he mostly left that to a salesman by the time Molly was at school. Growing up, Molly and her brother Jake would visit the showroom, make powdery hot chocolate from the drinks machine and climb into the driving seats of a beached Austin Maestro or a hatchback, sticky fingers on pleather. The ample, bright space smelt of newness: metal, plastic, volatile organic compounds off-gassing – a scent that Molly was forever to associate with safety and paternal love.

The problem with Molly's closeness to her father only revealed itself in adolescence. Alan didn't set out to thwart his adolescent daughter's nascent sexuality. Yet he told her regularly – and fervently believed – that no teenage boy would be good enough for her. Perhaps none of them was. Molly dreaded his judgement. A kind man, he was nonetheless quick to pronounce. She felt witnessed.

Some boys expressed interest, but none of them was quite right. Too many moles. Acned cheekbones. Ski-slope shoulders. A hyena's laugh. None desirable enough that they were worth bringing home to weather Alan's frank and voluble assessment.

By the time she left home for university, her inexperience had become a burden, her single most significant source of shame. She carried it around in the pit of her stomach. She was a freak. Frigid, perhaps. These things were whispered about girls like her. Jake was younger than her, but he had gone out with a girl called Amy for eighteen months. They never talked about it, but Molly sensed that he approached his own sex life with cheery and routine practicality that seemed unfathomable.

On her last night before heading up to London, Diana had appeared in her room. She was clad in the clothes she wore to do her evening stretches, her make-up removed. Her blonde hair was fluffed out, like a baby duckling's, her eyebrows almost entirely absent without pencil.

'It's all going to be different,' said Diana, sitting down on Molly's duvet. 'When you're away.' She smoothed the cover with her hand.

'What do you mean?' said Molly, stiffening. She and her mother never had such conversations.

'You're going to have your own life,' replied Diana. 'In

all regards. You've worked so hard at your studies, Molly. You've always been such a good girl. But there is more to life than making your father and me happy. You're going to find out.' This statement, possibly the single most perceptively maternal one that Diana had ever made.

'Thanks, Mum,' said Molly, leaning against Diana's jersey-clad shoulder. She wanted to hold on tight, to never let her go. If her mother could be like this, perhaps everything she believed to be true about their relationship was wrong. Yet Diana, as if overwhelmed by her uncharacteristic candour, broke the embrace first by patting Molly's back and standing. She gave Molly a little wave before leaving the room, leaving only the lingering smell of Cristalle and a juddering excitement in the pit of Molly's stomach. She was to be free.

Alan and Diana dropped her at the halls of residence – a tower block backing onto King's Cross. Molly's room was on the third floor, above a small car park. The surrounding buildings were so tall that her window only admitted a segment of dirty white London sky.

'Well. You did want to be right in the thick of things,' said Diana. She had dressed up for the drop-off, a belted blazer and heels. Molly had forbidden any kind of hat.

'Makes me feel closed in,' said Alan, whose burliness took up much of the small room. 'All this concrete.'

'It's OK,' said Molly. 'I like it. This will do me fine.' The halls smelt of sliced white toast and Fairy liquid: an English kind of comfort.

'I suppose this is goodbye,' said Diana. 'Ring us tomorrow. Make sure you eat.'

'Remember, if you don't like it, sweetheart, you can just come home,' said Alan, looking distrustfully around the room. 'You only have to say the word. There is always a job for you on reception.'

'Alan. Give the girl a chance,' said Diana.

*　*　*

Things didn't change as radically as Molly might have hoped in her first term. She was available, a taxi with her light on, but it didn't seem as if boys were noticing. Or, at least, not the ones she wanted. It was just how it had always been. She drank. Sometimes she kissed. But there seemed nobody just for her.

She started on the first year's reading list; The Wife of Bath's knowing bawdiness was a sustained taunt.

Alice's room was the next but one along the corridor. At first, Molly was wary of the girl with the hockey sweatshirts, hairbands and sashaying walk. But one night, she and Alice got talking in the laundry room, both going to collect their piles of damp clothes simultaneously. They walked back to their corridor together, and a friendship began, Molly slotting easily into the more confident girl's orbit. Alice had a frank seaminess that Molly desperately admired. Subsequent late-night conversation in their rooms, fuelled by plastic cups of toothache-sweet white, revealed that Alice's compact body had already weathered much. Multiple partners. An older boyfriend. A threesome. Her flesh contained multitudes.

For a long time, Molly didn't confess. She embroidered

past snogs to suggest there had been more to them, hinting that there had been a boyfriend back at home. She didn't lie outright, but she avoided mentioning the truth that preoccupied her.

'Have you ever had sex?' asked Alice, casually, one evening as they readied themselves for the student union's cocktail night. Her tone was kind, and, caught off guard, Molly admitted that she hadn't. 'We need to get you laid,' said Alice. 'Tonight.'

'Oh, I ...' mumbled Molly.

'It's honestly not such a big deal,' said Alice, arcing her eyebrows to apply another coat of mascara onto her eyelashes. 'You'll see. You've built it up.'

They drank Long Island ice teas and sat in the corner of the student bar. They had befriended Viv, whose room sat between theirs, by this point. Sensible Viv was their perfect foil. That night, Alice introduced Molly to a succession of boys, for Alice knew everyone already. As Molly grew progressively drunker, she eventually found herself playing pool with a chemistry undergraduate called Damon. He wore a white grandad shirt, his shoes encased in vast trainers, his hair falling in wings over his eyes. After she beat him, Damon held his hands up.

'I wasn't expecting that,' he said. 'I'll freely admit it.'

Molly laughed, awkward now she no longer had something to do with her hands.

'You've got beautiful hair,' said Damon, in a blunt non sequitur. Molly touched it. Nobody had ever once said that about her mousy waves. Really?

In the girls' toilet: a pep talk.

'He'll do,' said Alice. 'He's fit.'

'He's got big lips,' said Molly. 'I don't like men with big lips.' She was falling into her habit of anatomising boys to reject them before they had a chance to do the same to her.

'What are you talking about?' said Alice. 'Listen to yourself, Mol. Come on. Besides, this doesn't mean you are going to marry him. Right?'

So, later, Molly took Damon back to her single bed, and the deed was done. At last. She was so drunk that she couldn't really tell how it felt, or whether she had enjoyed it, or if she even had truly wanted to participate, but the following day she felt overwhelming relief. Alice was right; it hadn't been anything to worry about. She didn't need to perform; she wasn't to be judged. It didn't have to be momentous. The experience shored up the sense, one she was going to cling on to long after it had outlived its usefulness, that alcohol unlocked experience.

Alice and Viv pinned a gold paper star on Molly's door the next morning. After Damon was gone, they took her to a greasy spoon for breakfast, where they debriefed over beans on toast and mugs of builders' tea. Molly felt initiated, one of the gang. Her sensory dial was turned up: the squeezy ketchup and mustard bottles on the table in front of her frankly bright, the savoury smell of grease profound, the pattern of raindrops on the window like art.

Damon didn't contact her. She pretended not to mind. His lips were a turn-off, after all.

'One-night stands keep things simple,' said carnivorous

Alice. So, Molly tried to follow suit with other boys than Damon. Only it turned out she didn't feel the same way. She yearned to hold hands with someone when walking down the street. To sit together in one of the gated squares near their halls. She wanted to be someone's girlfriend. Her hunger for romance was a shortcoming. She craved sexual insouciance, knowing deep down that she would never achieve it.

The three girls knew of Lucas. He studied economics and lived on the tenth floor of the halls, a character on campus with his height and briefcase. By rights, he should have been a figure of mockery, but inexplicably he wasn't. Then they met Tommy and Noah, friends from school. Both were studying English like Molly and Alice. None of them could have predicted the romantic entanglements that were going to redraw friendship lines over the years to come.

Tommy seldom made it into seminars, but he got firsts in his essays without trying. Many of the girls admired his bleached, casual handsomeness. Molly could hardly look at him.

Once, they had a conversation at the start of a lecture about Coleridge. Tommy slipped in late and sat down next to Molly, who had been sitting on her own, near the back of the amphitheatre.

He sat down with a waft of tobacco and chewing gum, which she would later recognise as his trademark. His eyes were rimmed red, but he was glorious.

'Thought I'd come in for this one,' he said, coughing.

'Where's Noah?'

'Asleep. I said he could take my notes,' said Tommy. 'He's done the same for me enough times.'

'Oh right,' she said, looking ahead. *Oh right?* She wanted to dazzle Tommy, but that was the best that she could come up with. Still, he had chosen to sit next to her, when there were so many other empty seats.

Her stomach flipped and she remained aware of him throughout. His right forearm appeared to be a heat source, and she couldn't concentrate on what the lecturer said. At the best of times, she couldn't get on with the Romantics and found them too opaque and melodramatic, but glancing over, Tommy looked enthralled. He sat still as the lecture came to a close, resting his jaw in his hands as if not wanting the words to end.

'I love all this shit,' he said, finally, as other students made their way past, many girls giving him coy glances. 'Coleridge was something else.'

'I can appreciate it,' said Molly. 'But it doesn't really move me.' Tommy smiled and shook his head as if surprised at her philistinism.

'Catch you later,' he said, standing and slinging his record bag over his shoulder. He loped off, back to Noah and the student house they already shared. Molly carried the memory of his proximity with her for the rest of the day.

26

Medina, Marrakesh

Saturday night
Twenty-six years later

The crowd tired of them after ten minutes, despite Alice's increasingly energetic attempts to hold their attention. As she tipped her body forward, shimmying all the while, Molly began to worry that she might be preparing to launch herself into the Worm. Drunken breakdancing was one of Alice's favourite party tricks. Molly had lost count of the number of floors that Alice had wiggled upon: sticky barroom lino, reclaimed parquet in someone's new kitchen extension, the immaculate Berber rugs of her and Lucas's own living room.

'Al ... it's time to go.' Molly grabbed Alice's arm just as Alice was about to go down, her clutch stronger than she intended.

'Ow,' said Alice, shaking her arm free in annoyance.

'Look at them,' said Molly, looking at the crowd standing

in front of them. 'They think we are a joke.' As if to prove her point, a man let out a whoop and nodded encouragingly.

'All right. All right,' said Alice, stepping away.

Molly turned and nodded to the singer, who raised his hands in faintly mocking applause.

'We should go and get another drink somewhere,' said Alice. 'Let's not go back yet. They'll just be doing all the same things as always. Even our news won't have changed that. Let's do something else while I've got you. Before we have to go back to *normal*.' She shuddered at the last word.

'OK,' said Molly. 'What was that bar that Lilith was talking about? Rouge something or other. We could try that. It's not far from the medina. Look it up.'

Alice typed Rouge into Google Maps, and the name Maison Rouge flashed up. The women started to follow the route.

They were quieter then, both more worn out from the dancing than they cared to admit.

'This must be it,' said Alice, sighing in satisfaction. Another riad, the small scarlet door hanging open, cut inside a larger one and revealing a square furbelowed with fairy lights and crowded with plants.

They entered and found a table for two, slotted into the corner. A waiter approached the table.

'We'll have two of the Maison Rouge cocktails,' said Alice. 'When in Rome!' She laughed, coquettishly, and Molly looked away and outwards, in the direction of the bar. It was a place for tourists. Many of the guests were older than them, some seriously overweight, coronets of silver hair glowing in the dim light.

Alice's mouth puckered in evident disappointment as she surveyed the scene.

'This isn't what I was expecting,' said Alice.

'Never mind,' said Molly. 'We'll make the best of it.'

The waiter arrived back with their drinks: immense ruby-red goblets, each with a parasitical raspberry clinging to the rim.

'Wonderful,' said Alice, flashing another one of her flirtatious smiles. 'Look at that. So *pretty*.'

The cocktail's festive appearance only served to make Molly realise how little fun she was having.

'You're flirting!' she said. 'Look at you.'

'Sure,' said Alice, shrugging.

'It's just I've realised something this weekend,' Molly replied. 'I don't care any more about the male gaze. Getting dressed up like this ...' She gestured at the blue dress. 'It has really made me understand that fact. I've left that side of my life behind and it's really OK. It's liberating, in fact.'

'Good for you,' said Alice. 'But you always were far worthier than me, Mol. I want a future that involves the male gaze, no matter how deluded that might be.'

'I would have made different decisions, if I'd just been more confident about my own needs,' said Molly.

'Let's not talk about the past again,' said Alice. 'I just want to inhabit the future. That's all I want. That's what leaving Lucas is about – the future, full of possibility.'

Molly paused. 'One last thing then. I've been thinking about Star too. I feel so guilty for how I treated her. I accused her of something just before she went away. I always thought it was my fault she left to go travelling so impulsively.'

'You're always so hard on yourself, Molly,' said Alice. 'If it was anyone's fault, it was mine.'

'What do you mean?' Molly asked. Alice sighed.

'I accused Star of nicking some of my stuff. It wasn't working out, the three of us living together. Honestly, she was mooning after Lucas in a way that made it all a bit uncomfortable and I thought I was doing us all a favour in resolving the situation.'

'You lied?' Molly said.

Alice looked uncomfortable, leaning forward to stir the ice cubes in her drink.

'I was young and stupid, like I said. I had strong feelings for Lucas. And you know Star – she was pretty chaotic. Half the time she wasn't sure what was hers and what wasn't.'

'That's not true,' said Molly. She rubbed the gap between her eyebrows. 'I can't believe you did that.' She pushed her cocktail forward and stood. 'I think I had better head back to the riad.'

'What, to punish me for something that happened more than twenty years ago?' said Alice. 'Look, this is why I never told you. I knew you'd be ... purist about it.'

Molly turned to go and then turned back again, her hands placed on the back of a chair.

'She was my friend. I loved her,' said Molly.

'I did too. Do you think I didn't? But I had to make a choice,' said Alice. 'That's what life is, a series of choices. And sometimes they're difficult.'

Molly was about to say more, to argue back. But Alice's

phone – slim as a wafer, the slick grey of sealskin – started to chime. Alice picked it up.

'Hang on, how do I ...' Alice said to herself. Then there was a chime of acceptance as she swiped. It was a video call, and from where she sat, Molly could see an upturned view of Olivia's elegant face, with its leonine eyebrows and golden hair in a centre part. Fully grown, Olivia looked like an elf princess with a John Lewis store card. Olivia and Edward had always been alarmingly proficient children. Academic and sporting. Good readers. Good eaters. Precociously adept with a knife and fork.

Now Edward was at Bristol and Olivia in the sixth form, but Molly knew they were both at home for the weekend, holding the fort in their parents' absence.

'Mummy?' Olivia's voice was a filament.

'Sweetheart!' said Alice. 'How are you and Eddie doing? Look, we are just in the courtyard of this amazing bar. Can you see the stars?' Alice angled her phone up to the sky. 'We had dinner, and I've just come out for a drink with Molly.' Molly frowned. She wasn't prepared to change the subject that easily.

'Looks nice,' said Olivia, flatly.

'Is everything OK, Ollie, sweetheart?'

'Have you told them yet? All your friends?' said Olivia. 'Does Molly know?'

'Yes,' Alice replied. She cleared her throat. 'We did it tonight. It all went as planned.'

'I'm pleased it's worked out so *brilliantly*,' said Olivia. 'But listen, there's a problem here. Eddie and I decided to have some friends back tonight and – well – it's got a bit out of hand.' A door behind her juddered open as she spoke, and a boy appeared. He was topless and reeling, eyes flashing, lips wetly crimson.

'Ollie!' the youth said, moving towards the girl.

'Ew,' said Olivia, she stood up, and the phone's screen went black for a moment. When Olivia appeared again, she was under the bright spotlights of a bathroom.

'I've locked myself in the en suite,' said Olivia. 'Some people turned up that we don't know, and they're smashing things up downstairs. I thought it was in hand, but I'm a bit scared now of what they're going to do. I couldn't get hold of you or Daddy.' The last bit an accusation.

'You're joking.' Alice raised her manicured hand to her mouth.

Molly pictured her friend's double-fronted Edwardian villa. As Edward and Olivia had grown older, the house had become the focus of Alice's energy and drive. Every item in it, every surface, had been chosen with extreme care. It was a symphony of marble and porcelain and linen, of uplighters and discreet tech. Molly imagined the invaders splintering the side tables, shredding the canvas of the vast seascape above the fireplace, pissing on the Jeff Koons. They would undoubtedly find Lucas's treasured collection of wall-mounted skateboards, each worth a small fortune.

'I'm not joking,' said Olivia. 'I don't know what to do.'

'Where's your brother?' asked Alice.

'He's downstairs. He is trying to get them to leave, but I'm worried he will get hurt.' Olivia slumped on the floor of the en suite, her back against the side of the bath. There was the sound of someone beating on the door outside. 'I'm scared, Mummy.'

'You need to call the police,' said Alice. 'Right now. Ring off and do it now.'

'OK,' said Olivia, obediently.

'Do it and then call us back,' said Alice. The phone screen went dark. 'Fuck,' she added. 'I can't believe this has been going on while we're here, and I didn't pick up my phone.' Alice leant forwards and covered her eyes with her hands. Molly noticed them trembling. The anger she had just felt towards Alice leached away. What did it matter any more? Alice had made some bad decisions, but hadn't they all?

'Hey,' said Molly. 'Try not to worry too much. This happened to someone in Bella's class, too. It was shit, and there was a lot of damage, but nobody got hurt.'

'I've got to find Lucas,' said Alice. 'We've got to go back to the riad right now.' Alice stood, and Molly followed her out of the bar. 'I just can't believe it. The children. The house. All my things.'

27

Riad Mousseline, Marrakesh

Twenty minutes later

At Mousseline's front door, Molly and Alice encountered Noah, his hair skewed, his face ruddy and his special-occasion shirt untucked.

'Ladies!' he said affably. 'I was just looking for you.'

'I've got to get hold of Lucas,' said Alice. 'There is some kind of home invasion going on at our house.'

'He's still upstairs,' said Noah. 'He's in a bit of a state. A tad too much to drink, I think.' Noah winked, but Alice just pushed past him and disappeared inside. 'She didn't seem in such a good mood.'

'Olivia and Edward held a party, and they've got gate-crashers. I think she's frightened – Olivia was hiding in the bathroom. Besides, they have just announced their divorce, it's hardly the cause for celebration they've been making it out as.'

'Of course not,' said Noah. He paused. 'Did you know about the divorce?'

'Not a clue,' replied Molly. 'She didn't tell me even when I talked to her about *us*.'

'Well, trust those two to turn telling everyone into such a production,' Noah said, pushing his hands into his pockets like a schoolboy. They were awkward together; this was new. 'Hey. Have you seen Tommy?'

'I thought he was still with you,' said Molly.

'No. He disappeared about the same time you did,' said Noah.

Molly thought guiltily of the disappointing kiss, the futile reach for an earlier version of herself. That wasn't the answer to anything – she was sure of it now.

'Let's get a drink in the courtyard and see if he turns up,' suggested Molly. She longed to sit down.

She followed Noah into the corridor, and they sank into the low wicker seats under the fig tree, near a thick candle flickering under a glass dome. The air smelt of oranges and dust, plus the particular undertone of Mousseline: incense and cooking.

'So.' Molly looked at her husband in the dim light.

'So.'

'Do you love her? This Greta?' Molly laughed as if the very suggestion was ridiculous.

'No … I don't know.' Noah looked at his forearms. They weren't the arms of a man who spent eight hours a day reading different folio editions of Shakespeare, but more robust and capable, visible veins pushing up among golden brown hairs. Molly had always loved them. If she'd had to choose one part of Noah's anatomy, his arms would be it. When had she stopped noticing them?

'Tell me about her.'

'Are you sure?' Noah frowned. 'I don't think that's a good idea, Molly.'

'I want to know,' said Molly. 'No, actually – I *need* to know.'

'I don't know where to start.' Noah coughed.

'How do you feel when you're with her?'

Noah paused, grimaced and then visibly steeled himself. 'She is so optimistic about things. It turns out that I miss being close to that kind of enthusiasm. You've been so passionless, Molly. For so long. It's like you don't notice, but you don't seem to care about anything any more. You don't enjoy teaching these days. You don't even seem to enjoy being a mother. You definitely don't enjoy being with me.'

'That's not true,' said Molly, but she recognised the truth of his words. Somewhere along the way, she had lost the thread of pleasure. Life had become a series of obligations, even in its most intimate spheres.

'It's nice to be liked,' Noah was rueful but insistent. 'Fancied. Greta makes me feel good. I don't care if that makes me some kind of simplistic animal.' He shrugged. 'But I haven't stopped loving you. I never stopped loving you and the girls. What we have. It's everything to me. Say the word, and I'll end it with her. But I need to know that you want me. I can't go on as we have been.'

Molly was silent. She loved her husband too. But she no longer desired him, and this was a single, immovable fact which sat against her solar plexus, radiating out through her entire body. How much easier it would be if she did.

'Say it, Molly. Please.' Noah leant forwards, entreating. He looked close to tears.

'I love you.'

'But do you want me?' Noah whispered.

Molly couldn't stop herself from frowning. She resented the grovelling note of sexual pleading in his voice. The imposition of it. She tipped her head back and looked up at the stars. She would quite like to float away, leaving behind her body, so cumbersome and problematic, with its slow ebb and the expectations others placed on it.

'A-hem.' There was the sound of a throat clearing from across the courtyard. A voice called, '*I* want you, Noah. Surely that's good enough?'

'Tommy, what the hell?' said Noah. They hadn't noticed Tommy, but he had been sitting in the gloom on the other set of chairs beside a jasmine-wreathed pillar. He stood and lurched towards Molly and Noah. His pale hair stood out in the gloom, and in his right hand, he dangled a bottle of beer from his fingertips so casually that it looked as though it might slip and smash across the chessboard tiles.

'*Tommy.*' Molly was aghast, both at what he had heard pass between her and Noah and the fact he was holding a drink. How she regretted that earlier kiss.

'Cheers!' Tommy lifted the green bottle aloft, tipped his head back and swallowed. His eyes shone, and he had the dangerous looseness to his limbs that Molly recognised; this drink clearly wasn't his first. For so long, Tommy had drunk with them; before he had started to do it alone, she knew what it looked like.

'But that's beer?' Molly couldn't stop the surprise. 'You've been doing so well, Tommy. Don't do this. Just put the bottle down. You've got almost a whole year.'

'*Doing so well*,' Tommy mimicked. He spun round on the spot, spilling a little from his bottle as he did so. 'What a star pupil, I am.' He bowed. 'Tommy the lush.'

'Listen to her,' said Noah, tiredly, pressing his thumbs to his eyebrows. 'You're just going to set yourself back.'

'Too late,' said Tommy, closing his eyes in something like rapture. 'Too fucking late. Not that I want a lecture from you, Noah. How could you? I've been eavesdropping, and I heard it all. Pathetic, Noah. Screwing around on your lovely wife like that.' With this, he relinquished the bottle, and it fell onto the ground, breaking into pieces and scattering across the tiles.

All three were silent for a second. Molly thought of that time that Bella, aged five, had cut her foot on a piece of broken glass. The amount of blood had been surprising.

'It's not as simple as you might think,' Noah said, but he was cowed; he looked down as if trying to locate the shards of glass and piece them back together with his gaze.

'He's right; you don't know the full story,' said Molly. She looked at Tommy, begging him with her eyes. 'We have been trying to work it out. For the sake of Bella and Eve.'

'You should have better than that, Molly,' said Tommy. 'Somebody who would treat you with the respect you deserve.'

'It's not as straightforward as it looks, Tom,' said Molly. 'A long-term marriage takes a certain amount of compromise.'

Tommy didn't appear to be listening. He had turned away. Picking his way past the broken glass, he made his way towards the fountain at the centre of the courtyard before climbing onto its stone brim and then tipping into the water basin with a damp splosh, arcing his long frame around so that he could sit inside it. He dipped his face into the water and then lifted it out, pursing his lips and spouting out over the edge in a parody of the stone fish doing the same above his head.

'Tommy. What the fuck. Climb out of that right now,' said Noah, in his lecturer's voice.

'She chose you,' Tommy said. 'She chose you! And there wasn't a bloody thing I could do about it.' The man was quite obviously in a state, but Molly recoiled from his words. This was not good. This was very, very bad.

Tommy submerged his face again into the water, but this time he didn't lift his head. After a beat, Noah and Molly strode forward in sync and reached the fountain together. They leant over and dragged Tommy up.

'Tommy, come on. Out of there,' Molly said, like the mother she was. She could feel the artery on the left side of her head pulsing.

Tommy climbed out slowly and stood, dripping beside them both, a damp jasmine flower in the middle of his forehead like a bindi. The night was still warm, but he shivered extravagantly.

'Maybe it's time you went to bed,' said Molly, reaching out to touch him on the arm.

'All in good time.' Tommy shrugged her off. Even distraught, he possessed that carnival spirit that entered him when he drank. Even now.

'What did you mean?' said Noah quietly. '"She chose you." What were you talking about?'

'Tommy ...' Molly was beseeching. But Tommy looked as though he was somewhere else, his hair slicked close to his skull, his blue eyes distant, fixed on the past.

'You're blind,' said Tommy. 'You always have been.'

'Hush,' said Molly. 'Don't say it.'

'Say what?' asked Noah, looking between Tommy and Molly.

'We had a thing. Molly and I. Way back when. Before you had even decided you liked her.'

'What?' Noah looked at Molly. 'Is this true, Molly?'

Molly hung her head.

'I'm so sorry I didn't tell you,' she whispered.

'When did it end?'

'Long before we got married.'

'But not before we moved in together?' Noah frowned.

Molly shook her head. Her bones ached, and she knew herself to be pathetic. These were the shenanigans of the past. She wanted nothing more than to be in bed, on her own, head piled on cushions, a sheet pulled tight across her chest like a shroud. To rest.

'Molly got pregnant,' said Tommy. 'Not long after you got your first place. She didn't know whose it was, did you, Mol? Isn't that right? And so, she got rid of it.' He shuddered and then added, hysterically, 'A *baby*. It might have been mine.'

'It wasn't the right time,' said Molly, biting her lip and looking at her husband, reaching out a hand towards him. Noah backed away as if burned. 'Noah,' said Molly. She started to cry softly and looked at Tommy, who had a pool of water forming at his feet and was crying himself. 'What we've always had is so special to me. Tommy and I – that was so long ago. I was an insecure girl back then, but I've grown up with you. It never seemed worth hurting you for.'

The three stood, facing each other, the corners of an isosceles triangle.

'How *could* you?' said Noah to Tommy.

'I'm not sure,' replied Tommy, wiping his nose with the back of his hand. 'But it sounds like you've nicely evened up the balance sheet recently.'

'You're a waste of a human,' said Noah. 'I knew you'd end up back on the booze.'

At this, Tommy put his head down, like a bull facing a matador, and charged at Noah's stomach with a roar. He had the advantage of surprise, and he knocked Noah onto the floor with a thud. The men formed a ball of limbs, scuffling on one of the Berber rugs laid on the tiles, the starburst of broken beer-bottle glass dangerously close.

'Stop!' Molly shouted, but they continued wrestling, one gaining traction, then the other assuming momentary supremacy. Finally, Noah pinned Tommy's wrists to the ground and lay on top of him. Once he had done it, Noah seemed not to know what to do. He looked down at Tommy, blinking, a forelock of his brown hair tipping forward.

'Let me go,' said Tommy, eventually.

Looking embarrassed, Noah lifted his hands and held them in the air. 'My pleasure.'

Tommy rolled over and ran to the stairs at the side of the courtyard. Noah looked at Molly. His shirt was now damp, and its top button had pinged away during the fight so that Molly could see the creep of his chest hair. Her husband was so hairy, an amiable werewolf.

'Noah,' she said. 'I'm so sorry.' Noah said nothing. 'Oh, but you're bleeding,' said Molly. A poppy of red began to bloom against the sugary pinstripes on Noah's shirt, on the side of his belly.

'I am?' A note of panic flew into Noah's voice. He had always hated blood.

'We need to have a look,' said Molly, moving towards her husband. 'Come on, unbutton your shirt.'

'Keep your hands off me,' said Noah, but he started to undo the buttons and then let his shirt flop open. The blood was coming from a gash made by one of the shards of glass, a vicious cut in his flank, parallel to his navel. 'It's just a scratch,' said Noah. But he sounded panicked.

'I think it's OK,' said Molly, who had long been the one in their relationship to attend to the minor surgeries of parenting, the splinter removals and wobbly tooth yanks. 'But let's go to our room and clean it up. We can ask Lilith for a plaster.'

As she helped Noah stand, not worrying about his blood smearing on Alice's blue silk, there was a scream from the roof terrace above them. It was the type of sound normally reserved for nightmares, a note of absolute horror made by a woman in extreme distress.

'Alice,' said Molly, letting go of Noah and beginning to run.

28

Riad Mousseline, Marrakesh

Two minutes later

Molly's legs didn't seem to move fast enough as she made her way up the stairs to the first floor, then the roof.

Noah was behind her, moving more slowly and clutching his side. Molly turned to look at him and noticed a trail of red drops following them up the staircase, breadcrumbs through the fairy-tale forest.

'You all right?'

'Yeah.' Noah winced. His shirt was still undone, and one side oozed blood, the oxygenated red bright as paint.

Another of those guttural screams from Alice. The kind of ancient sound that Molly would be happy never to hear again for the rest of her life.

Molly turned back and took the final steps up to the roof terrace. She wove through the maze of plants and mirrors to the seating area. There were Alice and Lucas, Iona and Viv, standing in a row, all turned in the same direction. Music was still playing and the festoon lights swung in the breeze, but Mousseline's guests were no longer partying, they were in a rigid, horrified line.

Molly realised that the group was watching Tommy, who had climbed onto the wall at the edge of the roof terrace, at the point directly above the alleyway below, contemplating the drop beneath him.

Molly raised her hand to her mouth. She didn't say anything. She was worried that she might trigger a movement from Tommy if she spoke, which could prove definitive.

Alice turned round and looked at them both. Her eyes were wide, the lashes poking out in perfect curls. She looked like a furious china doll.

'He ... he ... he ...' Alice pointed, her customary composure stripped away. 'He appeared out of nowhere and just leapt up there.'

'Tommy.' Noah stepped forwards, hand still clutched to his side. 'Tommy, *get down.*'

'What's the point?' Tommy called over his shoulder. 'Nobody gives a shit.'

'Of course, they do,' said Noah, who took another step towards the wall, with its flimsy trellis covered in jasmine. 'Don't do this, Tommy.'

Tommy turned round then, swaying slightly as he did so. Molly balled her hands into fists, but he stabilised again and faced the group, silhouetted against the night. Behind him were pricks of white against indigo, the stars always hidden from view in their own city.

''Scuse me!' Tommy slurred the words and raised a finger as if to make a toast.

'Oh my God, he's *pissed*,' said Alice. 'Of course, he is.'

'Bloody maniac,' muttered Lucas.

'Just don't move again, Tommy,' said Viv, who was holding on to Iona's hand. 'If you turn round like that, you risk falling.'

'Come on, Tom, if I step forwards – do you think you could take my hand?' Noah had abandoned the fury of moments before and was entirely calm. Molly was reminded of how he dealt with Eve at her most impossible and felt a swell of gratitude towards him, the father of her children.

'Nuh-uh,' said Tommy. 'I don't think so. I can't take it any longer. You know, this must be how Star felt when she did it. I've spent twenty years wondering.' He extended his arms; his long fingertips seemed to brush the stars. His sodden shirt clung to his slender body. He was a scarecrow, a stick figure, their conscience.

'Don't be an *idiot*,' said Alice.

'Shhh!' Noah shot her a look and took another step forward. Molly could see that he was steadily getting closer to Tommy.

'You know, she would have been disgusted by the lot of us,' continued Tommy. 'What we've all become. Maybe especially you, Lucas and Alice. No offence.' Tommy giggled and wobbled again, righting himself. 'We've all prioritised the wrong things, wasted the opportunities we've had. What difference has any of us made?'

'Speak for yourself,' said Alice.

'Sometimes, I think she was trying to send us a message with what happened. I just wish I could have stopped her,' said Tommy. 'That I could have been there for her. The rest of you seemed to be able to move on from it, and I could never understand how you could.' His face crumpled, the momentary amusement leaving it. 'She committed suicide and what kind of friends were we then?'

'Star didn't commit suicide.' The voice was quiet but definite. Molly scanned. Who had spoken? It wasn't Alice or Noah. She looked around her friends and realised that the words had come from Lucas, who was standing slightly apart from the rest of the group. In the dim light, Molly struggled to make out his expression.

'None of us know what she did. That's the point,' said Alice, briskly. 'But this little ... re-enactment isn't going to do anyone any favours, Tommy.' She had recovered herself, her diction crisp, miles from the guttural utterance that had drawn Molly to the roof.

'I know,' said Lucas, simply.

'What on earth are you talking about?' Alice's voice was a blade. The rest of the group continued to look at Lucas. He had their full attention. 'Nobody was there with her on that roof garden, nobody knew what was going through her head and – knowing Star – it probably wasn't a great deal. She still had plenty of alcohol in her bloodstream from the night before. We'll never know.'

'But *I* do,' Lucas insisted. He took off his glasses and blinked, as if astonished with himself.

Star

5 a.m.

Star has screwed herself up for an hour and now there it is – a stripe of light on the horizon, the start of a new day. Lucas and Alice's wedding day. Trust them to get married in their mid-twenties.

If she had caught her flight as she was supposed to, she would be landing at Heathrow at this time of day. She would head into the grimy familiarity of the Tube and then catch a train directly to Kent. Together, she and Lucas could tell Alice what they meant to each other. And the rest of her life would have a chance to go in the direction she had always hoped it might.

It's not easy to stand up. Star is thirstier than she's ever been. It's now or never. She must do something. Pete's flat is still dark. It's as if he never really lived here at all and it was just a show home for the party.

Star walks towards the balustrade and contemplates it. This time, she cannot falter. She frowns. Without Lucas, is her life really worth living at all? With all this time on her own to re-member, she's reached the conclusion that it isn't.

She turns back and goes to the side table by the sunloungers, retrieving the lipstick which has been lying there alongside the glasses. The gold cartridge feels reassuring in her hands. She has long adored this shade, with its evocative name 'Cherries in the Snow'. She applies a coat to her mouth, a motion so familiar that she doesn't need a mirror. It's a comfort to make the motion over her Cupid's bow. She smacks her lips together.

Then, as an afterthought, she keeps the bullet of the lipstick ex-tended and goes to the glass doors, those infernal bifold that have imprisoned her, that have stopped her from going home when she was supposed to and claiming the life that should have been hers.

She holds the lipstick like a crayon and begins to write. A mes-sage in that red–black, the colour of ripe cherries, something she needs to say before it is too late. Just in case. A loop, a curve, that elaborate handwriting that Star perfected with the plan of one day signing her autograph, then she draws a star as a full stop: her signature.

Once finished, Star steps back to assess her handiwork. She nods to herself, then clicks the lid of the lipstick back on and lets the lipstick drop to the floor. No matter what, she isn't going to be coming back here.

Star turns. She has to be brave. She climbs back onto the cactus's pot and grabs the railing with both hands, hoisting herself up onto the edge of the tubular steel before she can think about it too deeply, as if she were just swinging herself onto the stile on the field behind the mill house. This time, she doesn't look down. Of course not; what kind of fool would do that?

The breeze strokes her face.

Star tips forward and drops onto the ledge on the outside of the balustrade. It's thirty centimetres or so wide, set with the same beige stone covered by the entire edifice, an externalisation of the bland, corporate luxury found within.

She sets off, inching along it. She has always been sure-footed; it's one of her gifts. She keeps her centre of gravity slightly to the side so that if she wobbles, she will meet the wall.

She moves. Time will tell if her feet are made from wood.

29

Riad Mousseline, Marrakesh

Saturday night
Twenty years later

Everyone was silent, waiting for Lucas to continue, but he said nothing more and turned, with the vague air of someone searching for a misplaced household object, scratching the back of his head. Then he took a step forward with a sigh, as if repairing for the night.

'You can't let him bloody leave!' Tommy jumped down from his elevated position and moved to grab Lucas's upper arms. Molly exhaled the breath she didn't realise she had been holding. 'What the fuck are you talking about?' said Tommy, adding, 'You supercilious prick,' seemingly as an afterthought.

'Sorry,' said Lucas. 'I shouldn't have said anything, at all. Not now. But you're safe, Tom. That's the important thing. I really couldn't have borne it, not if something had happened to you as well. On the anniversary too. Imagine – like some kind of awful echo.'

'Don't change the subject,' said Tommy, his knuckles white from the effort of gripping Lucas's arms. Tommy's clothes were still sopping, his white hair slicked back close to his skull.

'He's right,' said Noah. 'You've got to tell us what you meant. You can't leave it like that.'

Lucas sighed again, deeply. 'You don't want to know.' His voice was hollow, dredged from within. 'I think we've all had quite enough upset for one evening.'

'We do,' said Tommy, stoutly.

'OK,' said Lucas, drawing out the word, as if it were a caution. 'Star was coming back to see me, that's how I know. I rang and asked her to fly home, just before the wedding.' He looked at Alice. 'I'm sorry, Alice. It wasn't that I didn't have strong feelings for you. I was torn between the two of you back then and you wanted to get back together, I was flattered. But as it got nearer to the wedding, I realised my heart lay with Star. I'd let her down over that stupid accusation you made, using it as an excuse not to commit. I realised what a mistake that was and rang her and asked her to come back. I even paid for her ticket. She was set to arrive on the morning of the wedding itself and – if she had – I would never have gone through with it.'

Alice's mouth formed a perfect circle. 'You coward,' she said, at last. 'You're just saying that now that we're separating. It's absolutely pathetic.'

'It's the truth,' said Lucas, simply, lifting his shoulders into a shrug. 'I know it doesn't reflect well on me.'

'You're just being typically self-important. Classic Lucas!' said Alice. 'Even if you did ask her to come back, it still doesn't mean she didn't kill herself. It might have been that that pushed her over the edge entirely.'

'It wasn't.' Lucas's face was impassive, the only sign of distress in the deep grooves at the corners of his lips. He twirled his glasses in his right hand, his face naked without them.

'But how on earth can you know?' said Noah. 'Come on, Lucas. This is conjecture, and pretty tasteless if you ask me.'

'She wrote a message. For me.' Lucas spoke the words softly, maintaining eye contact with Alice as he did so.

'What?' said Molly. 'A letter?'

'No. On the roof terrace she fell from. She used her lipstick to write on the glass doors,' said Lucas. 'She wrote directly to me and so the Australian police contacted me about it. I didn't tell anyone back then. I thought it better for us all – as a group – if we didn't dwell on what happened. It wasn't going to bring her back.'

'What did she say?' Molly thought of Star's red lips: her trademark at a time when the prevailing trend for grunge made it all the more of a statement.

'That she had missed her flight because she was stuck and she was sorry. That she loved me ...' Here Lucas's voice cracked. 'And that she was going to try to come back, however she could. She didn't want to die. She must have tried to climb down to the flat below and ... tripped.' Lucas sobbed then, dropping to his hands and knees, but instead of moving to help, the others shrank from him, taking a step back in unison. He was a spectacle, writhing in his trainers and pristine clothes.

'No,' said Alice, her face carved with despair. 'That didn't happen. You never told me this. It's been twenty years. That cannot be true.'

'There are lots of things we neglected to tell one another, Alice,' said Lucas, raising his face to the sky, his eyes glittering. 'You were the safer choice. The more sensible choice. A choice I'd already made. There didn't seem to be any point in rocking the boat. But I've lived to regret it, especially in light of recent events.'

Alice let out a sound, a primeval roar saturated with the interior anguish of being human.

'What a fucking mess,' said Tommy. 'You've got blood on your hands, man. And you just carried on?'

'What else could I do?' said Lucas. 'Please try to understand.' He reached out a hand for Tommy, begging, but Tommy shook his head, taking another step back. 'Noah? Alice? Molly? Don't you see I had no choice? Once she was dead, what else could I possibly do?'

Just then, Alice's phone started to chime again in the gloom.

'Oh no, I forgot about the children,' said Alice, pressing her hand to her mouth.

Star

6 a.m.

Star is almost halfway across the ledge. She pauses. Her fingertips are bleeding from how hard she had gripped onto the wall behind her. She can't fully accept that she is engaged in this act of unwilling parkour.

Best to pretend it's not happening.

Think: red shoes, dancing shoes, all eyes on her. Applause. A spotlight's sweet pivot. A dress of carmine silk. Lucas's hands on her waist.

Star sighs. Her vision snags on something on the boardwalk far below. A neon running vest worn by an early-morning jogger. Without meaning to, she looks for a beat too long. She wobbles, rights herself with her hands, wobbles again. Realising she is losing her balance, she throws herself towards the balcony below. A last chance. But her body misses its intended mark, and Star is upended.

She drops.

Disbelief. But — also — a kind of inevitability. Of course, this was how it was going to turn out. Of course. It's almost as if she knew from the minute she found herself unable to open the door.

A spurt of terror as the air swills around her ears and the ground rises to meet her. Star screams, but the sound is swallowed back into her own throat.

She descends.

So, she won't ever see Lucas again, or Molly, or her mother. That's not how it's going to be.

Then a glittering second of something else. A familiarity. Wholeness. Clarity. A blissful pirouette in red shoes.

30

Riad Mousseline, Marrakesh

Saturday night
Twenty years later

'Uh-huh. OK. Thank God you're all right.' Alice spoke into her phone, her left hand cupped over her ear. She nodded and made sounds of assent. 'Olivia, darling. I'm going to get the first flight home that I can.' She hung up. 'They're fine,' she said to nobody in particular. 'The police have arrived and got rid of the uninvited guests.'

'That's something,' said Molly, her arms folded.

'Get the first flight back with me, Mol?' asked Alice.

'No. I don't think so,' said Molly, recalling their earlier conversation. 'I'm glad Olivia and Edward are all right, but, well, I don't want to.' She swallowed. In the history of their friendship, she had never openly defied Alice. 'I need to rethink a lot of things.'

'Molly? What are you saying?' Alice looked stricken. 'None

of us behaved blamelessly ...' here she glanced at Lucas and then back at Molly herself, '... but we're grown-ups now. What's done is done and we've got a history. That's important – it's everything.'

Molly shook her head. 'It's not everything. Sorry, Al. It's not even enough.' She met Tommy's eye and he smiled at her, a tiny hat-tip.

From his position on the floor, Lucas pulled himself to stand using a chair. 'I'll fly home with you. I think there's a 5 a.m. flight to Heathrow.'

Alice looked at Lucas, newly shrunken, who still gripped the chair, as if unable to fully support himself. She shook her head, disgusted. 'You can do what you want, but it doesn't change anything,' she said, pivoting to walk away. 'I'm going to pack.' Lucas followed her, head down.

'The irony is that they are perfect for each other,' said Tommy, watching them leave.

* * *

Later, Molly tiptoed downstairs from her bedroom, using her hand against the smooth plaster of the wall to feel her way. She wore her pyjamas, muslin ones that were perfectly respectable should she encounter anyone. She wasn't sure where she was heading exactly; she just knew that she couldn't stay in the room with Noah snoring any longer. They hadn't spoken any more after turning in, mutely, and then away from each other on the bed.

But the evening's adrenaline was still coursing through

Molly and experience had taught her that she was hours away from sleep.

She left the borrowed *cheongsam* outside Alice's room, folded neatly into a silken blue pillow, so that Noah's blood wasn't immediately visible. Alice's dry-cleaner would probably be able to remove it in any case. Then she walked past Tommy's room, relieved to see that the light was out. He had promised them both that he would seek help as soon as he got back to London.

'We'll see,' Noah had said, shaking his head, after Tommy had left the roof terrace.

'Only he can do it,' Molly had replied. 'That's for sure.' For so long, she had felt guilt about Tommy, in tandem with her guilt about Star, as though she were personally responsible for his decline. Yet something about the night's events had picked it away from the space between her shoulder blades where it normally sat. Tommy was responsible for himself. They all were.

Now Molly stood in Mousseline's courtyard, in the half-dark, listening to the sound of the fountain, and tipped her head up to look at the square of sky. She moved to a seat and sat down. Someone had swept up the broken beer bottle, discreet hands cleaning up their mess.

She had to make her decision and nobody else could do it for her.

Images of Noah flickered through her mind. That evening, pinning Tommy's wrists down and looking at his oldest friend in astonishment. Arriving on the roof of Mousseline, his rucksack on his back. Then spooling back earlier. That first walk on the abandoned railway bridge, the spontaneous piggyback that started things between them. Rocking Bella as a newborn, encased in her baby sleeping bag. Bathing the girls, testing the water with his forearm. Reading to them at night, answering each of Bella's questions about whichever book they had chosen as fully as if he were taking an undergraduate seminar. Taking Eve to her swimming. Bending over the dishwasher, muttering murderously about Molly's loading technique. Putting on the layers of his cycling kit in the morning, the luminous tabard, the bike clips, the ludicrous helmet with prongs to the front. The crack of his bones when they embraced, which had only started in his forties, as if he were made of dry kindling. The excitement on his face when he told her about the documentary series. The expectant pressure of his hands on her skin. The *ping, ping, ping* of his phone.

His dear body that she knew so well that she had long since stopped desiring it. Flesh and sinew; hair and bone. Blood and shit, spit and semen. Those angles and fluids contained within. So fragile and fleeting, all of it. She shut her eyes.

'Can't sleep?' Lilith stood over her in a robe, holding another mug filled with herbal tea. Even exhausted, she retained her elegance, as well as the air of aloneness that wreathed her like perfume.

Molly mutely shook her head.

'Too much drama?' Lilith asked.

'Something like that.'

'Well, drama can be exciting.'

'Trust me, not this kind.'

'Do you want to come and listen to a record?' asked Lilith. 'Sometimes, on the bad nights, it helps me.'

'OK,' said Molly, standing. The night couldn't get any stranger than it already had.

Lilith gestured towards her quarters on the ground floor, the part of the riad that Molly hadn't explored. She pushed open a door and led Molly into a large room that served as both Lilith's living and sleeping quarters. It resembled a junk shop, full of all the artefacts that hadn't made the final cut in the house: an embroidered wall hanging depicting a vast tree, branches bearing indistinguishable fruit, a giant upturned clamshell full of dried out starfish, beeswax candles, as thick as babies' arms, that looked as though they had been stolen from a church.

'Wow,' breathed Molly. 'All this stuff.'

'I need to sort through it,' shrugged Lilith. 'I've been meaning to employ someone to help me do it for ages. I just need to find someone I can trust. You don't want a job, do you?'

Lilith placed her tea down and moved over to a record player in the corner of the room. She pulled out an Edith Piaf record, blew off the dust on the cover, placed it on the record player and pressed play, turning the volume down so that the music was confined to the curious room full of treasures.

'You like this music?'

Molly nodded. She sat down and watched as the older woman swayed and sang along, her eyes shut, '*Non. Je ne regrette rien . . .*'

'I wish I could say the same,' said Molly, smiling.

Lilith stopped moving, looked at her sharply. 'Do you think anyone gets to your age without regrets?' she asked.

'Probably not,' said Molly.

'Let me tell you. It's impossible,' said Lilith. '*Impossible*. Regrets keep coming. But we're alive – isn't that the most wonderful and surprising thing, in itself?'

'I suppose it is,' replied Molly.

'You still have time, you know,' said Lilith. 'I see you and you think it's done, the good bit of your life. But you're wrong. Take it from me, someone further on. My life now is different – less drama – but I notice more. I thought I'd miss my own beauty, but I'm able to find more beauty in the world around me. I promise you this is true.'

Molly thought of the blue of the sky on the afternoon she'd arrived, the precise trigonometry of the plants at the Jardin Majorelle, her ache of recognition when she had stepped into Mousseline's courtyard, the irrepressible life force of her daughters, the relief of being absorbed in a piece of writing. There was still much to bear witness to, much to do.

'And you have time, to work out what you want to do next,' said Lilith. 'It's not all over, not nearly.'

'Do you really think so?' asked Molly.

'I know it,' replied Lilith.

'This is such a wonderful house,' said Molly, looking around the curious room. 'And the city itself – coming here has really been an eye-opener.'

'There is so much more you haven't got to yet. Marrakesh is magnificent,' Lilith agreed. 'I came once for a holiday, and after that, this place was constantly in my dreams. The light, the people, the smells. You know, in April, all those trees on the other side of the medina are covered in orange blossom.' She gestured. 'They smell like paradise. There is nothing else like it. I knew I'd have to come back. Of course, now with climate change, who knows how long this place will stay the same? It's all change.' Lilith shrugged.

'It must be wonderful to live here all the time,' said Molly, for something to say.

'It's like anything; you get used to it,' said Lilith. 'Sometimes, I see it afresh. Mostly, I could be back in Paris. Human nature, unfortunately. We adapt to pretty much anything. I had a husband, you know?' she added. 'I left him when I was fifty. Bertrand. I decided one day that I didn't want to spend the rest of my life caring for him. I was done with looking after him. Cooking dinner for him every night. One day – to wipe his bum, you know?' She crinkled her nose in amused disgust. 'But it was – how do you say? – a strong decision. There was still love there, a certain comfort. I miss him, even if I don't miss being a wife. But for me, it was the right decision.'

'But weren't you scared?' Molly made eye contact. In the background, Piaf warbled on.

Lilith was silent in response. She swayed to the music, accompanied the song softly under her breath.

* * *

Molly woke the next morning on the roof as dawn broke. After spending some time with Lilith listening to other

332

records, she had left the older woman's room when they got to the Johnny Hallyday part of her collection. But instead of heading back to the bedrooms where Noah and Tommy slept, Molly had gone to the top of the building in search of the stars. Once up there, she had been overcome with the sleepiness that had eluded her and had laid down on one of the sunloungers, using one of the heavy towels as a blanket, before falling into a deep sleep.

Molly stretched her limbs and looked over towards the spot from where Tommy had threatened to jump the previous evening. There were still splashes of Noah's blood by the plunge pool, an abstract pattern on the terracotta. Above her, the sky was turning the very palest blue and pink, a surge of brilliance lighting an errant cloud.

Star had probably died at dawn. That's what they had been told. Molly wondered what the sky must have looked like on that last morning for her friend.

Something like this?

Star had been coming home. Everything could have been so different.

Molly shivered a little and sat up, watching the colours of the new day crack open above her. The buildings of Marrakesh were progressively illuminated, glowing like salt lamps. A murmuration of small white birds bloomed above the palm trees, dipped, rose again and then moved away, a natural fluidity, like the undulations on a heart monitor. Molly strained her eyes until she couldn't see them any more. For some reason, it seemed important to watch them for as long as she could.

Then she stood and made her way downstairs. Noah was bustling around the bedroom, folding items into his rucksack. He had disposed of the bloodied shirt and wore a familiar T-shirt over the plaster, grey to match his poorly slept face, his hair skewed by the pressure of a pillow. He looked every one of his years, but also, remarkably, just the same as he had the first time that she'd seen him in the corridor of the English department, Tommy at his side. The boy and the man commingled together in a way that she was coming to realise was her privilege alone. To be the closest witness of someone's life a unique and precious prize, possibly worth the mistakes and irritations, the atomisation of desire. Possibly.

'Where did you sleep?' he asked.

'I took ages to settle, so I went up on the roof,' said Molly. 'It was gorgeous waking up there this morning.' She thought of her notepad, of writing down what she had seen, the rising sap of creativity. The shape of the birds, the delicate colours of the sunrise. The intimation that perhaps she might even thrive.

'What a night, eh?' Noah scratched the back of his head.

'You can say that again.'

'Tommy's downstairs drinking a coffee,' Noah said. 'He seems OK this morning. Calm.'

'Well. That's something,' said Molly, rubbing the back of her neck. 'Do you think he'll get help?'

'Who knows?' said Noah. 'Nobody can make that man do anything, but if he sets his mind to it …'

'Yeah,' said Molly. 'Right.'

'What about us?' said Noah. He stopped moving, and his

arms hung by his sides. The distance between them re-asserted itself. That trench that had been dug with a teaspoon through the minutes and years. Full of the secrets they'd kept and the minutiae of their daily lives. The moments they had supported each other and the ones where they had turned away.

Molly knew that she would have to be the one to breach it.

'Noah.' She stepped forwards and reached for one of his hands. Her husband looked faintly startled. 'I'm so sorry about what happened with Tommy. I'm sorry he told you like that. It must have been the most terrible shock.' Noah screwed up his face. Molly was reminded of Bella after one of the boys in her class had been unkind to her, or of Eve after they told her she couldn't go to a particular party. Their daughters were so like him. 'I should have been honest with you from the very beginning,' said Molly.

'Yes,' said Noah. 'You should've.'

'But the thing is that I chose *you*, Noah. And once I'd really done that, I was fully committed.'

'I know.' Noah looked down. 'I do understand.' He looked up and then pulled the little finger on her right hand towards him. 'We can work through it. Just like we can with the Greta stuff. We've been through so much already. We can get through this.'

'The thing is …' Molly swallowed. 'I don't want to. I don't think either of us has been that happy for ages. We were, but then we weren't. And I love you enough that I don't want you to be miserable. I don't want to be unhappy myself.'

'What are you saying?' Noah gripped her fingers, but she saw recognition – even relief – in his face.

'I'm going to stay on here for a bit, I think. In Marrakesh,' said Molly. 'I'll talk to Lilith. I'd like to explore a bit more on my own. Just for a couple more days to give me time to think. And she needs some help sorting out these antiques she's got in her room. You can go back for the girls?'

'I thought this was it. Us.' Noah spoke slowly. 'What comes afterwards?'

'After us?' said Molly. 'I'm not sure, but I've finally realised what comes next is overrated. We can resolve things in our own time when I get back. There isn't a rush.' She looked away from him towards the sunlight falling onto the floor, oblongs of gold. A beautiful day, and it was hers.

Acknowledgements

If writing a second novel is as tricky as they say, then writing one during a global pandemic really takes the experience to an *entirely* different level.

But I did it. And I'm still intact (or just about). And there are so many people I have to thank for this fact.

Firstly, my marvellous agent Sophie Lambert, who has nurtured this book from the first glimmer of an idea and provided oodles of insightful feedback along the way. And to everyone else at C&W – I'm so grateful for the work you do.

To my editor Charlotte Mursell, whose upbeat advice on drawing out intrigue had a huge impact. And the rest of the team at Orion Fiction – including Sanah Ahmed, Yadira Da Trindade and Ellen Turner. Also, my copy editor, Francine Brody, and Clare Hey, who initially brought me in.

To my friend and fellow novelist, Kate Maxwell, for Whatsapp-centric consolation and musings on all things writing.

To my book group girls – Hannah, Charlotte (x 2), Alex, Lou and Julie – for sustaining friendship.

To the Rosebery and affiliates crew, for twenty years of fun.

To my incredible yoga teachers Naomi Annand and Adam Hocke for Zoom classes that kept me sane in our 'interesting' times and a teacher training course that I wish I could begin all over again.

To my writing-course mentors – Richard Skinner and Louise Dean, who both excel at writing and teaching.

To my mum, Sue Turner, whose own love of reading and life has shaped me, and whose seventieth birthday party, held in a riad in Marrakesh, inspired this novel's setting.

To my dad, Peter Ley, whose absence is a thread running through my every creative endeavour.

To Andrew, for always, *always* listening (even in the middle of lockdown, with three children screaming in the background) and for being my partner, in the truest sense of the word.

To Isobel, Felix and Seb, my lovekins.

To Ellie, for reading an early draft of The Trip and communicating, via sisterly ESP, exactly what you needed to. I'm so lucky.

To my other siblings – Ruth, Naomi, Abi and Will – because we come as a package, don't we just?

And finally, a nod to the sadly now-disbanded Kneehigh Theatre company, whose knockabout magic enchanted a generation of Cornish schoolchildren, me included, and whose production of *The Red Shoes* provided a template for the one in this book.

Credits

Rebecca Ley and Orion Fiction would like to thank everyone at Orion who worked on the publication of *The Trip* in the UK.

Editorial
Charlotte Mursell
Sanah Ahmed

Copyeditor
Francine Brody

Proofreader
Jade Craddock

Audio
Paul Stark
Jake Alderson

Contracts
Anne Goddard
Humayra Ahmed
Ellie Bowker

Design
Charlotte Abrams-Simpson
Joanna Ridley
Nick May

Finance
Jasdip Nandra
Sue Baker

Editorial Management
Charlie Panayiotou
Jane Hughes
Bartley Shaw
Tamara Morriss

Marketing
Yadira Da Trindade

Production
Ruth Sharvell

Publicity
Ellen Turner

Sales
Jen Wilson
Esther Waters
Victoria Laws
Rachael Hum
Anna Egelstaff
Frances Doyle
Georgina Cutler

Operations
Jo Jacobs
Sharon Willis

If you loved *The Trip*, don't miss Rebecca Ley's emotional, heartbreaking and uplifting debut . . .

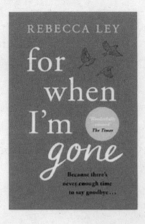

Because there's never enough time to say goodbye . . .

Sylvia knows that she's running out of time. Very soon, she will exist only in the memories of those who loved her most and the pieces of her life she's left behind.

So she begins to write her husband a handbook for when she's gone, somewhere to capture the small moments of ordinary, precious happiness in their married lives. From raising their wild, loving son, to what to give their gentle daughter on her eighteenth birthday – it's everything she should have told him before it was too late.

But Sylvia also has a secret, one that she's saved until the very last pages. And it's a moment in her past that could change everything . . .